Growlers
Moroi

John Black

DEDICATION

Thank you for buying this book and supporting my work.
I hope you'll enjoy it.

To my wife, who helped and believed in me.

CONTENTS

ACKNOWLEDGMENTS

Editing by Nicola Markus
Qualified Freelance Editor & IPEd Member
nicola@nicolamarkusedits.com

Cover art by Bogdan Bratu
https://www.facebook.com/bogdan.bratu.77

1 NORTH KOREAN MISSILE

The sun was setting over the hills to the west. It was not time yet, but soon.

The young officer was restless. His first rocket launch, all for the glory of his country. Wait until he told his mother. She would be so proud.

The door slammed open.

"Are you ready?" barked the colonel.

"Yes, sir!" His pulse raced.

"Okay then. Prepare the launch."

He started doing what he'd trained for, and stress was slowly replaced by focused duty.

Our country must be kept safe from those American dogs. They envy our way of life. Wait 'til I tell my mother. New Year is coming soon. I should ask permission to take some leave after this. I'll bring her a chicken. She's always loved chicken.

"Fuel the rocket! And keep the bay doors closed!"

Smart choice. The American dogs have eyes everywhere. They mustn't suspect anything. This will take them by surprise. Clearly the strike will be devastating. Hopefully it will hit one of their cities. This doesn't look like an exercise.

He'd seen all the exercises of the past showcased on TV. All had been important for the defense of his country, as a means of deterring the enemy. But this one was different. The special payload had come in a week ago. It wasn't a nuclear warhead, no. It was

1

something else. No one could get close. A new type of explosive, maybe. There were quite a lot of scientists roaming around it; that was for sure.

"Status?" came the bark, pulling the officer's mind back into the present.

The numbers and indicators on his command console looked good. The launch would be a success.

"Rocket ready, sir!" He felt the adrenalin pumping. His first launch, and right at the enemy! He'd sometimes wondered how he got this high-responsibility position, and why the previous officer wasn't doing this anymore. No matter. He deserved to be here!

The door opened and four people come in. Those scientists again. Even though they were not military, they looked focused and determined. *We are all here for the same reason: hit the enemy.*

They started checking a special control panel which seemed to be linked to the new payload, muttering between themselves.

"Refrigeration is on and energy almost full. Should be enough for re-entry."

"I estimate 80% of the bacteria will survive the high temperatures."

"I really hope the thermal shielding works."

"The math shows it's enough."

A lot of scientific talk. It did sound like a new kind of bomb. Probably a biological weapon, now he thought of it. Even better. *Wait 'til my mother hears about this!*

"Ready when you are," said the colonel in a strangely calm and supportive voice. "Give us the word and we'll launch."

"Do it," hissed one of the scientists. He was a small man, very skinny, and his eyes seemed to be incapable of showing any emotion.

The colonel nodded. He opened a small, gray envelope and then handed the young officer a sheet of paper detailing the target coordinates. The officer punched them into the guidance control system. He knew his coordinates; he'd trained intensively for this position. These were not heading toward the USA or one of its allies. They were somewhere in the North Pacific. At least the rocket would go over Japan; that would be a clear message to those dogs.

"Ready, sir!" he said, a little less enthusiastically this time, thinking it must be just an exercise again.

"Open bay doors! Fire up the engines!" yelled the colonel, speaking once more in his usual bark.

"Ready, sir!" He was doing it! He was really doing it! Enthusiasm returned.

"Launch!"

The tremor in the command center intensified. The noise became almost unbearable as the mighty rocket took off.

The indicators and figures looked good. Things were going well. The young officer checked his control panel, satisfied.

Oh, what was that? One sensor showed higher-than-estimated heat on one of the controllers aboard the rocket. Voltage seemed to be fluctuating a bit as well. That shouldn't be happening.

The young officer turned to the colonel. Upon seeing his face, though, he realized what reaction bad news would generate. He turned back. Hopefully it was a faulty sensor. That sometimes happened.

The big explosion was visible for miles. Silence hit the command center.

The skinny scientist left the building, silently followed by the other three.

"What have you done?" came a coarse undertone from the colonel.

Probably Mother didn't need to hear about this.

Up in the sky, a falling capsule opened and some dust got free, spreading in the air. The winds carried it away.

2 TRAVELLING TO A SMALL TOWN

"Is this everything?" said Andrei, looking at the luggage on the floor. "Can I start loading up the trunk?"

"Almost. You need to take the big suitcase from upstairs. I just finished it," said Lili.

"I have to do everything," he mumbled as he headed up the stairs.

"What was that?"

"Nothing, nothing. Just picking up the suitcase." He continued to climb the stairs. "I just said I love you," he added, giggling.

"Of course you did," said Lili, puffing. "But keep in mind I'm the one who needs to handle everything."

"Not true. Now, let's see. I have to think how to fit everything in our small car," he said, grabbing the suitcase. "You sure you've got everything? Slippers? Towels?" he continued.

"We're going to my parents, Andrei, not a shitty seaside motel. I'm sure my mother has towels we can use."

"Well, at least we'll eat some good food for once," he added, grinning as he stole a glance at her face, waiting for a comeback.

"I don't think anyone would ever suspect you're not well fed," came the expected answer.

"Ha, ha. I will have my revenge. But not now, later. Hey, Mat, come help!"

"What?" came a squeaky answer from upstairs.

"Come help! Is your backpack done? Can I take it to the car?"

4

"Yes! Yes, it's done! I just have to add a few more things in the backpack, Daddy."

"Then it's not done! Why did you say it's done? Didn't I say to have everything ready and take it downst—"

"Stop yelling, both of you! And you, don't talk like that to the kid. He's seven; you're seventy. Talk nicely."

"Pfft! We're the same age, you and I. If I'm seventy, you are as well. And the kid needs to learn to be organized."

"Yeah. Just like when you couldn't pack your own suitcase, so I had to do it for you?" said Lili. "Now be gone and let me finish this."

"Okay, okay, fine. You handle it. You just put everything you want to be transported to your parents' place right here in the hallway, and I'll take it to the car. Anything other than that is your responsibility."

Andrei moved down the stairs, mumbling toward the kid. "Okay, maybe I overreacted a little, but you can be such a dreamer sometimes. Structure and reliability are the keys to success. When you say you'll do something, you have to do it properly."

"Mat, put your things in the backpack and take the backpack to the hallway ASAP!"

"But Mom, my backpack is done. Why is he saying—"

"Mat, you can see your dad is cranky, and I am too. Don't answer back. Just do it!"

A few minutes later, Andrei stood surveying their small hatchback trunk. *Everything will fit,* he thought, checking out the available space.

He grabbed a rolling suitcase, pushing it into one corner of the trunk. "Man, this is heavy," he huffed, just as Lili came to the door, bringing Mat's backpack.

"Well, I've tried to squeeze things together, that's why," she said, dropping the backpack.

"You're good at this, I know. I always wonder how you can cram so many things into such a small piece of luggage."

"It's my superpower," said Lili, smiling briefly. "Can you fit all these in the trunk?" she asked, gesturing at the large pile of waiting luggage.

"Yes, of course."

"True, you've always been good at maximizing available space and making things fit," she said as she headed back to the house.

"That brings back some memories," said Andrei, trying a charming smile and a deeper voice, yet just managing to sound awkward.

"Pfft. Stop it. Good luck with these."

"Hey, do you have anything you need in the front?" he called out a few moments later.

"Yes, the bag with water and the one with food," came a yell from the house.

"Why do we pack food? It's just a five-hour drive, and we'll stop at least once for gas."

"Well, someone needs to eat those cold cuts we have in the fridge, and why spend money at the gas station when we have perfectly good food at home?"

"Fine, fine," mumbled Andrei, while trying to fit a large duffle bag in a not-so-large space.

They were running late. It was almost 1 p.m. and they were still not ready to go. There was no need to hurry though. Andrei liked to drive at night, and Lili was happy as long as Andrei was happy. Also, leaving this late meant traffic would be better, as everyone else in the city must have left hours ago.

"Ready? Should I warm up the car?" yelled Andrei. "Anyone?"

No matter. He still needed to connect the phone to the car's screen and wash the windshield, so this was a good moment to prepare everything.

As he set the destination, the radio turned on and a news bulletin could be heard.

"... *a kid got injured while using a fire cracker ... the flu epidemic, coming from eastern Asia, is spreading quickly ... in preparation for the new year, the President addressed a message ... a new rocket launch in a series of ... a new day, a new clash between riot and police in the streets of ...*"

"Ah, those bastards. Shut up!" Andrei pressed play on the music player, replacing the anchorman with his beloved heavy metal music.

* * *

Two hours on the road. It was already 4 p.m. and the sun was starting to set.

"We're almost at our first stop," said Andrei, checking the navigation system.

"Perfect! I do need a break. I want to eat," said Lili, who'd spent most of the trip so far staring out the window, her mind clearly elsewhere.

"Can I get the tablet now?" came a whine from the back seat.

"No, Mat, we've told you. You'll get the tablet after we make the stop at the gas station."

"But Mom, it's getting dark and—"

"No 'buts', young man! Look out the windows. You're staring at screens way too much!"

"Should we get some onions?" interrupted Andrei.

"What?" Lili turned to him.

"I said, should we get some onions?"

"What do you mean, dear Andrei?"

"I mean, let's get some onions. See? There!" He pointed to a spot coming up on their side of the road.

They were entering onion territory—the part of the country where people were famous for growing lots of onions, especially those yummy red ones.

"I really love onions. And your parents too. Let's get some. They must be good!"

"My dad loves them, my mom, so-so. Okay, fine. Stop and get some. But not like last time, when I had to throw away half. Get a string not a sack!"

"Yeah, yeah."

Andrei pulled in near the stall. "Hi. How much for this big sack over here?"

* * *

"Well, good thing you like this music. I don't. Can you skip it?" Lili huffed.

"I've told you, honey, every time you don't like a song, just skip it."

"Thank you. We should get some of my music."

"Well, your music sucks."

"Yeah, Mom's music sucks!"

"Mat! Stay out of this," said Andrei, laughing. "Look, we'll stop the music, as Mom has a say in what we do."

"Well, thank you. And as for you, young man. If I hear that again, I'll take that tablet away from you, you hear?"

"Yes, Mother."

"... *while a United States representative has declared that this serves no purpose and just shows the world how unreliable the Pyongyang regime's promises are ...*"

"Ugh, they launched another rocket," explained Andrei.

"Who?"

"The North Koreans."

"Ah," said Lili.

"Yeah, it seems they targeted some uninhabited island, but it exploded soon after takeoff."

"Mm. Fascinating."

"Well, they keep on flexing over there," continued Andrei. "I wonder why the US doesn't bomb their launch site and just stop all this."

"War is horrible. I hate this kind of talk. Put on some more music."

"Well, think! What if they try to launch again, then you bomb their site, make it look like an accident? They just said the rocket exploded mid-air, so accidents have happened before, right? And if it explodes right on launch, their site will be unusable for months!"

"I don't know and I don't care. Let me be. War is bad and it upsets me. Put on some music!"

"Okay, okay. I guess my heavy metal, *real* music as I like to call it, is not good enough for the princess, so I'll try some radio channels," he said, grinning.

"Whatever," said Lili, acting as if she didn't notice his sarcasm.

* * *

They crossed the town limit and entered Lili's hometown—a tiny community of about 20,000 people, including the surrounding villages.

The area was hilly, and mountains could be seen in the distance. A river split the town in half: the main part, with a large, round park at its center, and the other, smaller section, a bit poorer than the rest. Well, almost everyone here was poor—poorer than the country average, at least.

A few blocks from the park, close to the river, stood Lili's parents' apartment building.

"Life can be good here," said Andrei. "Every time I get here I realize how much I like the slowness of this small-town life. The crisp clean air, the smell of pine trees. It's so different from our crowded city."

"Yeah, I know," said Lili. "I loved it here as a child. It was better here for me than it is for Mat in the big city, that's for sure."

"Why don't we move back here?" said Andrei. "You know, we could slow down a little."

"Yeah, I know what you mean. But you'll never find an IT job nearby. And I don't like that there are so many stray dogs everywhere. Look," she said, pointing to the left, "there go a few of them now. And they don't look friendly."

"Yes, what's up with that? I wonder why the mayor isn't dealing with it."

"I don't know," said Lili just as her mobile phone started ringing in her purse. "I bet that's my dad."

"Dogs or no dogs, this is a nice little town," said Andrei, sighing.

"Hi, Dad," said Lili, answering her phone. "Yes, we're almost there. Yes, we just entered the town. No, the traffic is good. Now that you mention it, we've seen very few cars. Just a lot of snow. Well, yes, I'll ask. Andrei, you want Ma to make some mulled wine?"

"Yeah, that would be nice actually."

"Yes, Dad, mulled wine sounds great. Yes, for both of us. Mat? He's good. A few days ago he felt under the weather and coughed a couple of times. And so did I, actually, but now we're good. He's been on the damn tablet for the last few hours. Yes, we'll see you in the parking lot in a few minutes."

* * *

"Hi, honey! So good you're here. How are you? How was the

trip?" said Dan, Lili's father.

"Hi, Dad!" Lili threw her arms around her dad's neck and kissed his cheeks. "It was good. It's been snowing for the past couple of hours. Otherwise it was fine."

"Mat! How are you, big boy?"

"I'm fine, Grandpa."

"Hi, Andrei. Come here." He pulled Andrei toward him for a kiss on the cheek. "I hope you're in the mood for some whiskey. Let's go inside."

"You said you have mulled wine."

"Yeah, that's to wash your teeth with. Real men will get some whiskey. Let's go in. Mom is waiting."

The apartment was in a pretty old but sturdy building, with a ground floor and two others on top. There were two apartments on each floor—one large, one small—for a total of six.

Dan was a big guy, so he took half the luggage. He was a little over seventy but only looked early sixties at most.

Waiting in front of the door to the big apartment on the top floor stood Maria, Lili's mom.

"Where's my little Mat? Where's my grandson? Come here, Mat. Give Grandma a kiss."

"Grandmaaa!"

"Hey, Maria, aren't you sick?" said Dan. "Don't kiss him!"

"Oh, I'm fine! It was just a small thing. I'm okay now. Come here." She pulled Mat over for more smooches.

* * *

Following a hefty meal, the family sat quietly in the living room. The TV was on, and Mat was watching cartoons, eyes glued to the screen.

Andrei and Dan sipped whiskey, while Lili and Maria enjoyed some mulled wine.

"I've prepared a lot of food for the next few days," said Maria, smiling. "Just let me know what you want and I can heat it up for you."

"Indeed, my beautiful wife has prepared food for a hundred people." Dan grinned.

"Oh, stop it!"

"Well, it's true: you're beautiful! You have the most beautiful face, just as you did on the day we met!" continued Dan, which made Maria blush.

"Thank you, Maria, it's really nice. We're looking forward to relaxing a bit while here with you," said Andrei, before taking another sip from his glass.

"Indeed. Just relax," said Dan. "Sleep as much as you want. Do nothing all day. The forecast says the snow will continue for the next two days, right up to New Year's, and then a cold wave will hit from the east."

"That's how it usually is," said Andrei. "Here in eastern Europe, the cold usually comes from the east."

"Well, don't I know it!"

"Did you see the new rocket launch in Korea? And the continuing riots in Hong Kong?" continued Andrei, adopting a more serious tone. "I wish the US would take some concrete action, rather than just talk. Stop Korea and help Hong Kong. Bring peace to that part of the world."

"Well." Dan paused to sip from his glass. "I'm not sure the US has any real reason to help Hong Kong. On the contrary. But from another point of view, it's good this is happening way over there. It means the big guys are focused there and we have less noise in our part of the world."

"True."

"What they do over there is their business. Let them launch all the rockets they want. As long as it doesn't escalate, we'll be fine. We're living our lives peacefully. They don't impact us in any way, so why bother?"

Suddenly a loud noise interrupted their conversation.

3 HAPPY NEW YEAR, EVERYONE!

"What the hell was that?" said Lili. Her mouth remained open; it looked like she was gasping for air. "It sounded like... like... like a bear?"

"Well, technically," started Andrei, "it sounded like a bear... but I don't think it was one. Who would bring a bear here, in the building? I'd say it was a person who made this noise."

Despite his calm words, Dan knew Andrei was afraid from his sudden pallor. Lili just rolled her eyes.

A bear growled again!

Everybody in the living room froze. And several loud thumps came from the neighboring apartment, followed by a loud scream, sounds of a struggle, and a few more growls.

"We should go investigate, maybe call the police," said Lili. She stood and rushed toward the door.

"Don't! Mind your own business!" said Dan. "We don't get involved in other people's lives, as you well know."

"But maybe someone has been attacked or they are fighting. What if someone is dead? Don't you call the police then? Well, actually, you are the police, so maybe you should go investigate," said Lili, visibly affected.

"I've been on the force for over thirty years, but now I'm retired. I can't just go investigating. I don't know how things are done in that fancy big city of yours, but up here we don't meddle in each other's business, unless it's our business. And right now, our business is to enjoy our evening and not interfere with our neighbors," said Dan, slowly rising from his chair.

"These neighbors—husband and wife—have a rough relationship," continued Dan in a more relaxed voice. "They yell and even hit each other. I've tried to talk to them over the years. I even went to the authorities, but every time I involved the police, they both denied everything. And they blamed me for getting involved. They kept insisting what they do is their business. I will not have conflicts with my neighbors over their bad life choices!" he concluded, and moved toward the apartment front door.

He peered through the door viewer, trying to see if he could get a sense of what was going on. But the hallway was dark and he couldn't see anything. Not that he'd expected much, and, of course, no one else in the building would bother to come snooping around. That family's behavior was well known.

He returned to the living room and smiled, trying to release the tension. "Now, let's finish our drinks. Then you three go to bed and sleep as much as you want. Don't forget, we have the big family poker game on the New Year's Eve, so get ready to be squashed!"

* * *

The next day was awesome: snowy outside, warm inside. Mat was bothering his grandma, while Lili, settled in a large armchair, was reading her fashion and interior design magazines.

"Do you know a lot of people believe that 'minimalism' means something small and cheap?" she said enthusiastically to Andrei.

"Mm," answered Andrei, slowly browsing Facebook on his phone from the comfortable couch.

"Yeah! People actually believe minimalism means having one or two small pieces of furniture, usually cheap. And imagine, it's one of the most expensive interior design styles!"

"Wow, honey. That's great," mumbled Andrei. He noticed some images on TV and turned up the volume. "Hush, honey. Let me hear this."

"... while the flu symptoms are beginning to show up everywhere. The health ministry is informing the population to stay warm and hydrated, while making sure people avoid crowded places."

"Yeah, like that's going to work, one day before New Year's," muttered Andrei.

"What?"

"I said, like that's going to work!"

"Aha, yeah," said Lili absently, turning another page of her magazine.

"... *general flu vaccines are available at local pharmacies. This year it seems there will be a bigger than usual influenza epidemic, with multiple accounts being identified all around the globe, especially in the east-Asia region. There is no specific vaccine yet, but as the death toll is a bit higher than previous years, some areas have gone into full lockdown. The World Health Organization is still silent, while some research institutes promote the idea that we are, in fact, dealing with a bacterial infection. Please see your local physician for any kind of ...*"

The report was cut short as Andrei switched to a movie channel. "I don't understand how these people get sick so easily," he mumbled.

"What?" said Lili.

"Ooh, *Die Hard*. Awesome," continued Andrei, before going back to browsing on his phone.

Life was good.

* * *

Later that night, after another hefty dinner, they went to bed.

"Man, that onion salad sure was good! Not too spicy, not too dry. I bet I stink like a goat," said Andrei, grinning. He loved to raise opportunities like these with Lili.

"You always stink like a goat." Lili's comeback followed as expected.

"Ha-ha, never heard that one before. Good thing this double bed is small, as you will suffer all night."

"Ha-ha. I would have suffered even without you eating," said Lili, cracking open the window.

"Yeah, that's good. I love a colder room when I go to bed."

"I opened it to get rid of that onion stench, dufus," said Lili, getting into bed next to him.

"What was that?" yelled Andrei suddenly. He jumped out of bed and went to the window. "It came from outside. Sounded like that

14

man or bear or whatever growling again."

He moved the drapes a bit and looked out. Lili quickly joined him. From their room they had a direct view toward the bridge connecting their part of town with the other side. That part of town, spreading up a hill, was renowned for its shady characters: poor people prone to drinking, stealing, and minor violence. These carryings on had got that neighborhood the nickname 'Las Vegas'. Pretty ironic—but irony could sometimes be a strong feat in this town.

A few people were coming from Las Vegas, across the bridge. They seemed a little drunk, and they were chasing several other people who, even at this distance, seemed scared.

"What the hell happened to this town?" said Lili, closing the window again. "Okay, they're drunk. But why isn't anyone intervening? Where are the damn police?"

"Well, you saw General Dan, how afraid he was to—"

"My dad is not afraid. He just knows that some things are not to be messed with. You know very well, image is everything in a small town. You also know we don't like to pry in other peoples'—"

"Yes, but now?" interrupted Andrei. "Shouldn't we call the police?"

"I don't know," said Lili, thinking.

"If we call the police, we'll have to wait for them to come…"

"Yeah, and sometimes they take their sweet time. Then we'd have to give statements…"

"…and people from Las Vegas would see someone from this building is being interviewed by the police," said Andrei, shaking his head.

"Yeah, I'm not sure Dad would be happy about that."

"Ah, look, they got away. They're not in danger anymore. No need, probably," said Andrei.

* * *

Two hours till midnight. Two hours before the New Year began.

The TV was on a national station, playing some prerecorded show. The family mostly ignored it as they got ready for dinner.

"Pretty festive thing we've got going," said Andrei, smiling.

People were dressed casually, and if not for the bottle of chilled, sparkling wine, no one would have guessed an important event would be celebrated soon.

"Oh, come on. Don't tell me you would rather have gone to a club," said Lili playfully.

"I bet the clubs here are the bomb!"

"Pfft. You wouldn't recognize a hip club if you slid and hit your big head on a stool in its restroom."

"Finally, an original joke!"

"When I first met you, you were dressed like a hobo," continued Lili, ignoring his last remark. "You might actually fit in perfectly here."

"Well, at least we both agree on your humble origins." Andrei leaned toward the table and plucked up a carrot, pretty satisfied with the exchange. "But I still find you cute," he said, carrot in his mouth, trying to hug her.

"You're not bad yourself." Lili cuddled a bit in his arms. "Although a little fat."

"Ha-ha." Andrei laughed, taking the carrot in his hand and kissing her cheek.

* * *

January first. New Year had arrived half an hour ago and the poker game was well underway. Lili, Maria, Andrei and Dan were playing, while Matei was, finally, asleep in their bedroom.

They had agreed to end everything by 2 a.m., and judging by Lili's lack of enthusiasm, that time couldn't come soon enough.

Just as Dan was winning with a nice hand, the noise hit again. That noise. The same weird noise.

Now it came from the apartment below. The bear-like noise. The growl. Then a lot of rumbling, furniture moving and falling, all accompanied by growls.

"This is not normal," whispered Lili, looking at Dan. "You cannot tell me this is normal."

Soon, the same noise started as well in the apartment on their floor, which made everyone stand up, mouths open.

Dan always had an answer when directly asked a question. He

always knew what to say. Now, he was silent.

"This is... What the... I mean, what is..." Andrei struggled to articulate.

Eventually, the noise died down and then ended.

"Let's go to bed," Dan finally said. "Good night, honey. Good night, everyone. Happy New Year!"

* * *

It was noon and they'd just woken up.

The town was silent. It had stopped snowing, and no one could be seen on the streets. Not one person.

Everybody must be sleeping in, eating, or watching TV, Andrei thought, while looking out the window toward the bridge and Las Vegas. *January first, what would you expect?*

Then he saw it. It looked like a body, half hidden at the side of the bridge. Only the legs were visible, still on the pavement. Snow partially covered the limbs, but someone was definitely lying there.

"Lili! Liliii!!!" he screamed. "Come into the bedroom! You need to come here!"

"What? Why are you yelling? I've told you a million times not to—"

"Wait! Look over there. Do you see it?"

"See what?"

"There's someone on the bridge."

"Mm, like that's some incredible thing!"

"No, look! He's down, not moving. See, at the end of the bridge, right behind that concrete side."

Lili gasped. "We need to call the po— Dad! Come quick!"

Dan came, almost running. Upon looking out the window, he picked up his phone and dialed the emergency number. "Hi, yes. This is former police officer Dan Popovici. I would like to report a person, fallen on the— What do you mean 'when you can'? I'm telling you, as a former police officer, you need to send a— Yes, I understand, but what could be more important than a possible DOA or, even worse, a possible homicide? ... Yes, okay, but I don't think there were fifty homicides last night, right? Okay, some people got into fights, but we didn't have a homicide here in— Yes... Yes,

17

you do as you want. I'm just telling you that somebody is lying there, in the cold, outside!" He hung up. "These new guys in the force are brainless!" exploded Dan. "Apparently, they had a lot of calls today, and very few policemen came to work. This country goes to shit more year after year!"

Andrei gasped. "Where is he?"

"Who?" said Lili.

"The guy. Where is the damn guy?"

"He's not there anymore?" said Lili, audibly relieved.

"Ah, he must have been a drunkard," said Dan, visibly relaxing. "These guys must have a saint looking over their shoulder. He slept there for a few hours, in the cold, it snowed all over him, then he woke up and left while we were on the phone. That bastard."

"But where did he go? Shouldn't we see him walking either toward Las Vegas or toward town? The call wasn't that long," said Andrei.

"Hmm. He might have taken a few steps, then fell again, and is now fully hidden by the concrete side of the bridge," said Dan, and once more he became irritated. "That's why I told those foolish halfwits at the emergency number to send someone."

"Language, Dan," said Maria, approaching the group. "There's a child with us, so mind your language. Everyone, I've just prepared some cookies and warm milk. You can find them in the living room."

* * *

January first was nearing its end. The family had spent all day watching Blurays, while Andrei messed about on his phone, laughing at mediocre memes.

Then, Dan rushed into the room. "Switch to the news!"

There, they saw it.

In the nation's capital, hundreds of people were dead. Some video footage showed people attacking others. All were moving strangely, like they were drunk. None responded to police officers ordering them to stop.

And that noise. That man-made bear growl. That horrible noise was everywhere.

4 THE EXPEDITION

"Let's go out!" said Lili, trying to sound a little more optimistic than she really was. "Look," she said, pointing outside the window. "It's a cold morning, true, but the sun is up and the surroundings look magnificent."

Andrei stopped, holding his coffee mug in mid air, a few inches from his mouth, and let out a groan.

"Come on. We've been inside for three days now, and we need to get some fresh air and move around. You, especially, need to move, or you'll start to look like Maui. Minus the muscles, of course," said Lili, pushing a bit at Andrei's buttons.

"You guys are going out?" asked Dan. "You should be careful."

"Your dad is right. Did you see the news last night, Lili? Don't you understand that people are behaving strangely? Haven't you heard those noises through our walls, and on the bridge, just like the ones on TV?" said Andrei, becoming visibly scared. "I think we should spend more time trying to understand what's happening. What if we get atta—"

"Who can attack us? Do you see anyone outside? Look, the bridge is clear; Las Vegas on the other side is clear. There's no one around."

"Now I remember! I saw it on my phone. A lot of stupid things, a lot of sick people, but also news of attacks here and there around the world. More than usual. I'm telling you, my phone—"

"You always keep your nose in that phone. Move a little. You should be more active if you want to live a healthy life. Again, look out the window. This is not one of those big cities you read about. This is our tiny town, close to the mountains. People here are already drunk, so it's all quiet."

"Well, isn't it too quiet? Shouldn't there be some people out and about? It's the second of January. How much time do they need to recover?"

"Well, you don't know this place as I do. It's a small town. People just stay in, eat, drink, and watch stupid things on TV. So, move your ass. Let's go out and take our fat bellies for a stroll."

It was difficult to argue when Andrei's weight was, indeed, on the wrong side of the scale. He decided to try his last bullet: "What do you think, Dan? Is it safe to go out?"

"A walk is always good," answered Dan. "I usually go out every day, but right before Christmas we bought everything we needed for the holidays and then decided to stay inside. We didn't want to expose ourselves to that flu, so, unfortunately, I can't tell you how it is in town right now."

"But Dad, there's no one outside. We'll not touch anything, and if we see people, we'll just avoid them. And if we see a drunk person, we'll make sure we go five hundred miles away from them."

"Yes, if you pay attention you should be fine. I suggest you go by the river. There are fewer people there and the risk of getting anything is lower. Or you could even go to the park. It should be deserted at this time of day."

"Well, okay. But when we come back, I want some of that pork and mashed potatoes." Andrei surrendered and turned to Lili. "And tell your ma to make some mulled wine."

* * *

Mat was ready to head out. He liked going out to run and play in the snow.

"We have to fight with snowballs, Dad. You and me are one team. Mom is the other. Mom, you have to fight us, and we'll win. There's no way for you to win! We are the best team, right, Dad?"

"Yes, we're the best," muttered Andrei. "Now, let me be and get your shoes on."

"And after we win, Mom will beg for mercy. Right, Mom? You will have to tell us that—"

"Oh, shut your yapping!" Lili exploded. "Let me focus on what to take, otherwise I'll forget something."

"But Mom, we have to—"

"We have to nothing. Now shut up! Are you ready to go out? Then just go. I'll follow after. Andrei, you're ready; take Mat and get out."

"Make sure you keep that hat on properly," said Maria to Mat, coming out to the hallway to see them off. "You don't want to get sick. And did you get your scarf?"

"Mom, let him be. He's fine," said Lili, adjusting Mat's hat.

"But it's cold outside. Did you get a good hat? That one doesn't look too warm. Tell him to put on his hoodie, that would help."

"Mom, he'll sweat. Let him be. I remember when I was a child, you kept on pushing us to overdress, just like now."

"Yeah, my parents did the same," said Andrei, trying to calm Lili. "I think it's something with this part of the world. We pamper our children too much."

"Well, be it as it may," said Maria, "but you don't want a sick kid, don't you?"

"Of course not," said Lili, sighing. "No one wants that. But I do want him to feel fine. Just fine. That means one hat is enough. I don't want him to go through what I went through as a child."

"But you turned out *fine*, didn't you?" said Maria, scoffing as she moved away a few steps.

* * *

After opening the door, Andrei experienced a strange sensation as he looked at the door to the other apartment on their floor. He heard those noises again clearly in his head, and the memory sent small shivers down his back.

"Let's be quiet, Mat. People might be sleeping," he whispered, trying to make Mat silent. He wasn't sure about the sleeping part, but he was damn sure he wanted to get out of the building as quietly as possible.

Mat moved fast down the stairs, talking about the toy store, and

21

Andrei followed silently.

They left the second floor and reached the first. As they made it to the ground floor, Lili yelled down to them.

"Maaat! Did you take your gloves? I have your gloves here. Did you take the other pair?"

For a second there was silence. Mat looked up, opening his mouth to answer. Another second. Andrei caught him and covered his mouth.

Silence remained. Everything was fine.

Then that loud growling started everywhere.

There was movement in the apartments, thumps against walls and doors.

Everybody stood still: Lili on the second floor, blocking the door, and Andrei and Mat on the ground floor, right by the entranceway.

Slowly, the noises faded, then stopped. Behind Lili, Dan and Maria had emerged and were holding on to each other, all silent.

You could almost taste the fear as everybody tried to regain their self-control.

Mat looked up, opening his mouth to say something, but Andrei stopped him and whispered, "Shush. We need to be quiet. We need to go back up the stairs slowly and return to the apartment. Can you do that? Can you go slowly and quietly up the stairs?"

Mat hesitated a moment. "Yes."

"Shush! Don't talk, whisper. Okay, let's go, slowly."

They started up the first flight, taking them from the building's entrance to the first two apartments. They took each step gingerly, trying to be as quiet as possible.

The noise was strong in his memory, and Andrei was scared. He couldn't remember the last time he'd been so afraid. Maybe that day when a group of kids surrounded him behind the school to beat him up. Then, he'd been terrified. But he'd been twelve at the time. Now, he was thirty-eight. He shouldn't be this scared.

As they reached the ground floor, they saw that one of the apartments had an old, wooden door. That wouldn't hold back an angry person, let alone a bear, realized Andrei, and fear started to overcome him. *No, but there couldn't be bears in here really. I saw it on TV. There were no bears in the capital. Was it people making that noise, then?*

As they climbed the next flight, he began to feel like something was behind him. He now understood why Mat would run back to the living room after turning off the light in the bathroom: that ancestral fear that something evil was behind you, lurking in the dark, and that you needed to go where other people were as fast as possible.

Almost without realizing he was doing it, Andrei picked up the pace until they were almost running.

Mat let out a small shriek, his emotions clearly getting the better of him, while Andrei took two stairs at a time.

Despite their intentions, they were making a lot of noise.

And then, the real noise started again.

Bear-like growls. Bodies slamming against doors.

Andrei and Mat ran. They weren't thinking anymore. They just ran, both screaming.

"Run! Oh my God, come on!" yelled Lili, hanging on to the doorframe.

All of a sudden, there came the sound of splintering wood as the door to the ground-floor apartment cracked open. Andrei heard it distinctly as he and Matei tore into their own apartment two floors up.

Dan slammed the metal door shut behind them and turned all the locks, his hands visibly shaking. Then he looked through the door viewer, watching the corridor beyond.

After another minute or two, the noises faded, and their breaths slowed, even though tears continue to stream down Matei's, Lili's, and Maria's faces.

* * *

The family sat quietly in the living room. Mat was still crying; no one could stop him. He was in that place where he didn't hear anyone. He just cried.

"He'll fall asleep," said Lili. "Let him cry, Mom," she told Maria, who was still trying to calm him. "Hold him and he'll be okay."

Once Mat did fall asleep, Andrei and Dan began discussing their options.

"So," said Andrei, "it looks like what we saw on TV and read in the news is everywhere. It's spreading. People are drinking something or touching something, and they're getting really aggressive."

"That's no alcohol-induced aggression, Andrei," said Dan. "I've met hundreds, no, thousands of drunks and have had my fair share of violent and aggressive behavior, but this is different. Those noises and what we saw on TV give a different perspective."

"True. Do you think it's a drug, then?"

"If it's a drug it would have to be one hell of a distribution system for it to hit the capital, here, and other parts of the world all at the same time. No, this is something else."

"But what if the mafias and drug clans arranged to sell it at the same time?"

"What would be the point? If that were true, they would have to be really stupid."

"Why's that?"

"Well, for one thing, this kind of behavior puts law enforcement on high alert. No drug that does this would be tolerated, so why try to sell it? You know this would bring the full might of state institutions upon you anywhere in the world." Dan shook his head. "No. This is no drug. This is something else."

5 DECISION TIME

"Let's turn on the TV. Maybe there's something on the news," said Andrei.

As they zapped through the channels, things seemed bad. Most of the TV stations were either showing reruns or weren't broadcasting at all.

They couldn't find any network covering any kind of news.

"What the hell is this? No news? Nothing? It's January second, the news stations should be broadcasting," said Andrei.

"Let's try foreign stations. You know ours can be crappy," said Lili.

"Crappy, okay, but not non-existent."

As they continued channel hopping, all they got was white noise.

And that's when it happened.

The electricity went off without warning.

"Oh, God damn it," said Andrei.

"Language!" said Lili. "We have a kid around."

"A sleeping kid!"

"Well, still a kid. And you know how kids hear everything. He might hear in his sleep."

"This is stupid."

"You are stupid."

"Next level comeback right there," said Andrei, grinning.

"Stop that," said Dan. "Stop. First, let's keep it quiet. You saw what happens when we make too much noise. Second, let's work together. We have no power in the house, okay. It will probably get fixed soon enough. Until then, it's still daytime, so we can look for all the candles we have, to be ready for the night."

"Also," intervened Maria, "who wants some food? I was just heating something up. We'd better eat it while it's still warm, now that we have a blackout."

* * *

Life always looked better on a full stomach.

"Clearly something is going on," said Andrei, moving around the living room.

Lili entered the room, coming from the kitchen, where Dan, Maria and Mat were finishing their dinner.

"Moreover, I suspect that flu we kept hearing about has made a lot of people sick. And we all know how high fever can make people not think straight and even behave irrationally."

Andrei loved to hear his own voice, and sometimes he thought out loud. Just like now.

"But we have our police and armed forces," he continued. "The government, as bad as it can be, has some effective institutions. And they need those structures to keep them safe while they keep on stealing. So, I think they have it under control, and they will appear soon with a communication of some sort. So when the power comes back on, let's make sure we keep the TV on the national television channel."

He turned to Lili to gauge her response. She was looking out the window, toward Las Vegas, deep in thought, not listening.

"Well? What do you think?" repeated Andrei.

"Yes… yes… maybe."

"I love it when you're oozing with that much enthusiasm."

Suddenly, Lili came to life again.

"I should be enthusiastic about what? We have no electricity, no info on what's going on. For all we know, everybody is dead and they all turned into zombies! I should be in the office in a few days. Mat has school. Oh, and we don't have hot water anymore, because of the power outage. How long can we stay here? When can we go back home? Can we actually go back home?" said Lili, crying, almost yelling.

"First," said Andrei, "keep it down. Remember what happens when we make noise." He forced a smile. "Second, let's not lose hope. I don't think everyone is dead, and zombies don't exist. It has been scientifically proven that there can be no such things as zombies, and—"

"Who proved that? How can you prove that?"

"Why are we talking about zombies? Can you hear yourself? They're a figment of someone's imagination. If we keep on saying zombies, zombies, zombies, zombies, we'll just waste time, instead of focusing on the important things."

"Okay, Mister Supreme General, please tell us what to do," said Lili, fire in her eyes.

"Well, first," said Andrei, taking a deep breath and trying to find the best answer, "we need to understand what's happening."

"Oh, wow. Thank you for that insight. That's a good plan. Why didn't I think of that?"

"Yes, yes, thank you, honey. Sarcasm is always helpful."

"Well, Captain Obvious, then stop wasting our time with such observations!"

"Okay then, I don't care anymore. You let us know what to do, and we'll do it! How does that sound?"

"Definitely better that your bright ideas," said Lili, and she left the room.

Life could get crazy quickly, even on a full stomach.

* * *

Left alone, Andrei picked up his phone. This would give him the information he needed to show Lili he was right.

As he browsed, he realized things were odd to say the least. And one hour later, things were looking really bad.

"Honey," he said, as Lili entered the room.

"What?"

"Look, I'm sorry."

"So am I," said Lili, coming closer and kissing him.

"I have some bad news, I think," he said, trying to find his words.

27

"What is it?" asked Lili, pulling away from him and looking straight into his eyes. "Is it your back?"

"What? No, no. Something else. About all this. So I checked the Internet. You know how I use social media for fun, seeing memes, and all that stuff?"

"Yeah."

"So, I noticed there are fewer 'Happy New Year!' posts that usual."

"Yeah, who cares about those anyway?" said Lili, and they both giggled.

"Indeed. But the bad part is I found some news. That new flu is everywhere, not just in our country, and a lot of violence has erupted around the globe, mostly directed toward the civilian population."

"Oh my God," said Lili, covering her mouth.

"Yeah. And it's worse in the big cities, of course. There are some analysts who blame these events on some global terrorist movement, origins unknown, that somehow managed to build an international cartel—" said Andrei, breaking off as Dan entered.

"Go on," said Dan, waving his hand as he took a seat. "I want to hear too."

"Yeah, so the idea is that there might be this cartel that somehow managed to hit all continents roughly at the same time."

"I don't think that's possible," said Dan, shaking his head.

"Yeah, sounds a bit far fetched, not without some countries finding out in advance. Especially the ones with strong information agencies. But the worrying part is that almost all news, comments and updates are at least a few days old. I haven't seen anything new."

Lili, Dan and Andrei looked at one another, pondering.

"The good thing is," said Lili, sighing, "we are in back-country, in the middle of nowhere. If there were terrorists involved, they wouldn't bother to target this place."

"True," said Andrei, "but judging by what has happened over the last few days, I fear we are already being impacted by whatever this is."

* * *

When morning came, everybody woke to find the electricity still off.

And even worse, after more than twelve hours without heating, the once-warm interior was starting to cool.

"Oh, nice!" yelled Andrei through the bathroom's opened door. "Water's out."

"Great," said Lili from the living room. "Add 'no water' to the list. No heat, no water, no electricity. We do have some food, but for how long?"

"We need to do something," said Andrei.

"Stop yelling!" yelled Dan.

* * *

"What do we do?" asked Lili, looking at her husband.

Andrei sat on the couch and took out his phone.

"Let me check this. I'll find a solution. And if not, I'll call the police. Oh," he said suddenly. "My mom and dad. I forgot about them. I should call them. Why didn't I think to call them yesterday?"

As he unlocked the phone, reality hit.

"Damn," he said, looking at Lili, visibly scared. "The mobile network is not available."

"What do you mean 'not available'?"

"I mean, I have no internet, no network signal. I cannot call or browse. Basically, this is useless!" he said, throwing the phone across the couch.

"What's happening?"

"I guess some generators failed and the antennas ran out of juice. Such things should be bulletproof, you know, with enough fuel so it keeps them running for a few days, but I guess in our country nothing works as planned," he said, leaning to pick up his phone.

Lili looked down, tapping her chin absentmindedly, just as Andrei retrieved and unlocked his phone, browsing nervously.

"I should have moved to Canada," he muttered, as he threw the phone to the other side of the couch once more.

* * *

Everybody gathered in the living room, scared but determined. Something needed to be done.

"Well," started Dan, getting everyone's attention. "We need a way to keep ourselves warm, we need water, and we need to stay safe. Here, in the apartment, we are relatively safe. I was here when they installed our new metal door six years ago. It's solid, well mounted in the wall, and now looks like it was the best decision ever."

"Yes, I pushed for that," said Maria. "Before we only had the old wooden door that came with the apartment. Just like the one on the ground floor."

Silence reigned as they recalled the events of the previous day.

"We're out of water?" asked Matei, looking toward his mother. "Mommy, we need water! Let's go buy some water!"

"Shush, hon, relax. We'll be okay. We're discussing what to do, and we'll have enough water for everyone," said Lili, caressing his head. "Let us talk and try to be quiet, okay, honey?"

"Right," said Dan. "So, as I said, we're relatively safe here. What we don't have is water or heating, and what food we have will not last us forever. We need to do something."

"How about we go to a supermarket?" said Andrei. "We could take my car; it's right out front. We go in, grab as much food and water as we can, and we also pick up a generator and put it out on the balcony. That should buy us some time until the power outage is fixed."

"Well, you've seen what happens when you make noise," said Dan. "If we put a generator on the balcony, the whole building will hear it."

"True, but what can they do? You just said the door is impenetrable," replied Andrei with an annoyed huff.

"That's true," said Dan, "but do you want a group of people banging on your door for the next few days?"

"By the way," said Lili, "taking the car... wouldn't that make some noise? Okay, it's a small car with a small engine, but it does make some noise, right?"

"For all we know, we only have an issue with noise in our building," said Andrei. "Everywhere else should be fine."

"Not true," said Lili. "You saw it on TV: it's happening

everywhere."

Again, the room fell silent.

Finally, Lili spoke. "I think we have to assume people are dead. A lot of people."

"I don't think everybody's dead," said Andrei. "Did those noises coming from the other apartments sound like cats to you?"

"No. But they didn't sound like people. And I didn't say everybody's dead! I said a lot of people are dead."

"Well, you're the one who pushed for us to go out for walks and lose weight, so, yeah, I guess you're the one thinking everything is safe."

"I was wrong. Okay? I was wrong. It was a stupid thing to do, and now we need to be smarter."

"Mommy, I'm scared! I don't want people to die," said Matei suddenly, his eyes watering.

"Ugh, honey, don't worry. I'm sure it's nothing. We're just throwing ideas around here, and everyone is nervous because of this situation. Mom, can you take Mat into our bedroom? I'm not sure he should hear these things," said Lili, looking at Maria.

"It doesn't matter who's right or wrong," said Maria, rising from her chair and going toward Matei. "What matters is how we ensure we have enough supplies to last until they come and find us."

"They?" asked Andrei.

"The mayor, the police. I don't know. The priest! He should know what to do in this situation."

"Pfft!" Andrei scoffed, as Maria and Matei left the room.

They could hear Maria's voice getting dimmer, trying to soothe Matei.

"Anyway," said Lili, "we need to be smart. We need to find a way to survive, yes, as Mom said, until help comes. What do we know so far?"

"Well," said Andrei, "we know a lot of people all over the country became violent in the last few days. Good people like us were attacked. We also know there is no one on the streets, and in our building, we're the only ones who seem to be okay."

"About that... why are we okay?"

"Does it matter? Let's focus on the relevant information."

"Why is that not relevant? Huh? What if we just need to, I don't know, look at the sun every day to be safe? Or, I don't know, drink water during the night? Why?" asked Lili again, her eyes slowly watering. "What if we're not sick and just by getting close to a sick person, we also get it? We have to gather all the info, as you said a while back."

"Fine! Okay. Let's waste time. Why are we okay?"

Silence hit the group once more. Everybody was thinking, trying to put things together.

"I don't know," said Lili, breaking the silence. "I have no idea." She looked so tiny in her chair, with her eyes moving around the room, like she was trying to read the answer from somewhere.

"I love you honey," said Andrei, with a calm voice. "I'm sorry I yelled."

Lili smiled, looking into his eyes for a few moments.

"Okay," said Andrei, more relaxed. "Temperatures are decreasing, so tomorrow, or in two days tops, we'll have to do something."

"If the electricity is not back on," said Lili. "Otherwise, we can stay here for a few more days."

"Yes, yes, of course. If electricity is not back on."

"Lili's right!" Dan came out of his long period of reflection. "We have to assume everyone is dead."

"Well, I didn't say that. I said we have to assume a lot of people are d—"

"We have to assume everyone is dead. If not, and some are alive, then that's good news for us. But we must assume the worst-case scenario," continued Dan. "We need to either find a safe place that has everything we need, or we need to fix things here. And most importantly, we have to assume there are violent people around."

Silence returned.

* * *

"Okay then," said Andrei. "Let's see. If we go to a supermarket, we'd have everything there. If everyone is dead, we could just live there, for many months. Ah… but it's difficult to defend, if we need to do so. Or we can go, pick stuff up, and come back here." He paused. Not a perfect idea, clearly.

"But how do we heat up a whole supermarket?" asked Lili.

"We can't. They probably have the same issue, no electricity. And I bet those places are even less insulated than this apartment and will freeze in a few days. We need to go to somewhere that has heat. Water is secondary; we can find other solutions. Look, there's a river nearby," said Andrei, pointing at the window.

"There are a lot of wells around this area," said Lili. "In Las Vegas, at least, I bet there are a few wells. Same for the outskirts of the city, where a lot of old country houses have their own wells. Especially in the areas where the administration hasn't put water supply pipes in yet. We should be looking to move somewhere farther away."

"Well, now it actually sounds bad we are so close to the city center." Andrei smiled. "However, now it gets clearer. See? Being structured and focusing on important things pays off."

Lili rolled her eyes.

Andrei continued. "So, we need a place farther from here, with its own well, food supply and heat. Yes! A lot of people here still use wood burners. Isn't that right? I remember you could see the smoke coming from the chimneys every winter! We need a place without central heating."

"Oh," said Lili, gasping as she suddenly turned and ran toward the window.

The others followed her and looked out. There was no smoke coming from any house, as far as the eye could see.

"Oh my God." Lili almost fell while trying to sit on a chair. "They're dead. They're all dead! What... how... how did this happen? What are we going to do?"

"Stop, honey," Andrei moved closer to her.

"What are we going to do?"

"Honey, stop."

"This is too much!" yelled Lili.

"Quiet, honey!" said Andrei, hugging Lili, as a rumble started beyond the wall of the neighboring apartment.

Again, the bear growls could be heard, but it soon died down.

"Be quiet, honey. We don't know what we're dealing with. We don't want them to know we're here. Be. Quiet," Andrei said in hushed tones close to her ear.

Lili started crying, and Andrei kissed her head, petting her gently.

* * *

Night came.

The light from the candles in the living room flickered. Everyone was looking straight ahead, rarely making eye contact.

Maria was putting on a winter jacket, while Lili sat on the far end of the couch, staring absently at the floor, a silent Mat in her arms.

"He's usually so noisy and alive," said Andrei to Maria. "Look at him now."

"Well, he understands we need to be quiet. And he's such a good boy. He can feel our suffering, he's so empathetic." Maria's voice sounded full of adoration.

Again, silence. This was happening too often. And was usually a rare occurrence when Andrei was around.

"What about my mother's house?" said Dan, breaking the silence as a knife goes through butter.

"What?"

"My mother's house. That's where we need to go. She passed away many years ago, as you know, God rest her soul," said Dan, while Maria said a short prayer and made the sign of the cross. "But we still have that house," continued Dan. "It's not far, around ten miles out. But it has everything: a working well, stacks of wood for the fireplace, three good rooms, and a kitchen. There are some cans in there as well, if I remember correctly. Enough for a few days at least. Plus, there's an outhouse in the back. Okay, it's not the nice toilet we have here, but it will do just fine for a while, until we figure things out."

"And how will we get there? You said it's ten miles out. Do we get the car?" asked Andrei.

"Yes, we take the car. We go slow, or we go fast, depending on what we find on the road. Or around it." Dan stopped, his face showing the thoughts that were crossing his mind. "Hopefully, we can go slow."

6 ROAD TRIP

A t 8 a.m. on January fourth, they were ready.

Dan had his own police-style clothes that he loved to rely on during the winter, including his beloved winter boots, gloves, and a heavy jacket. All leather, of course.

Andrei was wearing his standard jeans, but he'd put on a pair of long johns as well.

Matei was fully dressed in warm clothes, including his gloves.

Maria and Lili both wore long coats and big fur hats.

"Not sure you can run in those clothes," muttered Andrei.

"Oh, stop it," said Lili. "Always with the jokes. Now's not the time."

"I'm not joking. What if we need to run?"

"Well, if we need to run, we'll run. What, do you think my mom will run faster if she wears professional sportswear?"

"Yes, I definitely will," said Maria, laughing. "That's what been stopping me running for the last fifteen years: not wearing training gear."

"Okay, then," said Dan, and everyone paid attention. "We'll open the door and slowly go out. Andrei, you hold Mat's hand and go together. Lili, Maria, you form another group." He paused, then added, "And everyone keep quiet."

Slowly, Dan unlocked the door. They were all sweating, even though the apartment was already cold.

Once the door was open, Dan went first, followed by the

35

women, then Andrei with Mat.

They emerged into the small hallway. The neighboring apartment was silent and still.

Things were also quiet on the stairs going down to the first floor.

Dan locked the door while the others waited in the hallway.

"Lock it only once," whispered Andrei, his face tense and his eyes wide.

Dan understood. He turned only one of the locks.

There were two flights of stairs between floors, and the group moved slowly downward.

When they got to the first floor, everything was quiet. They tried to move stealthily, but some small noises could be heard: clothes rubbing and bending, shoes and boots hitting the floor. Still, it was way less noise than people would normally make.

One more floor and they could exit the building.

Dan held the lead going down the stairs from the first floor to the ground floor. He made it to the landing, then turned to take the second flight, only to halt. Lying face down between the two apartment doors on the ground floor was his neighbor's body.

The man was a teacher who worked in the next town. His apartment door—the wooden one—was in pieces, parts of it littering the floor beside the body.

When Lili saw it, she let out a small cry. She never had been able to control her screams when faced with strong emotions, and it didn't look like she would be able to start now.

Everybody cringed and froze, remembering what noise could do.

One second. Nothing. Two seconds. Nothing.

Then, the growl came.

It was the same bear-like sound.

And it was coming from their neighbor on the floor.

* * *

One growl. Two growls.

The neighbor pressed his palms against the floor and started to push himself up. He craned his neck, trying to look at the people on the stairs, as he continued to make bear noises.

Now Mat, Lili and Maria were all yelling, and Andrei loosed his own cry, despite his efforts to control it.

The neighbor was almost up. Now they could see his face: white, very white, with spots of dried blood on it, especially around the mouth, where a few teeth seemed chipped and smashed. He was looking at Dan the way a wolf looks at a rabbit.

On his feet, he took a step toward Dan, letting out a stronger, bearlike growl.

Then a gunshot was heard.

Smoke was coming out of Dan's pistol, and the shot splattered the teacher's blood and brains all over the walls.

The body fell.

All hell broke loose.

* * *

Growls exploded all around. From outside the building and from behind the broken door of the teacher's apartment.

Someone was coming, closing in fast. The growling intensified and feet thumped on the wooden floors.

But maybe even more horrible was the body on the floor—the one with the gaping hole in its head, which was still squirming. Squirming and growling.

"Back! Up! Go up!" yelled Dan, climbing the stairs. "Everybody! Go back!"

They dashed up the stairs, Andrei pulling on Mat's hand violently as he climbed. Maria and Lili were running. Faster than they ever had. There was growling everywhere.

As they reached the door, they realized it was locked. But Dan was close.

He had the keys and tried to find the right one. Why the hell did he like to keep all his keys on one ring? That was stupid.

Meanwhile, the growls coming up the stairs were closing in. The amplified noise made what was approaching sound like it was only a few steps away.

Dan finally found the right key and scrambled to unlock the door.

They rushed in, and Andrei slammed it shut behind them.

They were still turning the locks when the banging started.

Dan looked through the door viewer. It was the teacher's young wife who was pushing at and banging on the door, all the while growling, just like a bear. Her face was white, dried blood here and there, and her eyes stared blankly.

For a while she pushed and banged. Then suddenly she stopped. She took two steps back. Looked once more at the door. Then fell, like a plank, to the ground, facedown. Frozen, not moving at all.

Next to her, doing the same thing a few moments later, was the couple's five-year-old daughter.

* * *

Silence. Good, blessed silence.

Silence everywhere.

They slowly moved down the hallway to the living room.

Mat was already sleeping in his father's arms.

"What's wrong with him?" asked Andrei.

"It's a defense mechanism; I read about it," answered Lili. "When sudden, big, emotional events happen, they sometimes fall asleep."

"Poor kid," said Andrei, as he settled his sleeping son on the couch.

It was safe inside. But two of those things were right at the door.

* * *

"What do we do? Dad, you were a policeman. You fought bad guys, you handled tough situations. Tell us, what do we do?" said Lili. She was crying, but her voice was almost a whisper.

"We go out again," said Dan.

"What? How can we do that? Don't you know there's a zombie mother and child right outside our door?"

"We don't know they are zombies," said Andrei. "There's no su—"

"Then what would you call those things out there, Andrei?" Lili turned her burning eyes to him. "What would you call them? Fireflies? Ducks? Bees? Whatever we call them, we know one thing:

they seem dead, they look dead, they should be dead, but they are not. And they attack at every noise we make!"

"Then we have to go," said Andrei. "No other option. We cannot stay here. We are surrounded by these things. We have to go."

"And," said Dan, "we need to learn how to kill them."

"What do you mean?" said Andrei, his eyes widening. "Isn't that a bit harsh?"

"You saw the body I shot," answered Dan. "He was still moving. I've never seen anything like this before. I took a good shot. He should be dead. And it's not harsh. What if a larger group attacks us? We need to be ready to put them down."

"Maybe... maybe you... I mean... maybe you missed?" continued Andrei, trying not to offend Dan. "Like with that guy missing half his brain from the news?" he said, trying to come up with a possible explanation. "I don't know how this works, but what if the important part of his brain was okay?"

"Impossible," came the answer like an axe. "No one could survive that shot. Point blank range, right in the head."

They all stood there quietly, considering the implications.

"I still hope that guy had a strange brain," said Andrei.

"I hope so too," answered Dan. "But if I'm right, we need to find another weak spot. We need to be able to kill these... these... these people if they attack us."

"How can we do that, Dad?" asked Lili. "You see how aggressive they are. You see how afraid we are. I cannot go around killing people, especially when we don't know how! I have a small child. What will he learn? That it's okay to kill people? And he'll never sleep alone again, if he learns these people are unkillable!"

"They are not people," said Andrei.

"Oh, now they're not people." Lili turned to him. "Now they're not people. I guess they're not zombies. So what are they? Is it 'they'? Or should we use 'it'?"

"Honey, look, we—"

"Don't honey me! Don't you do it!" said Lili, and started crying.

* * *

"We need to try again," Dan whispered to Andrei later that evening. "That's the only way. There's nothing else we can do. Look at Lili and Matei. See how beautiful they look while sleeping. We need to do this for them."

"Can we fight?" asked Andrei. "Do you have another gun I could use?"

"I don't think guns are what we need," said Dan. "They make noise. We need other weapons. Some clubs, like baseball bats, maybe. Some knives even."

"They are starting to sound like zombies," said Andrei.

"Well, doesn't matter how they sound like. Personally, I don't care. All I care is to understand if we can kill them, and how. If they're like those zombies in the movies we've seen on TV, fine. It means I missed that shot and we'll have to kill them like that. If it's something else, double fine. We'll kill them nevertheless," said Dan, with fiery determination in his gaze.

Andrei stood there, silent. What could be done? How could they manage this?

"We have to try again," concluded Dan, and then he went to bed.

7 SECOND ROAD TRIP

"**O**kay, now, be quiet," said Dan, as he slowly unlocked the door.

Everybody was ready, just like the previous day. Backpacks, clothes, and now also weapons. Dan had a big baseball bat, as did Andrei, while the girls had long meat knives. It was a good thing Maria loved to cook and had the right tools on hand.

"Take Matei in the living room," whispered Lili to Maria. "I'll tell you when to come back."

Matei followed Maria silently, looking back and forth between his mother and grandmother.

While turning the locks, Dan cast frequent glances through the door viewer, to see if the woman and child moved. So far, everything seemed in order.

But as he opened the door, the little girl rose, growling, looking toward the noise.

The group froze and Lili loosed a small screech.

That's when the girl attacked. She charged toward them, and in six little steps she was right in front of the door.

Dan pushed her with his baseball bat, while Andrei jumped around, adrenalin pumping.

The little girl's growls started to wake the mother.

"Let's hit them!" said Dan, with a confident voice. This helped everyone eliminate their fear a bit and focus on their objective.

As the girl came forward again, Dan thumped her with his bat,

41

right in the head.

With a horrible noise, the skull broke, changing into a mushy thing, and the little girl fell. Her chest continued moving, though, the growling still coming from her throat. Even if her head was smashed in, she still seemed to be alive. Dan was certainly onto something.

The mother was up. This was a different enemy—way bigger and stronger. But Dan promptly hit her as well. She didn't fall after the first hit, even though the right half of her head was smashed in.

She came forward, mouth open, attacking the group. Dan swung again, but he missed, his baseball bat only clipping her shoulder.

A crack was heard as her bones broke, but this didn't stop her.

Andrei pushed her away with the other bat; he couldn't swing due to the door frame.

This kept the group safe and allowed Dan to try again.

* * *

The fight woke the entire building, and growls and thumps could be heard everywhere.

Luckily, everyone else had upgraded their doors to metal ones at some point and no other people could come out. Soon, the noise settled down.

When the growling stopped, they took a look at the bodies.

Heads were smashed in and their chests had stopped moving. They looked dead.

As they moved around, Dan's boot made a noise near the mother, who a few seconds later came back to life.

Even with no head, the body tried to get up, albeit without success. It remained active, aggressive, like a chicken right after you cut off its head.

These sounds woke the little girl as well, who added her own growls to the growing noise.

The rest of the building quickly followed.

After a while, they stopped and lay still on the ground.

"It's clear that hitting their heads halts them, but not fully," whispered Dan. "They still seem to have some *life* in them, and they try to attack the source of the noise."

"Should we try to stab their chest?" asked Andrei.

"Why the chest?" whispered Lili.

"Well, it's where the heart is. You know, like in the movies, when they hit the head and the chest... the two vital organs."

"I see. You do it," said Lili, holding out her knife.

"Yeah, we should try," said Dan. "Give me that knife."

He inched closer to the dead mother and touched the body. Suddenly, like an electric shock goes through a lightning rod, the body shook and came back to life, more aggressive than ever.

Hands and legs flailed, scratching and touching everything around them. And, as always, the bear growls were present, even more intensified. This brought to life the whole building once more.

Dan held her down until everything slowed. Then in one swift move, he turned the body face up and pushed the knife into its chest.

He took out the blade and moved away. The body struggled, just like last time, hands in the air, clawing at his police jacket. Fortunately, this didn't do much damage, and his skin wasn't touched.

The body gradually slowed, until, right at the end, it let out a longer-than-usual growl, then slumped.

This was the first time they'd really killed one of these things.

* * *

"To the car!" said Dan, confident. "We know how to kill them. We don't know how many they are. But we know how to kill them. So that's good."

As they reached the ground floor, they saw the teacher's body. Clearly it had moved from when they last saw it.

"Careful. He's still alive," whispered Andrei to Dan, nodding toward the body.

He was right. The noise they made triggered a response from the body, which started squirming.

"Shouldn't we kill them all, to make sure we have a safe return home?" asked Andrei. "What if we need to come back to the apartment?"

"Don't worry about that," said Dan. "We'll not have to, and if we do, we can navigate around them… or kill them then."

As they passed the smashed door, Lili said, "Should we go in and take some food?"

"Well, we have taken a lot in our backpacks, but why not," said Dan. "We could manage a few cans; they would last longer. But we need to be careful. Who knows what else we may find inside."

* * *

Twenty minutes later, they were ready to go. They had found some nice canned fish, and, to Andrei's delight, a small sack of fresh onions.

"Imagine this! All these perfect onions, and those poor bastards didn't get to eat them!"

"Oh, yeah," said Lili, "anyone who doesn't eat onions with every meal must be an idiot."

"Truer words were never spoken."

"Let's go out," said Dan, as they finally reached the building's main entrance. "Lili, go get Maria and Mat."

"Quietly," added Andrei.

* * *

They were out!

Dan stopped, right at the entrance. He looked around carefully.

"The snow is untouched. That means no person, animal or… thing has walked here for a few days."

"This is it? This means we're safe?" asked Andrei, who was a few inches away.

"Come," whispered Dan a few seconds later.

As they headed toward the parked car, their confidence grew.

"When we get to the house, can we play with snowba—" started Matei.

He was immediately shushed by all the adults.

"You need to learn to be quiet," said Lili, whispering. "We cannot make any noise if we want to be safe. Okay, sweetie?"

* * *

All the backpacks were in the trunk. Andrei couldn't resist a proud smile.

"You can all see that, as the average person would have managed to fit only three of those backpacks, by using my—"

"Yes, yes," interrupted Lili. "You're a genius. Now, let's go!"

Andrei got in the driver's seat, mumbling again about the world being unfair to elites, connected his phone to the car by reflex, and then turned the key partway in the ignition.

He didn't want to turn on the engine until everyone was in.

But suddenly, even though the engine was off, the audio system switched on and heavy metal music poured out, all while the car doors were open.

He quickly reduced the volume to zero and looked around guiltily.

"Idiot!" whispered Lili.

One second. Two seconds.

Growls came from everywhere, especially from the building next to the parking lot, on the right-hand side of the car.

They could see people behind some of windows, hitting the glass, trying to get out to the car.

On the first floor, a guy managed to break the window and climb out. There was no blood gushing from his arm, although the window pane was stained red.

"It's like cutting a flank of red meat," said Maria in a faint voice.

Then, he fell to the ground. One leg was clearly broken, but he still got up and started toward them. He was trying to run. And he was gaining speed.

"Quickly, in!" yelled Andrei, as he turned on the engine.

He didn't wait for seatbelts, not even for everyone to properly close the doors. He put the car in Drive and floored it. The motor purred for one second, then the wheels started spinning. Unfortunately, there was snow everywhere and the car couldn't get any traction.

"What are you doing?" yelled Lili. "Let's go!"

"It's the snow!"

The guy, their neighbor, really, reached the car, and went straight toward the right front window, where Lili was sitting. He charged head first. They were lucky that, due to his injured leg, he didn't have too much momentum, so the strike didn't smash the window. It did leave a big smudge on it, though, as his forehead slid down.

Andrei tried to accelerate again. The car engine revved louder, but to no avail. The car started sliding left, without advancing.

The neighbor scratched along the car's side, snapping his teeth, trying to bite Lili through the window, all the while making those terrifying growls. His teeth scrapped against the window, the sound horrible.

Matei was yelling and crying, and pushed his face into Maria's chest. She held him, looking scared herself.

"Stop! Press the break and hold! Okay, now activate winter mode," said Dan calmly from the back seat. "Now, press the accelerator gently."

His commanding voice gave Andrei confidence.

He did just that, and, finally, the car started moving.

The neighbor was left behind as the vehicle exited the parking lot and entered one of the main streets.

A 'main street' in this town didn't mean too much. It was basically like all the other roads. One lane going, one lane coming. Not a big town, so no large boulevards.

Luckily, everywhere seemed deserted, as if the people had all been inside their houses when this happened.

"Poor kid, he fell asleep," said Maria suddenly, with pity in her voice. "These things are too much for him."

"They are too much for us, let alone a young boy," said Lili with a trembling voice.

In the rear-view mirror, Andrei could see their neighbor trying to follow them. But after a few turns, he finally lost sight of him.

"Relax," Dan said to Andrei. "We're good. And slow down, the roads are slippery. Plus, we'll make less noise."

This helped Andrei calm further, and he relaxed his foot on the gas pedal.

Another left, and they were heading straight for the bridge they could see from their bedroom window: the bridge that linked their neighborhood to Las Vegas.

And there, on the left-hand side of the bridge, was a body.

That body. The one they saw a few days ago through the

window.

"What do we do?" asked Andrei, stopping the car a safe distance from the bridge. "Do we go on?"

"Yeah, we can go," said Dan. "Just go very slow. As little noise as possible."

"Make sure you don't wake him," said Lili.

"Yeah, that's the objective," said Andrei, irritated. "Why do you think I asked what to do?"

"Well, I just wanted to make sure you know what *not* to do."

"Well, thanks a lot. That information changes everything." He released the break.

As the vehicle crept forward, the adults watched the body. It didn't move. But it also looked very frozen. The man's clothes were covered in snow, and in some areas there were little icy parts.

Then the body shake, and that sound they'd come to know so well could be heard.

But this time it was a bit different: less powerful, colder maybe, with a bit of hissing added. More like a bear and snake mixed together.

The body tried to move; it was clear it wanted to get up. But it couldn't.

"It's frozen!" said Maria. "It's like a frozen piece of meat!"

Everybody shivered at the thought.

Andrei accelerated and they crossed the bridge.

Only ten more miles to Grandma's house.

* * *

As the road wound its way up the hill, through Las Vegas, they passed houses with tall fences to the left and right. All were silent; there was no movement anywhere.

Snow covered the road—there was no one around to remove it—and as the path curved left and right, it became less and less accessible.

The small hatchback, now loaded with five people plus luggage, was barely making it, especially once they'd left the town behind and the snow got even deeper.

Finally, the car stopped moving entirely, wheels spinning, stuck in the snow.

     "We have to walk," said Dan.

     There were still seven miles to go.

8 ON FOOT

It was midday. With snow everywhere, you could barely distinguish the road.

The group was one mile out of town. Straight ahead, seven miles away, was the small village where Grandma's house was located.

"Should we turn back, get some shovels, and dig the car out of the snow?" asked Lili.

"No, we should go on to Grandma's house. A few miles out we should find the place," answered Andrei, looking confidently in the direction of the village.

"I don't think you can walk seven miles, uphill, in deep snow. Remember how enthusiastic you were when we wanted to go for short walks?"

Andrei was an IT guy. He had worked at a multinational company for many years, basically sitting on his ass in front of a computer all day. He was chubbier than he would have liked—according to the medics, he was at the entry point for obesity—and sports for him meant going to the kitchen to get the next beer. But, contrary to what reality had shown him over and over again, he held the strong belief that he could accomplish any sporty feat he wanted, if he had the inclination.

Now was a good time to start wanting.

"Of course, we can!" said Andrei, his face warming as he threw a few quick glances towards Dan. "Why do you say that?" he added, trying a very serios face. "We just go that way, step by step, until we reach the house. You know, the average speed of a walking person is about three miles per hour, so in two to two and a half hours we should be there."

"That's not on snow, and not uphill," said Lili. "But fine, okay, you can do it. How about Mom, or Mat, though? They are not in the best of shape."

If Andrei was borderline obese, Maria was clearly overweight. She really liked to cook, and you cannot be a good cook if you don't like food. When she was not in church, she spent most of her time in the kitchen, cooking and tasting.

She'd been born and raised and had spent all her life in the hilly town behind them. She used to walk out of town, up the hills, especially in the summer, but that was thirty years ago. Now, aside from going out for the much-needed groceries, she was in no shape to trek seven miles up a snowy hill, at temperatures way below freezing.

"True," said Maria. "I can try, but we'll have to walk slowly. I walk around the city every now and then, so I should be able to cover some distance." She didn't sound confident.

"Okay, Mom, you'll try, but what do we do if you cannot walk anymore? We can't carry you. We can barely move ourselves. We might have to carry Mat, and he's already pretty heavy."

Mat was seven and a half, and, luckily for their current situation, he was a little small for his age. He was athletic and very energetic. But still, like all active kids, he was used to burning his energy fast and then becoming depleted and generally a burden to others. Plus, his energy was strongly linked to his enthusiasm. While he could run up and down a hill if, as a result, he could hit his father with five snowballs, the motivation was completely different if he had to climb the hill just because. And he had already started whining about the cold.

"Maybe it's better to get back, sleep somewhere in town, and then return tomorrow with a better car," said Lili.

"What better car?" Andrei asked immediately. "What, my car's not good enough for you?"

"It looks that way," said Lili, smiling.

"Pfft. I wanted a smaller car," he said, again throwing quick glances at Dan. "So what? It's really good for a crowded city, and it has fantastic mileage."

"Yes, I'm not challenging that. It *is* a good car," said Lili, in an appeasing tone. "But it's not built for offroad adventures. You said it yourself, it's built for the city."

"Fine, we'll do as you want. We'll return, we'll get past that dude on the bridge, and get a better car," he said, and turned his back on the group.

"Fine!" said Lili.

"What's 'fine'? Aren't you the sporty one? Why aren't you up to this challenge? Weren't you the one that was all like"—Andrei started moving his hands around his head—"'Ugh, oh my Goood, let's goooo. Let's go walk around the hotel for no apparent reason. Woo-hoo.'"

True, Lili was a little sportier. She was average height, thin, and really stressed about keeping fit and eating well.

"Well, yeah! I want to be healthy, not like a certain slob with his annoying ass glued to a PC chair!" she said, glaring.

"Language!" said Andrei, happy he'd managed to catch his wife using bad words for a change.

A few seconds of silence descended.

"What do you think we should do, Dad?" said Lili, turning to her father.

Really, Dan was the only one up to the task. On top of his morning routine, he walked for miles almost every day, taking trips into the hills around the city. He loved doing this. And as an ex-police officer, he strongly believed a fit body was the key to a happy life.

"There's a house up there, I think," said Dan, looking uphill along the road. "More of a cabin really. It's somewhere midway. We could go up there, slowly, no rush. We still have a few hours of sunlight, so we should be fine."

"What house, Dad?" asked Lili.

"A woodsman's cabin, where the guys who manage the forests have a small HQ of sorts. They should be making sure people don't illegally cut the trees, but as you can see, they're not doing a very good job of it... Anyway, it's two of three miles up, and if we go slowly, we should be able to reach it safely."

51

"Ok, Dad." Lili surrendered. "We'll go on."

And so, they made their way up the hill.

* * *

Twenty minutes in, Andrei started to realize the task might be a bit more difficult than he'd imagined. He was sweating abundantly, and he soon found himself out of breath.

As his breathing and heart rate accelerated, his legs also began to hurt—way more than when he went up the stairs to other floors around his big corporate building.

He was not ready for this.

Lili had already challenged the plan, though, so how could he now turn around and say the idea was bad? He had no choice but to push on. It couldn't get any harder than this. He remembered from when he was young and used to run, that after a period of low energy and low confidence, somehow the body found a way. So, yeah, he could do it. He just had to push a bit more.

Ugh, this hill was steep though. And the snow kept getting deeper, already halfway to his knees. Still, he couldn't show weakness in front of Lili.

That said, so what if he did show weakness? He was just an IT guy; he was not prepared for this sort of thing!

Why wasn't Dan going alone? He could take a nice SUV or a 4x4 from the town, find the cabin and check things out there, and then come back and get them? Why should Andrei be the one to suffer?

He looked back at Lili. Her red face told him she was going to call a halt soon. She'd be the first to say it, not him. He could continue a bit longer, and when she finally stopped, he could propose the solution of Dan going alone.

That way, he would be the one to stay behind to defend the women and children, while Dan took the easy job. Easy as he'd be the first inside a warm vehicle.

That's when Maria started coughing.

* * *

"You okay?" said Dan, moving closer to Maria.

"I'm okay," she answered, while still coughing a few times. She was out of breath as well, but the coughing was something else. "I guess the cold I had a few days ago came back. I'll have to rest this evening, maybe take some pills. I have a few with me."

"Well, let's pause for a bit," said Dan, looking around to find a place to rest.

There was nothing but snow and a few trees here and there.

"Use the backpacks. Let's sit," said Dan, removing his backpack.

"Mom, I'm hungry," whined Mat. "What can we eat?"

"I've brought some of the soup you liked and some of the meat you had yesterday. Actually, I have most of the food I cooked for you," said Maria. "We also have some cans with fish, meat, some beans…"

"But I don't like beans," lamented Mat. "I want baked potatoes!"

"Yeah, and I want a huge T-bone," said Andrei, breathing heavily. "Unfortunately, all we can give you now is a fresh, juicy and healthy onion." He grinned. He liked to joke this way with the kid, just like he did with Lili.

"Stop! I don't want onions! Mommy, why is he—"

"Andrei, let him be," intervened Lili. "Yes, honey, he was joking. We'll give you some real food. We cannot bake potatoes here, but I have a few meat sandwiches for you. Will that be okay?"

* * *

As they were finishing up their food, Maria had another coughing episode.

"You should have some of these onions; they've got vitamin C," said Andrei.

Lili looked at him, arms crossed. "Would you please stop with the onions? We get it; you love them. Now let us be!"

Andrei huffed. "Sorry for promoting a healthy habit."

"Perfect. Now, Mom, you're okay? How do you feel?"

"Not too well. It's clear my cold is coming back. I can still walk, but I think I'll get a fever soon. Not sure how much more we have to go," said Maria, turning to her husband for an answer.

"We're about one mile out," said Dan. "On a normal, summer's day, we'd cover the distance in a few dozen minutes. As things stand, I guess we've got about an hour to go," he said, lifting his backpack off the ground.

They continued onward and finally reached some sort of hilltop. The barely visible road continued a bit downhill, and then began to climb once more.

Below them, they could see the woodsman's cabin. Next to it, on the right, there was a shed. A metal mesh fence, about six foot tall, surrounded the property. The place looked deserted. There was no sign of any vehicle, and the snow looked untouched.

"Good," said Dan. "No one's home."

They all shivered, understanding the meaning of those words.

"Come on, then," he continued. "Let's head down."

Seeing the destination helped, as it gave them the energy and motivation necessary to make it to the cabin, and the group reached their destination just as the sun set behind another hill.

9 SETTLE IN

Dan went in first. The door squeaked when he slowly opened it.

Once his eyes had adjusted, he could make out the small cabin's interior. It looked as though the place had been in use, but there were no signs of any recent visitation.

As he advanced into the room, he had an idea. He started hitting the walls and furniture, especially the wooden support beams, while carefully looking all around.

"Hey! Anybody here?" he yelled.

He waited a bit.

"Heeeey!" he called again.

Nothing.

"Well, I guess you can come in," he said, and the rest of the group happily entered.

The cabin was small. It consisted of a main room with two desks, a cabinet off to the side, where the woodsmen kept their things, and a toilet in the back. There was also a small stove in a corner of the room and a coffee machine. On the other side stood a nice, big fireplace.

"This will do," said Dan, and he dropped his backpack.

* * *

Warmth was good!

The family sat huddled around the fireplace.

The light from the fire danced over their faces. And they were happy.

They felt safe for now.

Dan had found a way to lock the door from the inside. He'd also checked the shed outside. It was a flimsy structure with wooden walls, and the wind whistled through the holes and cracks in the old planks. But what was inside was way more interesting.

Besides tools ranging from axes to shovels and pliers, he'd also found a fixed electricity generator, with enough diesel to run for a few days, and he managed to turn it on.

They were well fed, as Maria and Lili had put together a good meal, and their other needs were also solved, as the toilet had water pumped by the electricity coming from the generator.

Things were looking up, until Maria started coughing again.

"That doesn't sound too good," said Dan. "You should go to bed. I suggest you sleep close to the fire, to be warm. A good sweat should help you feel better by tomorrow."

"Yes," said Maria. "I'll take some pills as well. Ugh, I don't feel that well. I'm so sorry. I'm such a burden now," she added, almost crying.

"Don't worry, honey," answered Dan quickly. "We're all burdens from time to time. It's just a matter of sticking together." He continued, smiling. "Go to bed and you'll be better tomorrow. Actually…" He turned to the rest of the group. "Let's we all go to bed and get some rest. Tomorrow we have to walk several miles again."

* * *

They didn't walk the next day.

Maria took a turn for the worse. She coughed all night, her breath heavy, and in the morning, she had a fever.

She couldn't move.

"We can stay here for a few days, until you get well," said Dan. "We still have food, there's enough firewood to last us a few weeks at least, and the generator has a few good days-worth of diesel. Lili, can you put out some breakfast?"

As they ate, Andrei checked his phone.

"Damn it," he mumbled.

"What?" asked Lili.

"I hoped maybe out here we'd have a signal. But no, nothing, not even internet. At least I can use the electricity from the generator to charge it from a wall socket, to add some extra juice. In case, you know, we get to a place with internet connection."

"Mom, do you want something to eat?" asked Lili, turning to Maria.

Maria, who was lying by the fire, was paler than usual. She glanced up. "No, I'm not hungry. What are you guys having?"

"I've put together some of the cold cuts with some cheese, and, of course, a few bell peppers, onions, and some green salad. You know, the healthy stuff, as we need our vitamins. Are you sure you don't want some peppers?"

"Wow, you outdid yourself," said Andrei, taking his eyes off his phone and looking at the table for the first time. "How did you manage to bring all this food?"

"You know how good I am at squeezing things into luggage," said Lili, smiling at him. "Why do you think our backpacks were so heavy?"

Andrei looked at Lili in admiration for a few seconds, as she turned again toward her mother.

"So, Mom, do you want some peppers, salad, anything?"

"No, no, thank you. I don't like the smell of it. Especially those onions. They really stink," said Maria, and she turned her back to them.

"Well," said Andrei, feeling targeted by that remark, "they're fresh. That's how onions smell, and..."

Lili looked at him, her expression urging him to shut up.

"... anyway, let me move them to the side, away from you," he ended, a bit grumpily.

* * *

"Let's go out and stretch," said Lili to Andrei and Mat, a few hours later. "We need to move. The fresh air will do us good."

"Ugh, I'm not sure that will help," said Andrei, who was sitting on a chair. "I mean, we walked a lot yesterday. I've even got muscle cramps from all that walking in the snow."

"You call a few miles a lot?" asked Lili, grinning.

"Pfft," said Andrei. "But I guess you're right. Fine, let me get dressed."

"We can throw snowballs and maybe build a fort, Daddy," said Matei, eagerly putting on his jacket.

"Yeah, I guess," said Andrei.

* * *

"How are you, my love?" said Dan, gently caressing Maria's forehead once they were alone in the cabin.

"Ugh, I'm sick. I don't feel well. I'm sorry," she said, tearing up.

"Don't be. Really. It's not your fault. We pushed you too much. If it's anyone's fault, it's ours."

"I should pray," she added, sighing. "And I fear... I remember what the priest was telling us. These things, what happened to—" Maria suddenly stopped talking, interrupted by a long coughing episode.

"Hey, relax," said Dan. "Don't talk. Just relax." He continued to caress his wife. "You need to rest."

* * *

"You're dead!" said Matei, as one of his snowballs hit Andrei's chest. "Five–nil to me."

"Yeah, well, I just let you win," said Andrei, throwing a snowball but missing his son by a few feet. "Eh, this snow is not good for snowballs. Look, it sticks to my gloves, that's why I miss you so often."

"I don't think so," said Mat, hitting his dad once more. "Six–nil!"

"Okay, let's stop," said Andrei, panting as he bent to grab some more snow. "I'm starting to feel some pain in my back."

"But Dad, I want to—"

"Hey, leave your dad alone," said Lili, who was walking around the yard, taking deep breaths. "You know he has a bad back."

"Ugh," said Mat, throwing his last snowball to the ground. "What do we do now?"

"Why don't you tell me the last thing you learned in school."

"But I don't want to."

"Come on," said Andrei, squatting and kissing him. "I bet I already know whatever they taught you, since, you know, I invented all science."

"You don't know."

"Try me."

"Okay… did you know that tigers are so rare now they have to ask them to make babies with lions?"

"Really?" asked Andrei, moving his eyebrows. "Is that a joke?"

"No. A friend read it in a book."

"What friend?"

"A friend. You don't know her. She's in my class."

"Oh, a girlfriend," said Andrei, smiling.

"No, she's not my girlfriend," said Mat quickly.

"Why not?"

"Dad!"

"Hey, let him be," said Lili, who was now moving around them, as if she wanted to hear the story.

"Hey, why are you so protective of him?" asked Andrei, looking at her. "You're the one who pushed your mother not to 'put four hats on him when going out'," he said, trying to mimic her voice. "And you always complain about how our parents were overprotective of us."

"Yeah, I do believe people in this country pamper their children. But that's different."

"I do remember," said Andrei, seeming not to hear Lili's last sentence, "about one of my trips to France. In a town much like this one. Oh, okay, it was *definitely* different," he added, smiling, "but I mean it was a small town in a hilly area next to some mountains. And it started snowing. And I was the one with the biggest winter jacket, all zipped up, and I felt I needed the hoodie *on top* of my beanie. While the French, oh my God, most of them couldn't be bothered to even put on a hat. And their jackets were partially unzipped."

"Yes, that's exactly it," said Lili. "That's unfathomable for a lot of people here. And as for my mother, you would never see her outside if it snows or rains. I guess we tend to do that, to fear the elements and to overprotect our children. It's how we were raised. We probably do it to our son as well."

"So maybe we should stop doing it." Andrei nodded with a superior smile.

"Yeah, well, we've talked about this a lot," said Lili, "and I think we're already trying. We're doing better than our parents, that's for sure."

"Hey! I was telling you something," said Matei, pushing his dad's shoulder.

"Yes, yes," said Andrei. "Sorry. You said tigers are now making babies with lions? So what do they get, umm, tigons?" he asked, with a smirk.

"No," said Matei, pondering. "I think she used a different word."

"Ligers then?"

"Yes!"

"Really?" said Andrei, his brows drawn together. "Are you mocking me?"

"No. Really!" said Matei, nodding. "She told us that. She knows everything about tigers."

"Hmm," said Andrei, still not certain about the truth of the information. "I don't know. I've never heard about that."

"Should we go in?" asked Lili. "I think we've had enough fresh air and exercise."

* * *

"I need my priest," said Maria, as her latest coughing episode ended.

"Come on, don't talk like that," said Dan. "You'll get better, you'll see. I don't even want to think about an alternative."

"You know our priest said this could happen?" said Maria, now in a different tone.

"What? That old—"

"I know you don't like him," said Maria. "But he talked about this. He said the devil works his evil and he's never tired. And what happened to our neighbors—"

"We don't know what happened to our neighbors," said Dan, kissing her. "We still don't know."

"Well, he knew," she said, tearing up. "He told us to be ready for the Last Judgement. And I think now it's my turn."

"Don't worry about these things," said Dan gently, as Lili opened the cabin door. "You'll be fine. You'll see. Just rest and all will be okay."

"How are you, Mom?" asked Lili once she'd entered the room, followed by Andrei and Mat.

"I'm fine," said Maria, holding in a few coughs. "Don't you worry about me. I'll be fine."

* * *

When night came, things weren't looking good. Maria was sick. Really sick.

She had a fever, and she was white as a sheet.

She'd had no food the entire day.

"Hey, Mom," said Lili, approaching Maria with a large plate. "You need to eat something. I have some cheese and vegetables."

"Ugh," said Maria, shaking her head. "It stinks. Something stinks horribly."

"What? Nothing stinks. Everything is fresh. I picked the best pieces myself. Here, try a bit of cheese."

Maria took a few bites, yet she pushed away the rest of it.

"Have some veget—"

"Those vegetables stink! Especially the onions! They are rotten. Take them away from me! Are you trying to poison me?"

Andrei and Lili looked at each other, startled.

"All the vegetables are fresh," Lili repeated in a soft voice, after a moment of hesitation. "Why are you so angry?"

"Let me be," said Maria. Then she turned her face away, continuing to mumble a few things until she was interrupted by a long coughing episode.

"The onions are fresh. Why is she so angry?" whispered Andrei to Lili.

All Lili could do was shake her head.

* * *

In the morning, things were worse.

Maria's fever was running high, and no medicine seemed to help. They didn't have many options available, besides what they had taken from home and the few bits they'd found in the cabinet.

"Honey," whispered Andrei to Lili. "What if… you know… What if your mother…"

"Don't you dare say it!" said Lili, her eyes watering. "Don't you say it!"

"I mean, sorry, honey, of course we don't want that to happen! But what if…"

"What if what? She's just sick. It's the flu, and we'll probably all get it. We'll all be worse until we're better. And that's that."

"Okay, fine. I mean… I think we need to understand what happened to everyone else. And why—"

"Why what? Why are we okay so far? Is that what you mean? As far as I recall, that was a stupid subject and we needed to focus on the relevant things. So, what are the relevant things?" said Lili, with anger in her eyes.

"Well, we were both right. Now it seems it's relevant to understand why this… this thing didn't happen to us in the first place."

"Pfft!" scoffed Lili, and walked away.

* * *

That evening, Maria felt even worse.

Her breath was heavy and accelerated. She was making a cavernous sound, and for every breath she took a snarl came out of her throat.

She sounded kind of like—

Andrei quickly pushed that thought away.

Dan was clearly concerned. He sat beside Maria, covering her forehead with a wet cloth. Sometimes he talked to her, trying to give her strength.

Lili moved quietly in the background, trying to find things to do and keep her mind busy. She put some food on the table, but just like for the last few dinners, she kept the onions away.

"Don't we get some onions?" asked Andrei.

"No," came the short answer.

"Me and Dan, we can eat them outside," he continued.

"Do as you wish."

No way around it.

He took a few pieces and shared them with Dan, who seemed happy to get a few bites with his sausage.

Matei didn't quite understand what was happening, but it was clear to him that he needed to be quiet.

Maria's fever was very high. So high, you couldn't even talk to her. Mostly she slept, sometimes twitching.

And those breathing sounds.

The end was coming.

* * *

As he opened his eyes early the next morning, Andrei looked around.

Dan lay next to Maria, sleeping. Lili and Matei were in each other's arms, in their sleeping bag on the floor, right behind the table.

And Maria... Maria was whiter than ever. Maria wasn't moving. Maria wasn't making a sound.

Maria was dead.

As the reality settled in, a thought crept into Andrei's mind.

He slowly reached for his baseball bat, pulling it closer.

And he waited.

10 REALITY HITS

D an was the first to move.
He turned face up, yawning heavily while scratching his chest.

As he shifted around in his sleeping bag, a noise rose.

It was a growl. That bear-like growl.

And it was coming from his left.

"Maria?" he said, and turned.

* * *

Maria tried to get up. She was on her side, facing Dan. Her hands were inside her sleeping bag, and she was trying to push herself up.

Her face was white. Her eyes were blank, looking past everything and everyone.

Matei awoke, saw his grandma, and started screaming. Lili followed suit.

This made Maria fully active, and it was a good thing for everyone that she was locked inside the sleeping bag.

Andrei, however, was already up, bat in hand.

"Don't you do it!"

Dan's voice was deep and commanding, and Andrei froze.

"She's not dead; she's not like them. Give that to me!" he said, and took the bat.

Maria was squirming in her sleeping bag. Sooner or later she would break free.

The growls were relentless, and it felt like the small cabin was amplifying the sound even further.

"What do we do, then?" asked Andrei, looking around for the other bat. "Should we hold her down? Maybe give her a sedative?" He was uncomfortable speaking his mind. Maria looked and behaved just like the teacher's wife, but they didn't want to hear that. Especially not Dan.

"Let's be quiet. All of us," said Dan.

A good thought, really. This would prove Andrei's fears. Or not. Silence fell.

Silence was usually good. Not now, however, as the proof was there. Everybody thought it, though no one said it: Maria had turned into one of those things.

"Do we—" Matei asked.

"Shh!" Lili covered his mouth.

But it was enough to start Maria moving again.

Matei started crying, and Lili quickly took him outside.

Once Maria settled, the others crept out of the cabin.

"What do we do?" asked Andrei, taking in gulps of the fresh morning air.

"We need to find a way to save her," said Lili. "There must be a cure." She then turned to Matei, who was squeezing her leg. "Hush, Mat, it's all right. Grandma is a little sick, but she'll be okay."

"What can we do? You saw how all those pills didn't work. And we don't know what's causing this. Therefore, we don't know how to fix it."

"Well, good thing we focused on relevant information!" snapped Lili.

"Look," said Andrei, peacefully. "We've all been thinking, for quite some time now, on what could have caused this. And, especially, why we're safe. More precisely, why we used to be safe. And none of us has any idea. So, I'm not the enemy here. Really, I know as much as you do."

"Yeah… you're not the enemy," said Lili, collapsing into his arms, crying. "My mother is dead."

"I know, honey, I know."

Squeezed between them, Matei started coughing.

"Hell no!" said Lili, crouching next to him. "Matei, how do you feel?"

"I'm fine. I'm okay, Mommy, really," he said, while coughing, tears coming down his little cheeks.

Reality suddenly sunk in, and Andrei was hit. He looked around. This was his family: Lili, Matei, even Dan. Maria was also his family. And she was in the cabin, dead. Or transformed. Or whatever you wanted to call it. But she was no more.

Something needed to be done. And quick.

"We must get her out of the house," said Dan suddenly.

They all turned to him.

"Why?" asked Lili.

"She's... she has this sickness. And with us around, making noise, she won't stop until she's out of her sleeping bag. And we need the cabin to take care of Matei. There's no other way; we need to get Maria out," answered Dan.

Lili nodded.

"How? And out where?" asked Andrei.

* * *

Dan snuck into the cabin. Maria started squirming as soon as the door squeaks woke her.

He looked around, not moving. How could he take her outside?

He could release her from the sleeping bag, but that would mean they'd have to chase her. And then somehow hold her until she settled.

In that scenario, he might eventually be forced to hit her, just like he did to the teacher's family back at the apartment. And he couldn't do that to Maria, ever.

Then he had an idea.

* * *

The door opened and Dan emerged, pulling the sleeping bag with him, his right hand holding Maria's head. In the bag, Maria squirmed and growled, trying to bite. It was a good, tough sleeping bag, though, and it held things together in a way that allowed him to advance.

She was heavy, but he was strong.

He looked around for a moment, then spotted a suitable place.

"Where are you taking her?" asked Lili.

"I first considered placing her in the shed, so she would have some protection from the elements, but the generator would have kept her awake. And this sleeping bag isn't indestructible. So, I'll take her to the left of the cabin, near the forest."

"Yeah, at some point she would break free," said Lili.

"Indeed. I feel better knowing she'll be sleeping, rather than growling and squirming, eventually injuring herself," said Dan, sighing.

"She would have frozen in that flimsy shed as well, anyway," said Lili, stepping toward her husband.

Dan stopped for a few moments, following his daughter with his gaze and taking a deep breath. *She'll probably freeze, but she'll survive, just like that one on the bridge. She'll be alive. Won't she? And then, when the cure is found, we can come back and save her. But what if freezing her reduces the chance for a cure? What if the only way to keep her curable is to keep her warm?*

As these thoughts went through his mind, he lost his focus. His grip on Maria's head slipped, and she bit his right hand, right at the thumb joint.

"Ahh!" yelled Dan.

"What's wrong?" screamed Lili, turning around. She, Mat and Andrei were by the right-hand side of the cabin near the shed, holding one another.

"She bit me!"

Luckily, he had his trusty gloves on: thick, heavy, leather gloves. Maria had a strong bite, but not strong enough for her worn teeth to go through the material. However, the bite *was* powerful enough to cause acute pain in his right hand.

He swung his arm, trying to break free, but Maria did not let go. Growling, pale, empty-eyed, she simply moved her head to match his movements, grinding his hand with her teeth.

"I'll go help," said Andrei, breaking free from Lili's arms.

"Take care," she said, getting down and hugging Matei.

Andrei arrived, but he seemed afraid to touch his mother-in-law, so he just moved around awkwardly, while Dan tried to break free.

Dan let go of the sleeping bag and used his free hand to push against Maria's forehead, while pulling his right hand away from her mouth.

He finally got free, and now, with Andrei's help, dragged Maria to that place he'd chosen for her. Then they all moved back into the house.

"Ugh! This really hurts," said Dan, while carefully locking the door behind them.

When he took off his glove, he could see the bruise already forming. The teeth hadn't penetrated, so there was no blood, but the hand looked swollen and was very painful.

He tried to feel his bones, slowly, to see if anything was broken, but the pain was too strong. He'd ice it for now and would check again later.

As he headed toward the door, to get some snow from outside, Lili started coughing.

* * *

"Oh my God," said Andrei, sinking into a chair. "Honey, are you okay?"

"Yeah, I'm fabulous."

"I mean... how do you feel?"

"Well, I'm coughing. And I feel a bit sick. So, yeah, I'll die in about three days, I guess," said Lili, faking a smile.

"Wow, honey, your best joke yet. What you've got now might be a completely different thing."

"Yeah, keep telling yourself that."

"We'll find a cure. We'll find a way to stop it. See, me and Dan, we're fine. We'll find a way!" said Andrei, looking at Dan.

Dan was staring into the fire. He wasn't listening.

11 CREEPING DEATH

The day passed by, and the next morning, Lili and Matei were visibly sicker.

They lay by the fire, coughing, in high fever. And their faces were white—way paler than usual.

Dan was lost. He barely ate, and he was useless.

Andrei paced the cabin. He had ideas. He ran scenarios in his head. What was he doing that they were not doing? Why was he okay when everyone else was turning into those things? What had changed with Maria, Lili or Matei that stopped them from being protected?

All good questions.

All without an answer.

"Why am I okay?" he asked himself aloud.

"What was that, honey?" asked Lili.

"I said, why am I okay. I was thinking out loud. Sorry, hon. Relax."

"Well, that's simple," came the answer, followed by a short giggle. "It's because you're fat."

"Ha-ha," said Andrei. He looked at her fondly. He really loved her jokes, even if they focused mostly on one subject.

* * *

When evening came, Andrei remembered he was hungry.

"Do you guys want to eat something? Lili, Matei, you need sustenance," he said, with hope in his voice.

"No, I'm not hungry," said Lili, coughing. "Maybe Mat is."

"No," he said, in a tiny voice.

He was usually so alive. Even when he'd had a high fever in the past, he'd been more active. Now, he just lay there in his mother's arms.

As Andrei set out some of the food on the table, he realized they were running out of supplies. They had enough left for about three or four days, but out here, in the middle of nowhere, there were no options for finding extra. Food was becoming a precious commodity.

When they reached Grandma's house, there should be plenty of other houses around, and probably most would have food.

Okay, they might need to fight off some of those things, but between him and Dan, they could do it.

Dan still looked vacant. He kept touching his injured hand, absentminded, unreliable. For now. He'd be back. He'd be okay as soon as Lili and Matei got better.

But they didn't look better. They were paler, sicker, and the coughing was getting worse.

Their breaths seemed to be more and more like a snarl.

Don't think that. Don't think that. Think of a way to fix this.

As he opened one of the food containers, Lili said with disgust, "What the hell is that stench?"

He looked at her. Then he looked at the casserole dish. Then back at her.

Can it be that simple?

He took some of the cucumbers and bell peppers, put them on a plate, and moved closer to Lili. "How do they smell?"

"Better," she said. "But that onion stinks. It went rotten. You should throw it out. God it stinks!"

"So, this stink?" asked Andrei, bringing the fresh onions closer to her nose.

"Yes, idiot. What have I told you? Take that shit away from me!"

He returned to the table.

It is that simple!

"It's the onions," murmured Andrei. "It's the onions!"

"What?" Lili grumbled.

"It's the onions. Don't you see?" He jumped out of his chair. "You now hate them! Maria hated them when she had the fever. People who get sick hate onions."

"So? This is stupid. You hate tomatoes, but is that the reason you are not making any sense?"

"What have Dan and I done this entire time?" continued Andrei, ignoring her. "We ate onions. I had onions every day, with almost every meal. Dan as well! He loves onions, so he ate them daily. And we are fine."

"I had some onions as well," said Lili, coughing.

"You also had onions *at first*, but not for a couple of days now, right? You, Matei and Maria are not so fond of them, so maybe you didn't have any recently."

"We all had. We had that stew, and it has a lot of onions in it."

"Yes, but I think they need to be fresh, not cooked. You didn't eat any fresh ones, did you?"

"No, now that I think of it, that's true, I didn't. But why were we sick a week ago, then less sick, and now sick again?" asked Lili, trying to turn toward him. "You remember we got it and then it went away. Now we have it again."

"Well, think about it. You and Matei both had what looked like a minor cold right before coming to visit your parents. We had that big onion salad with the roast lamb, and you guys had a few bites of it. Luckily you are so fond of the greens and eating healthy food that you had some even though it was clear you didn't like it that much. And remember how you had to push Mat to have a few bites?"

"True. I remember it tasted a bit funny. That onion was turning bad."

"Not true! It was good and fresh. I think this is it," said Andrei enthusiastically. "You probably threw away good onions."

"Okay," said Lili, ignoring that last part, "so we got better, but—"

"Yes, so, the next day, you're better. Then we get here for the holidays. It all makes sense."

"Okay, but how about Mom?"

"Remember, we heard Maria had been a bit sick before our visit, and I bet they had some onions, fresh onions, and she got better right after. Then, shit hits the fan, with the neighbors and the bear noises and the zombies and everything."

Lili seemed too focused and too sick today to tell him he needed to mind his language. She did catch another word though.

"I thought you said zombies didn't exist."

"Yeah, I used the term just for you to understand what I'm talking about," said Andrei. "Anyway, getting back to our topic... We ran away from the town and ended up in this place. Here, we probably spent less time thinking about healthy food. We were all worried about Maria, and you stopped giving us onions, not wanting to annoy her with the 'stench'. The same with Mat. You probably let him be. While me and Dan, we had some on the side."

Lili was quiet, clearly thinking it through.

"It all makes sense," pressed Andrei. "Maria didn't have onions for a while and she got sick. Then, she hated them. Remember how she said they were rotten, just like you did?"

"Okay, but why isn't everybody else better? I mean, we're not the only ones eating onions in the entire town, right?"

"True, but even I'm not quite in the mood for onions like I used to be," said Andrei. A revelation hit. "I think we all have some sort of disease which is kept in check with onions. That's why it makes us stay away from them, as a simple yet effective defense mechanism."

"Defense mechanism?" asked Lili in a skeptical tone. "Is this from a game of yours?"

"No! Look. The disease is eradicated by some substance in the onions. Fresh onions. It takes over your body and makes you hate said onions, so you don't want to eat them. That's the defense mechanism."

Lili continued to look at him, her lip wrinkled with distrust.

"For me and Dan, who are extremely fond of onions and are in the habit of eating them with every meal, we've continued to do so. A little less, I agree. But for others, like you, Mat and Maria, not so much. When the sickness kicks in, the effect is even more powerful and you think they stink," concluded Andrei, victorious. "You perceive them to be rotten, even though they are fresh."

"Feed them onions," said Dan, life back in his eyes.

12 FEEDING TIME

"You have to eat it!" said Andrei, shoving a forkful of onion in Lili's face.

"No! This stinks. It's rotten. You cannot expect me to eat that."

She was sweaty. Her fever was high and wasn't going down with medication. She was getting close to that point in which you either fainted or started speaking nonsense. She couldn't be reasoned with. At least not easily.

"Look," said Andrei, peaceably. "I just walked you through my argument. Okay, it's not a perfect rationale; it has issues. If you want, we can take some time and go over them later. Until then, please, have some onions. Look at them. I swear to God, they are fresh. They are not rotten. Look!" He pushed the fork closer to Lili.

Lili stopped for a moment; it seemed like he was finally getting through to her. She looked at the onions, then back at him.

"No!" she yelled. "No. You are trying to feed me rotten food. You are trying to poison me. Why are you doing this? Why?" As her strength left her, she fell back onto her sleeping bag.

Andrei looked around, searching for help. Mat lay beside Lili, in the same sleeping bag. He was quiet, and it looked like he was having trouble keeping his eyes open. His breathing was getting worse as his sickness advanced.

Dan stood nearby watching. "Look, honey. Maria... Maria is how she is because we didn't know that onions would help. This

73

will help you." He grabbed her by the shoulders and continued. "We are your family. I want you to live. I cannot lose all of you." His usually powerful voice trembled.

Lili stopped fighting again, looking at him and then at Andrei. Andrei smiled, trying to be charming, while Dan had tears running down his face.

"Fine," she said, reaching for the fork. "Give that crap to me. I swear to God, you'll pay if it doesn't work." And she took the whole bite.

She started chewing, but immediately gagged. As she almost vomited, Dan covered her mouth, holding the onion in until she swallowed.

"You... you... you bastards!" yelled Lili, eyes wide, surprised by the move. "How dare you give me that rotten shit?"

"It's not rotten!" said Andrei, losing patience. "It's not rotten. We're saving your life, and you need to take some more."

"Take some more? Take some more? When I get better, I'll kick your lying ass. Just wait and see."

While she was spitting out those words, Matei's head drooped to one side. His eyes were closed, his breathing accelerated, and a soft snarl could be heard.

Time was running short.

"Let's take him," said Andrei, and he moved toward Mat.

Lili watched them with hate in her eyes. For a moment, it looked like she was assessing whether to hit them. Andrei started to pull Mat out of the sleeping bag, slowly, keeping an eye on Lili, trying not to make any sudden moves.

Man was he hot! Matei's body was so warm it was little wonder he'd passed out.

"He's out! We're too late!" said Andrei, almost crying. "What can we do?" he turned frantically to Dan.

"Well, that's easy," said Dan. "We need to feed him onions."

"Now I know where Lili gets it from," said Andrei, trying a quick joke in a vague attempt to calm his nerves. "How do we feed it to him though? He's passed out. Should we try to lower his temperature first? We can't make him eat anything in this condition. And you saw how Lili acted when we tried to reason with her. How can we expect to get through to a seven-year-old?"

"Let's feed him, nevertheless," said Dan. "How do you feed small children?"

"But they want to be fed," Andrei protested; however, it gave him an idea. "How about we mash them into a paste?"

"Yeah, that could work," said Dan. "But he needs to swallow. And he doesn't look like he can do that."

"Okay then. What if we make it less dry; actually, very close to a creamy soup. Then we just feed him teaspoons, and that way, he'll swallow," said Andrei, more and more confident in the idea.

"Right. But make sure you don't really make a soup. The onions need to be fresh. Maria had plenty of food with cooked onions, and we all know what happened to her," said Dan.

They cut the onion into small pieces. It was the smallest slice-and-dice Andrei had ever done. *A world record for sure,* he thought briefly.

Now it needed extra water. Not too much. Just enough to make it soupy.

Perfect. The smell was strong; his eyes were hurting. But no matter. His son would get better.

He inched the teaspoon toward his son's mouth. Mat was lying over Andrei's legs, his head raised and his mouth open.

Andrei maneuvered Mat's head a little higher; then he poured the onion-liquid into his mouth.

There was a small interruption in Mat's breathing as he swallowed, and then he resumed snarling.

A few tears stung his eyes, but he pushed himself to think positively. *This is easy. We can do this!* Andrei forced a smile and moved the second teaspoon toward Mat's mouth.

Ten minutes later, all the onion 'soup' was gone. The operation had been a success.

Now, they had to hope they were not too late. And they still needed to deal with Lili.

For the last half an hour, Lili had watched as they prepared the concoction and then fed it to their child.

The entire time, she didn't seem to get any worse. In fact, she looked slightly better.

Just slightly, as her temperature remained high, her breathing affected.

But still, slightly better.

"Do you have any more of those shitty, stinky onions?" she said in a defeated tone, looking at her husband.

His smile filled the entire room.

* * *

"This was a bad idea!" She pushed the fork away once more.

"Look, we've been through this. You can see you're a little better. It's because of that bite we forced you to have. You can see it actually helped you. Just take this," said Andrei, and thrust the fork toward her again.

"What if I throw up? You know I hate vomiting. I hate it!" yelled Lili, resisting.

"Well, honey, you won't. And even if it happens, you still need to eat this. This will cure you," said Andrei, growing ever more exasperated.

"How do we know this actually works? This is a stupid idea. Don't you understand it stinks? It stinks! It's the worst food ever. It's rotten, and it's not helping anyone."

"Mommy?" chimed in a tiny voice behind them.

"Mat! Mat! How do you feel?" Andrei ran to him.

"I'm okay, Dad. I feel okay."

Indeed, when Andrei touched his forehead, it was obvious his temperature, though still high, was dropping. His breathing sounded normal, and his eyes were alive again. He was slowly returning to his old self.

"Well, we gave you quite a lot of onion, big guy. I guess we cured you," said Andrei, really proud of himself. "As we all know, onions are really healthy, and everyone should—"

"Stop yapping and give me those onions," said Lili, with a heavy sigh but one laced with clarity.

Andrei rushed the fork to her, and she chewed and swallowed. Her gag reflex kicked in, but she forced the mouthful down.

"One more," she said, and it was the best thing Andrei had heard in what seemed like forever.

* * *

The two men sat by the fire, lost in their thoughts.

Dan had unearthed some bottles of whiskey—a hidden stash. Probably given to the woodsmen in return for turning a blind eye to people stealing wood, thought Andrei. It wasn't the best whiskey, but it was certainly better than nothing.

As they sipped from their glasses, a feeling of contentment and safety surrounded them.

Lili and Mat were sleeping; they were taking those good, deep breaths that a healthy sleeping person takes. God, how nice it was to hear that breathing.

"That was… intense," said Andrei, breaking the silence. "We've been through so much in such a short time. Especially them." Then he saw Dan's expression and realized his mistake.

"Look…," tried Andrei, hesitantly. He wasn't good at connecting with people. That was always Lili's job. "Look… we know what happened. I can only scratch the surface of how you must feel… but what you did, what she did… meant these two have a chance now."

Dan's eyes slowly came back to life as Andrei continued, a little more confidently. "If it weren't for her sacrifice, the sacrifice that made us understand and find the cure, if it wasn't for your determination and willpower, we would all be dead. Or maybe something even worse than dead. All three of us." He gestured toward Mat and Lili. "And for this, for this gift, we'll always be grateful."

It was a good speech. A little on the mushy side, but still, he'd tried.

And it seemed Dan got the message. He even smiled, raised his glass in the international sign of 'Cheers!', and took a bigger sip.

"Thank you, too, Andrei. You found that cure, you and your stupid onion obsession," he said, and they both laughed.

"Now," said Dan, becoming more serious, "we just need to make sure we have enough onions."

13 TRIP TO GRANDMA'S HOUSE

"Who wants more onion?" said Andrei the next morning, offering the plate around. "Take them while they're fresh."

The whole family was gathered around one of the desks, which they were using as a dinner table.

"I want some, thank you," said Lili, smiling.

"Matei?" said Andrei.

"No, I don't want onions."

"You need to eat onions at every meal, honey," said Lili, taking one piece from the plate. "Look, have a smaller one."

"But, Mom, I don't want onions now. I like onions, but why do we have to eat them all time? I don't want them!" Mat wrapped his arms around his body. "No more onions! No more onions! No more onions!"

"Look, son. You need to eat onions to stay healthy. There is a… flu going around," said Lili, while looking at Andrei with a question in her eyes, "a flu that…"

"A flu that makes you very, very sick and can even kill you," took over Andrei. "We want you to be happy and live a long life, so it's important you eat one piece of onion at every meal," he concluded.

Lili stared at him, full of criticism.

"Well," said Andrei loudly, "Mat is a big boy now and he needs to hear the truth."

Lili seemed placated by that explanation, and she moved on to quarrel with Mat over who should cut the pieces of meat on his plate.

* * *

"So, what do we do?" said Andrei. "This is not a bad place to be," he continued, looking around the cabin. "Okay, it's small, and we could use an extra room. But we have heat, water, and there are no… sick people around."

"We don't have food," argued Lili, closing the fridge and coming to sit with the others.

"There is that, yes," picked up Andrei. "I realized it yesterday, when you guys were sick. We have enough food for three to four days."

"We're out of food, Mommy?" asked Matei, turning his cute eyes toward her.

"Maybe only three to four meals." Lili turned to her son. "Don't worry sweetie; we have enough. We just have to eat a little less, so we have enough for a long time."

"Well, big guys eat a lot," said Andrei, proudly.

"You sure are big," concluded Lili, grinning.

Andrei scoffed, but he tempered it with a smile. "And you sure are small. And annoying. Yet, cute. So, we need food. Other than that, we have everything."

"And some diesel," intervened Dan. "That generator won't go on forever with no fuel. I'm impressed it's lasted this long. And finally, even if there are some unwanted neighbors we have to… get rid of, it's always better to have other houses, stores, and preferably storage places around. And let's not forget: we need onions. Lots of onions. That means we need to leave as soon as possible."

"Yes, but still," said Lili, "we've just been through a horrible experience, me and Mat…" She trailed off, hesitating. A few seconds later, she came back from her thoughts. "We need to stay a while and make sure we're okay. Especially Mat. We can't traipse through the snow with a kid who just had a very high fever. I guess two or three days should tell us if we're okay."

"But what do we do about food?" asked Andrei.

"Figured you would be the one to ask," said Lili. "If we eat smart, we can even squeeze close to one week with what we have left. We should be fine. It will be like following a diet. And I'll make sure the portions are the right size. Being warm will help, as we'll need fewer calories, so let's make sure the fire is always burning."

Andrei muttered. Now she wasn't that cute. He always ate 'normal' quantities. "Just make sure you keep in mind the weight we have when you size the portions!" he said, frowning.

* * *

The next three days passed by fast.

Andrei tried his phone every now and then. He was an only child and wanted to reach his parents. They had mentioned they had caught some cold when he spoke with them the day before they left for Lili's parents' place. *What if they had what Maria*— No, he needed to push away that thought. Unfortunately, he didn't have a network signal, so he couldn't reach anyone. But he kept on trying.

During the day, Lili spent more and more time playing outside with Mat, moving around, trying to relax. They were taking it slowly, but Mat seemed fully recovered, and so was she. She was always careful to play quietly, on the far right side of the property, though, not on the left where her mother was.

At night, Lili spent a lot of time in Andrei's arms, crying herself to sleep. She was so small and tiny, and Andrei used a lot of his strength not to cry as well.

Dan didn't cry. Dan, as far as Andrei was concerned, was lost. He seemed to be thinking, but he looked haggard and Andrei would bet anything his mind was blank. It was as if someone had taken his happiness and replaced it with emptiness.

* * *

At the end of the three days, they prepared to depart.

"Should we leave the cabin unlocked, in case we need to come back?" asked Andrei.

"Yeah, it's better, I guess," said Dan. "We never discussed if we're the only 'normal' people around. But if we are, it looks like these things don't move unless there's a noise. So, it should be okay to leave the door unlocked."

"About the noise..." intervened Lili. "Shouldn't we stop the generator?"

Dan went to cut the power, and as the generator turned off, a growl, together with a hissing sound, started from where they'd left Maria.

Lili and Andrei, who were in front of the cabin heard her faintly. They looked at each other, and Andrei experienced a thrill of fear.

"What if something is closing in and Maria heard it, like a guard dog?" he asked, inching closer to Lili.

They looked around, but they couldn't see anything.

"Maybe it was a strong burst of wind. Or maybe a bird," said Lili. "I don't hear anything else out of the ordinary."

As Dan closed the shed, Maria fell silent again.

"I think he didn't hear it," said Lili, whispering quickly. "Let's not tell him anything. He finally looks more like his old self."

"Yeah," said Andrei quickly, "good idea. Let's keep it that way. Hey, Dan. Ready to go?" he said louder, as Dan rejoined them.

As they exited through the gate, they took a good look at their surroundings. The road to Grandma's village lay to the right, the one to their old town on the left.

It had started snowing again, fresh snow settling atop the existing layer.

"Bye house," said Andrei out loud as they started walking.

"Where is Grandma?" asked Mat suddenly.

"We're going there, sweetie," answered Lili.

"No, I mean Grandma Maria."

"Oh... she's... sick and cannot come," said Lili, looking to Andrei for help.

"Well, why don't we give her some onions then?" continued Mat.

The group stopped.

Dan, who was in front, turned and looked back toward the cabin.

"Well, why not?" pushed Mat.

"Well." Andrei felt the need to answer. "We... we're not... I mean, we don't know if..."

Dan started walking back to the cabin with a heavy and

confident step.

"We'll think about it," concluded Andrei. "Thank you for the idea, Mat!" and he also turned back, followed by the others.

* * *

"She seems... frozen," whispered Andrei as he and Dan surveyed the body a few moments later.

Maria lay in the snow, inside her sleeping bag, face up. Fresh snow was already settling over her, and in a few hours, it would be difficult to see where she was.

"I guess... we take her in?" he continued. "Maybe let her dry out and heat up, then, just like with Mat, feed her some onions?"

Dan nodded, and slowly approached the body.

As he moved closer, snow and ice cracked under his heavy boots.

One step, two steps, inching towards Maria.

That's when the body came back to life, growling and hissing cutting through the silence.

The sound cut their hearts as well, and Mat, who stood some distance away with Lili, started crying, "I'm afraid! I'm afraid, Mommy, I'm afraid!"

Andrei tightened his grip on the baseball bat in his hand, while Lili tried to calm Mat. His wife and son were far from Maria, but clearly not far enough.

* * *

Dan picked up the pace and got close to the body.

Just like the guy on the bridge, Maria couldn't move, being frozen.

However, just like that guy, there was shaking. Something inside her was very much alive, and it was pushing the body to move.

Dan moved next to her head. He was now facing the length of the sleeping bag, looking down at what used to be Maria.

He took out his scarf, and with it he removed some of the snow from Maria's face.

What he saw paralyzed him. Her face, her beautiful face, was frozen. It was very white, mouth and eyes open. The mouth had some powdered snow in it, while the eyes... The eyes were cutting right though Dan. Her bright eyes, the ones he loved to get lost in, were now like two round pieces of ice. They were milky-white and empty. They looked like toy marbles. How can he ever expect to see them alive again? Dan shivered.

* * *

"So, everyone, what do we do? Do we get her inside?" said Andrei loudly. Everyone was confused, some were crying, and they all badly needed a reset. "Let's get her in where it's warm."

Andrei's words pulled Dan from his daze, and he grabbed the sleeping bag with both hands and started dragging his cargo toward the cabin.

But his right hand pained him and he couldn't keep hold. On top of that, the sleeping bag was stiffer, because of the ice that had formed inside, making it even more difficult to handle. "I can help," said Andrei, and he put down his bat. "You need to take care of that hand."

* * *

An hour later they were sat around the fire, Maria lying closest to the flames.

"This is going to take a while," said Andrei. "Maria is insulated in the sleeping bag, so parts of her will heat up and defrost slower."

Everyone else kept quiet, staring at the flames that were pulsating from behind the large, frozen package.

"We could open the sleeping bag," he continued, "but we need to make sure we put her back in once she's at normal temperature again. And maybe we'll have to restraint her. I mean, we don't want to be attacked while we sleep, right?

"Or, we can wait it out. Maybe it's better to defrost her slower, the same way she got frozen? For example, what if parts of her core are not frozen yet? For all we know, when they come back to life, something in the chest turns on. What if that part never froze? It's been what, five days? Maybe it makes more sense to reverse the process, basically, that's what I'm saying." He slowed his verbal assault as he realized the others were not willing to be part of the conversation.

"On the other hand, five days should be more than enough to fully freeze a body, or at least that's what I've learned from movies. Oh well, let's wait," he concluded, smiling.

No one smiled back. Maybe also because, due to Andrei's talking, Maria had been growling, hissing and squirming all this time.

* * *

"We cannot sleep in here!" whispered Lili to Dan, so that Mat didn't hear. "At every little noise we make, Mom wakes up. And those sounds... We cannot do it. Mat is just a boy. It's not okay to make him go through this. We need another solution."

Andrei saw them talking and approached. "What's happening?"

"We have a problem," answered Lili. "We cannot live here, not with Mom in this state."

Andrei understood immediately. He'd had the same thoughts; he just hadn't known how to raise the subject, especially following the impact of his 'how to defrost an insulated dead body' speech.

"Indeed. We need to do something."

"Well," snapped Dan, "then do something."

Andrei froze, taken by surprise. Involuntarily he took a step back, throwing startled glances at his father-in-law.

"Yes, *Dad*," said Lili, enunciating carefully, "we need to do something. All this has a big impact on Mat!"

"What do you propose?" said Dan, fire in his eyes. "We take your mother out in the cold again? She just got a little warm, and now we freeze her back up? It's your mother! I cannot believe you're saying that!"

"That's not what I'm saying! However, I'm proposing we take some kind of action, together, so that we can prepare a safe environment for Mat while also helping Mom recover! She's my mom and I want her back. But not at the expense of my child's wellbeing."

Everyone stood quiet. The solution was there. It was simple, but risky at the same time.

"You all need to go on to Grandma's house without me," concluded Dan.

14 ALONE

"Bye, Dad! Take care of yourself! And please, come to Grandma's house as soon as you can. If we find a good 4x4, we'll come pick you up," said Lili, tears in her eyes.

"Bye, Dan. Take care," said Andrei, not being an expert at goodbyes.

"Oh, and mind that drinking. You'll be alone, and drinking can cloud your judgment," concluded Lili.

"Take care of each other. You have the keys, and you'll find enough food for a couple of days. Don't forget, look in the pantry for some canned food. They might be frozen already, I know, but if the cans didn't break open, the food should be okay. You'll need to forage for more supplies afterwards," said Dan. "You might have to fight, so be effective at it. Do not be afraid to hit them. Try to think that they're not human."

"Yes, we will," said Andrei, his eyes widening at the thought of what might lie ahead.

"What happened back there?" asked Lili once they were a few dozen feet away.

"Where? With Dan?"

"Yeah."

"Nothing! I mean... he's always so calm. He just took me by surprise, I guess," said Andrei, carefully selecting his words while not looking at his wife.

"You're afraid of my dad, aren't you?" said Lili, smiling. "Well, don't be," she added, seeing Andrei's face turning red. "He's one of the good guys. Come on, relax. I love you."

* * *

Dan is alone. But not alone. Maria is with him. His beloved wife of over forty years.

Exactly as it should be, she has always taken care of him and now he is taking care of her. Hopefully, sometime in the future, it will be the other way around once more.

It was a long and beautiful life they'd had together. She was beautiful. She still is. He can remember the first day they met, and every day after that.

He was always faithful to her. Even if, as a police officer on the beat, he had a lot of opportunities to meet other women. And you could always tell which ones fancied a man in uniform, especially a man as fit and strong such as Dan.

But Maria was all he needed. And even now, she's all he needs.

* * *

As night advanced, he shifted in his chair. It was enough noise for Maria, lying very close to the fireplace, to become active. She started squirming and, for the first time, turned her head toward him. Her mouth moved, slowly biting the air in front of her.

The bear noise and hissing were still there. Although, the hissing was barely audible, while the growls were stronger than before.

"How are you feeling, honey? Do you still feel cold? Do you want me to turn your other side to the fire? You'll have to eat some onions soon. We have some other food, not too much, but we'll start with onions. When you get better maybe we can cook something? I could try to find a rabbit. You know there are rabbits around here. And then maybe you can make a stew? I've always loved your stews," he said, smiling at the glass next to him.

Maria squirmed, while he kept talking about food, movies, and some nice memories they once shared.

* * *

He woke. When he looked toward the fireplace, he saw Maria, in her sleeping bag, face up, by the fire. It was clearly still the middle of the night, maybe 3 a.m. or thereabouts. He'd fallen asleep at some point, and the whiskey was partly responsible.

He slowly rose and drew nearer to Maria. Her open eyes were looking up, but still they seemed empty. So empty.

Her mouth was open and he could see her tongue lying in an odd position inside.

Her skin was white, oh so white, and she looked… dead.

As he had this thought, in a moment of weakness, he even wished she would stay dead.

He shuffled back a couple of steps and that was enough to rouse her.

She was moving. Boy, was she moving! Like a fish suffocating on dry land, she squirmed and growled.

Her face turned toward him, although she seemed to look through him, and her teeth snapped and snapped.

"I'll start preparing the onions, honey," he said. "You're ready."

The chopping noises kept Maria active. It was incredible what a racket she could make, and for how long.

He took all the steps Andrei had: he cut the onion into very small pieces, put everything into a bowl, and then added some water.

His own version of onion soup was complete!

"It's ready," he said, rising from the chair. "The medicine is ready."

When he reached Maria's head, something strange happened: her aggressiveness disappeared.

She stared at the onion soup, and although her face remained void of expression, Dan could have sworn she looked scared.

He paused. Then he started moving the soup around, and Maria's gaze followed his hand. She wasn't attacking anymore, she was… observing.

He took a spoonful and slowly moved it toward Maria.

A different kind of growl erupted. It was a long, painful scream, like the one you would image a bear making when injured.

His heart melted. How could he let his wife suffer so much?

He couldn't do this.

* * *

It was quiet again. She faced up, mouth open, not a single noise in the room, except maybe the crackle of burning wood from the fire.

In his right hand, he still held the onion soup. He moved, slowly, toward Maria. As he almost reached her mouth, she came to life! She looked at the spoon and another long, painful growl erupted.

She clearly sensed it. The smell was powerful, and if you ask him, it wasn't the most appealing one, even to him at present.

"We have to do this, honey!" he said, then he quickly poured the contents of the spoon into Maria's mouth.

The end of the world, or the closest thing to it, hit the cabin.

His ears had never experienced anything like this before.

It was the most powerful, horrendous, and painful scream he'd ever heard. The walls seemed to tremble, the windows vibrating, as Maria poured out waves of screams.

Dan froze, but soon he pushed through. Spoonful after spoonful, he poured the soup into his wife's mouth, holding her head and fighting through his tears until the soup was finished. And most of it had ended up inside Maria's stomach.

Her screams were slowly reducing. She was squirming, but it was another type of squirm. It was like a fire was beneath her, or inside her, and she was trying to escape the pain.

There came one last growl, and she stopped.

Dan sank into the chair and closed his eyes. The sun was coming up, and the first ray hit Dan's cheek right as he fell asleep.

* * *

When he woke up, Dan realized it was over. Maria was no longer sick.

She was in her sleeping bag. Dead. No, not dead—he had to push this thought away—but anyway, not moving.

The fire was out, but the cabin was warm. The day before and throughout the night he'd kept a double- or even triple-sized fire to help heat Maria.

The whiskey bottle—almost empty—stood on the table, alongside a few scattered remnants of onion.

He moved. The chair screeched. He immediately checked Maria.

One second. Two seconds. Nothing! Three seconds. Four seconds.

She wasn't moving! Was she dead? Or was she just sleeping?

He moved closer. Her mouth was open, but her tongue was somehow in a better position. A more natural position. Not off to one side like before, but settled neatly between her teeth. Clearly a sign of improvement!

And the eyes had lost that milky-color. They were now closer to how they used to be.

"Ha!" said Dan. "You look better, honey. How do you feel?"

No answer, as expected. But he wasn't perturbed.

"Well then," he continued, more enthusiastic, "let's see how you feel."

And he touched her head.

She was cold. Like a dead body. No, not a good thought. Dan shook a bit.

As he continued to feel her face, he realized she was somehow more mobile than the bodies he used to see during his time in the force.

Maria would soon be back, alive and well, just as she used to be.

He eased down the zipper on her sleeping bag. As he removed the top part of the bag, he could see shreds of the insulation material under her nails.

She'd clearly dug through the fabric while squirming, trying to get out.

But she was cold. She was cold all over.

* * *

As the day went on, Dan made sure the fire was always strong. She needed warmth to recover.

He listened to her heart, which unfortunately couldn't be heard.

He tried CPR, even mouth to mouth. No result.

A strong smell of onions surrounded her, but Maria was

completely inert.

She needed time. And time he would give her.

* * *

When night came, the body started to develop an odor: the smell of dead bodies he was so familiar with. Okay, not too familiar, but he recognized it.

It couldn't be coming from Maria though. Her clothes were dirty, and all this freezing and defrosting surely hadn't helped. It must be the clothes.

When she's up, she'll take a nice long bath using melted snow and everything will be okay.

* * *

As the next morning dawned, the smell became even more powerful. The strong fire next to Maria wasn't helping. And the onions in her stomach must have started to go bad, as now he could smell dead body smells combined with those of rotten onions.

He moved around a bit, making a quick inventory.

The refrigerator was out. Probably the generator was out of fuel, so now there is no power.

No matter. He had heat and he could make water by melting some of the snow outside.

Food was scarce. He only had two cans left, and one onion. That onion was important, but he'd soon get more. And he needed to keep half of it for Maria.

The third and last bottle of whiskey was empty. No alcohol remained, and he slowly started to realize he might have been fully drunk for the last few days.

As he looked around, he realized Maria was in very bad shape. Her body... she looked like a dead person. That couldn't be! He'd given her onions! Weren't onions supposed to cure her? Well, she'd had a strong dose of onions, and now she was worse.

The fire needed to be stronger, he realized. Otherwise, there was no way for her to get warm again.

* * *

He was in school. His teacher was his ex-C.O., that small and stupid guy who'd made his life miserable twenty years ago.

The guy was asking him to get out of the classroom, as he was no longer in the police force. Dan was afraid to answer back.

As he stood from behind his desk at the back of the classroom, the smell of bad onions hit him. He looked around, but he couldn't tell where it was coming from.

His ex-C.O. stared at him, opened his mouth and let out the now-well-known bear growl. Again. And again.

When Dan opened his eyes, he saw Maria standing on the other side of the room. She was taking small steps toward him, while slowly vomiting all the onion soup he'd fed to her. Soup which, in the meantime, had turned rotten.

But now she was different from before. She looked dead. And she smelled like a dead body too.

She *was* dead.

But she was also alive.

15 NOT ALONE

"We can do this," said Andrei, looking to Lili for support. He was actually trying to motivate himself, without realizing it.

Lili nodded and silently followed, holding Mat's hand.

Once the gate was a few dozen feet behind them, the strong, clean air hit their lungs.

The road ahead was difficult. The snow was deep, almost knee deep in places, and they had backpacks with them as well. But more importantly, Mat was small, too small for this snow, and he was slowing them down.

"I'm cold," said Matei suddenly. "I want to go back to the cabin!"

"We need to go to Grandma's house, honey," said Lili. "It's not far. We'll be there soon."

"But I'm cold."

"You're properly dressed. You should be fine. Come on, put some muscle into it. You're too heavy for me to pull at every step." Lili looked around, as if trying to find a solution. "Look, I'll cook something nice for you once we reach Grandma's."

"I'm hungry now. What food do you have, Mom?"

Lili looked at Andrei, and he understood.

"Hey, Mat. I have an idea. For every five minutes we walk, you can throw a snowball at me. But from behind. Don't hit my face."

"Really? Let's do it every minute."

"No. Every 3 minutes. And that's final. Mom will tell you when you can throw."

Thud!

A snowball struck Andrei's back a few moments later.

"Hey!" he said, turning around. "You didn't wait for the go!"

A young, squeaky 'He, he, he' could be heard as another snowball hit its target.

* * *

They had been walking for an hour, and Andrei was tired. He had been tired for the last forty minutes already, but nevertheless, now it felt worse.

"We need to stop," he said, almost falling to the ground while taking off his heavy backpack. "I can't take it anymore."

He could barely see, as snow was melting on his overheated forehead and then streaming down his face.

"Let's stop for a bit," confirmed Lili, and Mat seemed in the mood to make a few snowballs and start a new war.

"Leave your father alone," said Lili, when she saw what he was planning. "We're not walking anymore, and he needs to rest. Here, have some water. And be quiet!"

"How far away do you think it is?" asked Andrei, experiencing a moment of concern. "We left late, and the sunlight might fade sooner than expected."

"Well, I guess a couple of miles," answered Lili after thinking for a few seconds. "I know my dad used to take us up here to Grandma, but that was way back and by car. The bad thing is the house is on the other end of the village, and you know how villages are around here."

Andrei nodded. "Yeah, I do. I hate that about our villages. People in this area love to build their houses on the main road. Which means, no matter the size of the village, most properties are located either side of the main street," he said, moving his hands around. "And usually there is only one street to begin with, only one," he continued, raising a finger, "which means a small village might spread on for miles."

"Yeah," said Lili, shaking her head. "It's a favorite subject of yours. You've complained about this at least ten times."

"But am I wrong?" said Andrei, continuing to breathe heavily. "And every time we have to drive to your parents' place, we spend half the trip following the speed limit."

"Yes, yes, I know."

"Villages in our country are stupid," he said, still trying to catch his breath.

Ten minutes later, Lili started sending subtle messages that it might be time to go.

Andrei understood, and he dragged himself up and retrieved his backpack.

As he fastened it on his back, a noise caught his attention. He stopped, raised a finger, and told Lili, who was talking to Mat, to shush.

"What?"

"Silence!" he hissed.

They stilled and listened.

"Did you hear that?" asked Andrei.

"What?"

"You didn't hear it? I thought I heard howling."

"Howling?" asked Lili, in a tremulous voice.

"Yes, howling... like dogs or wolves."

"Oh no! Oh no!" said Mat. "Mommy, I'm scared!" He hugged Lili's left leg.

"Relax, there are no wolves in this area. Deeper into the woods, closer to the mountains, maybe," said Lili. "But what do you mean you heard howling?"

"I mean it sounded like a pack of wolves, or dogs, in the distance."

"You sure it wasn't a train or something?"

"What train? Do you think trains are still in service, that everything else is okay, and we're the only ones who lost electricity, network signal and running water?"

"No, I mean... I don't know. I have no idea what you heard. But you're scaring the kid," said Lili, as she tended to Matei.

"Well, supposing I heard properly, what could it be?"

"I don't know. You're always seeing or hearing things. You hear everything that happens beyond our apartment or our hotel walls.

And then it takes you hours to fall asleep just because you thought you'd heard something."

"You're right, but now it's different," he said, and he moved on.

As they advanced uphill and made a small turn, they finally saw the outskirts of the village.

"There it is!" Lili's enthusiasm was almost tangible. "We're here!"

"How far to your grandmother's now?"

"Are we there yet?" whined Mat.

"Please don't start," answered Andrei, no patience left.

"About a mile to go, I think," said Lili, fighting through the snow, which was getting deeper.

Then the howling began.

They froze.

Lili barely stifled a small yell, while Mat started crying.

"Cover his mouth!" urged Andrei in a whisper, as he ducked in an attempt to take cover.

Lili smothered Mat's cries, whispering for him to be quiet, to relax, and not make any noise.

"Something's there," said Andrei. "Wolves, or dogs, or… Dogs!" he exclaimed, having a eureka moment.

"Dogs!" came at the same time from Lili.

"Jinx!" mumbled Mat behind Lili's hand.

"Shut the hell—"

"Language!" exclaimed Lili. "Why do I have to keep repeating this?"

"I mean, sorry… There are dogs. Stupid of me to believe they were wolves. Just think. I guess each household has at least one dog. And this little village had quite a lot of strays in the streets, just like your hometown."

"Yeah," confirmed Lili. "this whole region is the same. And we also had dogs. One of them was mine. We kept him at Grandma's when he grew too large for the apartment. She took care of him, and I would play with him whenever we visited. He died many years ago though."

"But what do we do?" asked Andrei. "How can we fight off a pack of possibly famished dogs?"

"Let's hope there are no stray ones," said Lili.

"What's that got to do with anything?" snapped Andrei. "What should we do about this problem we have?" he continued mockingly. "Oh, I know! Let's hope the issue doesn't happen. Pfft! You sound just like our prime minister."

As if in answer to the howling, another sound rose from the village in front of them. This time, it was the bear growling they knew so well.

"Do you hear that?" asked Andrei. "Do you hear that? What the hell do we do? There are dogs *and* dead people down there. And the dogs probably bring the people to life with their barking."

Lili was staring at the village, their destination, and didn't answer.

"Well?" asked Andrei in a yelled whisper. "Did you hear me?"

"Yes, I heard you... I heard you... I don't know... I don't know what to do!"

Stress and fear overwhelmed them.

They had nothing. No solution, no idea. Nothing.

* * *

As minutes ticked by, Andrei started talking. It was his way of working things out.

"So... what do we know? We are on the main road, heading toward the village. There are clearly some dogs down there. They could be in peoples' yards. But there could potentially be a pack of stray dogs roaming around the streets. And there are clearly some transformed people as well. We need to get across the village to reach your grandmother's house. That's a distance of one or two miles, and the sun is setting in about an hour. Did I miss anything?"

"No... no, that's about right," said Lili.

"I know!" Matei jumped up "We can go around."

"Yeah," said Andrei impatiently, "but the sun is setting soon, and I'm not sure I want to go around such a village, filled with dogs and bad people, in the dark. Plus, it would take too long."

"Then why don't we go straight, and we'll fight the dogs. I can fight, Daddy. I will keep them away!"

"You cannot fight them, Mat. Come on! How could you say that? You always say stupid things and move the discussion away from the actual subje—"

"Hey, relax! The kid is only trying to help. He's just a boy. Let him be."

"Well, if he's just a boy then he shouldn't get involved in grownup talk, should he?"

"Well, maybe you should have more patience with him, Mister Know-It-All. We're all throwing in ideas here. Why should he be prevented from talking?"

"Because he's saying stupid things!"

"Well, then you say the smart things, please. We're waiting."

As they fought, Mat tugged on his mother's clothes.

"What?" Finally Lili snapped. "What do you want? I've told you not to interrupt when I'm in the middle of a conversation."

Mat tugged her down to his height and then whispered into her ear. As he spoke, a smile came to her face.

"Well, why don't you tell your 'stupid idea'," said Lili, with air quotes, "to the Supreme Leader over there?"

"What is it, then?" asked Andrei.

Mat was silent.

"Come on." Lili encouraged him gently.

"If we can't go around, and we can't go straight, and we don't have enough time, why not go to the first house we find? Then we can wait for Grandpa Dan to come and save us."

"I love it! Of course, not the part about Dan saving us," he added quickly. "I love it because it gives us a place to rest and plan our next move. Hmm. We'll need a property with a good fence around it," he continued, looking toward the village, trying to spot the best option.

"First, thank you, Mat, for the wonderful idea," said Lili, directing a pointed look at Andrei.

"Yes. Indeed. Thank you, Mat. Sorry I yelled at you," said Andrei.

Mat grinned.

"This could work," continued Andrei. "We need a good fence around a nice property. It has to be too high for the dogs to jump and should have no gaps in it, so the dogs can't enter."

"In this area, people are pretty careful about not letting stray animals enter their yards, as they often keep chickens or even goats. The fences may not be beautiful, but they'll be well kept," answered

Lili.

"In that case, it's just a matter of heading to the first house we see, before any dogs find us," concluded Andrei. "Let's go."

They moved slowly.

"God damn it," said Andrei, puffing.

"What?" whispered Lili.

"I remember seeing in the movies how the wind carries the scent of prey to the predator."

"And?"

"And the wind is blowing from behind, dufus. It's wafting our scent toward the village."

"Then make sure you don't stink," said Lili, making Andrei's eyes laugh for a moment.

They continued to advance. As they got closer, Andrei stopped once more. "I say we go to the one on the right," he said, pointing.

"It looks better," agreed Lili.

"Yeah. The fence looks more solid than the one to the left. And the house on the left looks unfinished," he said, continuing to point as the three of them squatted together.

"True," Lili agreed, and they started to advance once more. "The one on the right is finished and will make for a better shelter."

They were about half a mile from the property when the howling recommenced, again accompanied by those bear-like growls in what seemed like a hundred voices.

They paused.

"The howling is coming from the same general direction," said Andrei, "so it appears we are in no immediate danger."

"True," said Lili, "but the sun is setting and we need a solution fast."

"Let's move while they're making noise," said Andrei. "It might be better, as they can't hear us when they howl."

They advanced faster. The road was to their left, but in their fear, they kept moving further to the right, until they were heading toward the back corner of the property.

"We'll have to jump. The gate is probably at the front," said Andrei pointing toward the main road, "but I don't want to go where the dogs are. Can you jump, Lili?"

"I think so, yes. It doesn't look that high."

As they drew closer, they could finally get a better look at the fence in front of them. It was a wooden construct over six feet high and it looked solid. The top part had two horizontal planks facing each other, positioned at an angle, like a small roof. This way, the fence was better protected against the elements.

There was snow everywhere, knee deep on the path and gathered on top of and all around the fence, and it slowed their advance. They had to pull Matei with them at every step, while also trying to keep quiet. And Andrei was struggling to catch his breath, barely managing to pull up his feet, knees trembling from the effort.

He was exhausted.

* * *

Finally, they were a mere thirty feet from the fence.

But then the howling increased, this time closer than before.

When they looked to their left, toward the main road, about ninety yards away they saw a pack of eight dogs. They were clearly strays, medium-sized, all gray, and a mix of breeds.

The dogs raced toward the group, barking.

"Run!" said Andrei, as adrenalin hit. He pulled Mat vigorously, and all three leaped through the snow.

Upon reaching the fence, it seemed way taller than it had from afar.

We should have gone for the left one, thought Andrei, but it was now too late, as the dogs were nearly on them.

The snow was slowing the dogs as well, but not by much.

"You go first, then I'll push Mat over, and then I'll jump," said Andrei, out of breath.

"No!" said Lili. "You can't jump the fence alone, and I can't pull you. However, I can jump. My aerobic classes should help."

"Fine," said Andrei. There was no time to argue. His ego had told him he was the strongest and the fastest, but maybe not this time.

"Throw the backpacks first!"

They threw the bags, and then Andrei said, "Okay, now I'll jump."

But he had no idea how.

He was the non-sporty type. He'd played some soccer in school, even some basketball, but he was always picked last. He felt deep down that he could play sports, but in reality, he was bad at it. And jumping over fences... Well, he had never tried that before.

"Grab the top with both hands, then jump and pull yourself up while I push you over. Get a leg over the top of the fence as soon as you can. Now go!" said Lili, with confidence.

He grabbed the top, jumped, and pulled.

He was heavy and already out of breath, and on top of that he didn't have the strongest arms.

He tried stepping on the wood, as Lili pushed, and he was slowly getting over. He finally got his right foot a top the fence, and as he realized he would make it, Lili's next push made him tumble over to the other side, while releasing a vigorous scream.

Thank God for the snow, at least three-foot deep, way deeper than on the other side, which safely broke his fall.

As he rose and brushed himself off, he heard Lili speaking to Mat. "Stay on the fence, like you did when riding that pony. You can do it!"

* * *

Lili got Mat onto the fence with only minimal difficulty. He seemed secure there and looked down at her with a grin. Then his expression changed as his gaze flashed to a spot behind her.

"Mommy!" he screamed, and Lili turned to see the front-runners among the pack were barely two leaps away.

She had two options: face the dogs or try to jump.

They were so close! In two easy jumps, the first two dogs—both rather skinny and therefore likely to be very hungry—would grab her.

She could face them, try to fight them off. But what could a thirty-eight-year-old woman, with no training whatsoever, do against eight famished and bloodthirsty dogs? And without a weapon. Maybe they would just be aggressive, barking a lot, but not biting. There are many such dogs that made a lot of noise but never acted. Hopefully, these were the same.

She could try to jump, but they would grab her before she

reached the top of the fence. And if they pulled her back, seeing her fallen in the snow would just make them more aggressive and more likely to bite.

She was, unfortunately, very bad at making quick decisions.

Asking her for a quick decision put a lot of pressure on her, and she was never in the position to give a good answer. She would basically freeze, unable to do anything as her mind raced, trying to cover various options, alternatives, pros and cons.

And this was one of those moments. She needed direction.

"Come on, honey, jump! You can do it!" yelled Andrei, his voice full of confidence.

* * *

Of course, Andrei couldn't see the dogs from behind the fence. He didn't realize that in two jumps they would reach Lili. He thought Lili needed to hurry, but assumed she had enough time to make the jump. That's where his confidence came from.

He would help her a bit, even though she probably didn't need it. So, he started hitting the wooden fence hard, while growling as menacing as he possible.

* * *

Andrei's actions helped.

The first two dogs, caught off guard by the sudden noise and probably also educated by recent events to be wary where growls were involved, reacted in confusion. They abruptly side-jumped away from the fence, and this gave Lili the half a second she needed to get on top of the fence.

Over their confusion, the dogs leaped up, snapping at her left leg, but she quickly swung it over the fence to safety. As she passed Mat down into Andrei's waiting arms, she realized what she'd dodged, and a strong feeling of relief engulfed her.

As she descended to join her family in the deep snow, she pulled Andrei into her arms and squeezed him tight.

Their hearts were racing. They'd barely escaped the bites of eight famished and bloodthirsty dogs. Life was becoming too much.

"Mommy? Daddy?" said Mat.

"Come here," said Lili in a loving voice, trying to get him close to them. A three-way hug was in order.

"Mommy. Daddy," continued Mat.

The dogs were barking loudly behind the fence.

"Mommy! Daddy!" yelled Mat.

"What?"

Lili and Andrei turned to him at the same time.

A tall man was coming toward them across the yard. He had already covered half the distance.

He was running.

He was growling like a bear.

And he should have been dead.

16 AT THE RIGHT MOMENT?

"Maria? Honey? Are you okay?" asked Dan, jumping out of his chair. He took a few steps toward her, reaching out. "You need rest, honey!" he said again, with tears in his eyes.

Maria growled as she walked toward him with small, slow steps. She was looking in his direction, but right through him.

When he tried to hug her, she bit his left shoulder.

The bite was strong, but somehow weaker than the one on his hand a few days ago.

But the pain was a wakeup call. This was not Maria.

The smell of dead corpse and rotten onions invaded his nostrils, now even stronger. This was not Maria. Maria smelled nice, like a flower. And when not like a flower, at least she smelled like delicious food. Not rotten onions!

And the growling... That growling is not Maria. Maria was kind, supportive, and she always had a loving voice, even when she was mad.

The pain, the smells, and the sounds made him wake up from the terrible dream that had lasted for several days.

And it finally hit him: Maria was gone. Was she now like their neighbors? Or did she transform into something else? It didn't really matter. The Maria he knew was no more.

He pushed against the body with both hands. The creature took two steps back, tripped, and fell on its back.

As it struggled to rise, he spotted a small piece of fabric from his denim jacket stuck in its teeth. Just like last time, he was lucky the bite hadn't reached his skin. He needed to be smarter.

The body was back on its feet, always looking toward Dan.

He didn't have his baseball bat—both the bat and his heavy winter jacket were on the chair beside the fire.

As the body closed in, Dan looked around, searching for a potential weapon.

In the end, he had no choice but to open the front door and escape the cabin.

The cold hit him instantly. It was almost evening and the temperature had dropped below freezing. A chill wind was making it worse.

As the dead body that used to be Maria stumbled out of the cabin, relentlessly pursuing him, growling and biting the air, he realized there was a simple way to get rid of it.

He started walking backwards, making sure he made plenty of noise.

Sure enough, the creature followed.

The snow made them both fight for each step, and what used to be Maria stumbled and fell a few times.

But every time, it got up and continued the chase.

Still, its reactions were slower, way slower than before the onion soup, and Dan had little difficulty keeping a safe distance.

He was about a couple of hundred yards from the cabin now. He was freezing, but the dead body still followed, moving really slowly.

"This is far enough," said Dan. His voice sounded odd over the growling coming from the creature. "This is where you'll sleep," he continued, and then he sprinted.

He was old, but he could still run. That thing was between him and the cabin, so he had to go around.

He raced to the right. The body started turning, but it was slow, and Dan sprinted past it, heading back toward the cabin.

Two hundred yards was easy, and Dan reached his refuge in good form, despite the lag created by the deep snow. As he entered the cabin, he looked back.

The body was coming after him, though its progress was halting.

And then it happened again.

Dan stood there, stunned. The memory of the teacher's wife and daughter sprang back into his mind. The same thing had happened to them.

The creature stopped. It staggered on its feet for a few seconds, still facing the cabin.

And then it fell. Without any reflex to break its fall, it dropped like a rock and hit the snow.

Just like falling into a deep slumber, thought Dan, and he closed the door.

The howling wind covered the squeak of the hinges.

He carefully locked the door behind him.

* * *

It was six a.m., and Dan was already up.

Being on the force had had a good influence on his schedule. Maria always said he was like a soldier.

He didn't like the comparison. That's probably why she'd kept on using it, just to tease him.

He had a lot of respect for any man or woman in uniform, of course. They were all serving their country or the community. And he knew the army had a strong influence, building character and making people love and embrace efficiency. But he also knew military men were rarely pushed to their limits as a result of actual need. Of course, this was a good thing, he agreed, especially here in the Balkans. On the other hand, policemen were always kept on their toes.

Hence, the comparison should be the other way around, he used to explain: military men are like policemen.

He did his morning routine: fifty pushups, fifty crunches, and fifty squats. He washed in the sink with some cold water from melted snow, and then he got dressed.

He ignored the pain in his right hand and left shoulder. True, his right thumb was really swollen and a bone was probably broken. He'd have to take care of that; Andrei was right. But a little bit later.

The coffee was ready, so he poured it into a mug. As he opened the fridge, reality hit: only a few bites of yellow cheese remained.

And there were no more onions.

No matter. He would join Lili, Andrei and Mat today.

He slowly unlocked the door, fully equipped: backpack on his shoulders, big baseball bat in his left hand, and his trusted gun in the holster on his hip.

As he emerged, the fresh air of the morning hit him. He took a deep breath and then headed right, toward the village, making sure to keep clear of the thing that had once been Maria.

The body was still there. Fully frozen, facedown, buried in the snow.

* * *

It was a good walk. Just what he needed! That cabin had been good for a while. Until he'd gotten lost in what happened with Maria. And all that alcohol clearly hadn't helped.

He wasn't an alcoholic, that's for sure, not even a high-functioning one. He could spend weeks or months without touching a bottle. He sometimes liked his whiskey, just like any guy would, but that was it.

However, when sorrow hit, if there was no one to pull him up, he could spend a few days drowning in drink.

And Maria had always been the one who saved him.

* * *

There it was! The little village in which he'd grown up lay ahead. He picked up the pace, in anticipation of meeting his daughter and nephew. Ah, and his son-in-law. He ought not forget about Andrei.

The snow was deep, right up to his knees. It had been snowing for the last few days, so he couldn't see footprints or any other traces to know which way they'd gone. But not to worry. They'd be together soon.

As he got closer, he spotted the first houses, to the left and right of the road. Others followed in the same symmetrical pattern. Two of them had smoke coming from their chimneys: the second to the left and the first on the right.

"What is this?" he mumbled, and he picked up the pace.

Then, right in the middle of the road he noticed seven or eight gray spots. Dogs! This wasn't good. But Dan had grown up around here and knew how to handle a few dogs.

He continued to walk. Five hundred yards. Four hundred. What was that? Three hundred yards.

He stopped about two hundred yards from the dogs. The snow around them was bloody. And a small body lay there, torn apart, almost fully eaten. Next to it was Mat's winter coat.

"MAT!" he yelled.

The dogs turned to look at him.

"MAAAATTTTT!" yelled Dan, starting to run forward.

And in the same moment, the pack ran toward him.

17 TOGETHER

"Oh God!" exclaimed Lili, her voice full of fear. "Oh God, Andrei. Oh my God!"

The big man, the monster, was coming, plowing through the snow like it wasn't even there. His legs were throwing snow with incredible speed. And he drew closer with every step, showing no sign of tiring or slowing.

Andrei looked around nervously, trying to find his baseball bat. The sun was setting, the bat was beige, and snow was white. He couldn't see it. He couldn't find it.

As the monster approached, Andrei realized this was it. This was the moment he'd sometimes fantasized about. This was when he must fight evil, overcome some big danger, while his family got away thanks to his noble sacrifice.

"Run! Get out of here!" he yelled, as he grabbed his backpack.

* * *

Andrei had told Lili what to do. That was good, as her inability to make a decision had almost frozen her again.

She had to save Mat, so she took his hand and start running, away from Andrei and the growling enemy. At the back of the property there was a shed. That was where they'd hide.

As they dashed through the deep snow as fast as they could, she glanced back, only to see Andrei had vanished. And the growling man seemed to be eating something on the ground.

* * *

Andrei held the backpack in front of him and struck the man with it. At least, that's what he'd wanted to do. As the man was running, the impact went differently than Andrei had predicted. In his mind, the runner would have been stopped, and they would push against each other, Andrei keeping him away with his big backpack, like a shield.

Right before the growling man reached him, Andrei had the reflex to raise the bag even higher, instinctively covering his face from danger. The man came fast, he was heavy, and he didn't feel any fear. He was also not quite alive, so he had no reflex to slow down or dodge. He slammed, face first, into the backpack, and then he advanced into Andrei.

They fell on the ground, the big man on top.

There was one good outcome though. Even if unplanned, that backpack was well positioned so the man started chewing and biting on that, instead of Andrei's face.

As he growled and munched, Andrei was pushed deeper and deeper into the snow. The man was heavy. And while Andrei was bulky, this guy was clearly another breed. He was muscular, strong—a different body-type altogether.

And he was on top of Andrei, chewing and biting.

It was just a matter of time.

* * *

To Lili's eyes, it was clear her husband was lost.

She loved Andrei. He was her rock. He was funny, smart, and he adored her. Some of his jokes could be ill-placed, but she loved their little quarrels, sometimes pushing for them on purpose. Fine, he had his downsides—he could be snappy and irritating, and the last few weeks had brought out the worst in him—but she'd planned on getting old next to him, and preferably dying peacefully together in their sleep.

She couldn't lose him like this! She had to do something.

As these thoughts went through her mind, she saw there are more enemies. Behind the big man, three more of those things were coming! The wife and two children: one girl, probably around twelves, and a young boy around Mat's age.

The mother seemed injured, bloody all over her chest and arms, like she'd been attacked and bitten before turning into this. She must have turned after the others. The children had blood around their mouths. *Her death must have been terrible,* Lili realized.

This was not the moment to worry about that, however. This was the moment to save her husband. But also save herself and Mat.

"Go, Mat!" she commanded, looking at her kid. "Go to that shed and stay there!"

Mat clearly didn't want to. He stared up at her, his expression beseeching.

"Go!" she yelled. "Listen to me. Run!"

Lili spotted the baseball bat in the snow nearby.

She'd use that.

* * *

Andrei was sinking. Was this it? He couldn't breathe and his strength was leaving him.

The man was too heavy. And Andrei was wasting a lot of energy pushing and thrusting against the body. Even in the MMA fights he sometimes watched on TV, during a clinch, the fighter below used lots of energy to shove away the one on top of him. While the one on top, if smart enough, just used his body weight to wear his opponent down.

Even if the thing on top of him wasn't particularly smart and had no objective save biting and scratching, Andrei was clearly losing this fight.

This was it. This was the end. He was so tired and so out of breath, he didn't even have the energy to think about how much he loved his wife and child. His beautiful, smart and witty Lili. His full-of-life little kid. His boy.

As he sank, he felt the body on top of him making a few different moves, like something was distracting it.

What could it be? was his last thought before he fainted.

* * *

Lili ran two steps, baseball bat raised, and hit the little girl right in her forehead. What a good strike! The girl's skull cracked, brains and blood spilling out.

With another step, she was in range of the little boy, who was having a hard time moving through the deep snow. She thumped him hard, and then she turned to the mother.

The mother was slower. Clearly the injuries she had suffered before dying were impairing her movement. She also smelled like she was rotting, unlike the other monsters Lili had met so far. That was something to investigate, but later.

She struck the mother on the head. And again. And a third time. As the mother fell, Lili hit her once more, squishing her head into a pulp.

Her hands hurt.

She turned around. The big man was still on top of something, biting and growling.

She ran over toward him, adjusting her grip on the bat.

She couldn't see Andrei, but he had to be somewhere down there, under that bag of his. And, more importantly, under that huge, growling man.

She squeezed the bat. It was rather heavy, but very efficient.

She started hitting almost instantly. *Andrei is there. Let him be, you monster!* She struck the huge man's back. First on the shoulders. One. Two, Three. Hitting hard. Four. Five. Nothing happened. The man was too big, her strength was no match, and he continued to bite his target, showing no reaction.

She needed to think. His head. That was the weak spot. She started whacking his skull. One. Two. Three. The man was still there. Still moving. Still chewing.

She managed to crack the skull. She heard it shatter. She could see the blood and brains spilling out. But still the man was moving, squirming, and biting.

Four. Five. Six. His head was so tough!

She stopped. She needed a new plan. But fast-thinking and swift decision-making were not her strengths.

Where else to hit? What were the weak spots?

She knew a few people, including Andrei, who suffered from back pain, and she had studied the subject. She knew which area of the spine was responsible for taking nerve impulses to the lower part of the body. It was a weak spot, and she could target that area. But what would happen? Probably the body would lose control of its legs, but the biting wouldn't stop. The hands would still try to scratch and pull at Andrei's flesh.

No, something else...

That area around the cervix connected the central nervous system with the rest of the body, and issues there could lead to atrocious pain, including headaches.

Suddenly, she remembered how a knife in the chest had killed the teacher's wife. On top of that, her fully smashed-in head, although it hadn't stopped her, had made her behave in an uncontrolled manner. But why was that relevant?

Lili had a feeling.

Yes, that was it! She was certain she had the answer! She didn't know why, but the cervical area at the back of the neck played an important role in all of this.

She must hit the growling man on the back of his neck!

One. Two. Three. The hits fell. Four. Five. The neck made a strange noise. Six. Seven. Eight. The neck was almost pulp. Nine. Ten. Hits fell like pouring rain as Lili screamed her anger.

The growl was there, still present. But after a dozen hits, it was clear the biting had ceased. The impulses, wherever they were coming from, weren't reaching the mouth anymore.

But still she struck. She swung and hit until she couldn't anymore.

When she stopped, breathing heavily, she realized the big man was still squirming. However, his movement seemed uncontrolled. She grabbed his clothes and started to pull. She needed to get this thing off Andrei.

They were close to the fence, where the dogs were still barking on the other side. The snowfall was higher near the fence than where she was standing. This made the pull a little easier, as she was downhill.

Slowly, the big man slid to the side and she could finally see her husband, under his backpack.

"Oh, no," she said, and tears filled her eyes.

Andrei was out, and he was barely breathing.

"Honey," she said, tapping his cheeks. "Honey, do you hear me? Andrei? Come now, honey. Please, Andrei. Please," she continued. "Please be well."

* * *

Mm, what a good feeling. He was so comfortable.

It was just like his bed back home. He had a huge bed, almost fully square. And it was oh so comfortable. He loved sleeping in a comfortable bed. *Who doesn't?* he thought, and he smiled. *Mm, this is nice. This is perfect. I could sleep like this for hours and hours.*

"Honey." He heard the call, distantly. "Andrei, honey, wake up."

Ugh, what now? Why couldn't everyone leave him alone? He wanted to sleep, not take care of whatever stupid chores he'd forgotten to do yesterday.

"Honey!"

The cry was so loud he opened his eyes.

Lili was on top of him, crying, and then she started kissing him violently.

"You're okay! Oh my God, you're okay," she said.

"Yeah... I... am... fine... I... guess," said Andrei, his words interrupted by kisses. "Stop it... stop it!" He pushed at her. "What's gotten into you?" He smiled. "I know what you want." He was trying to be charming, but, as usual, he only managed to sound clumsy.

"Stop with that," said Lili, pushing herself away from him. "Come on, get up. We need to get M—MAT!" she yelled, suddenly.

* * *

They ran to the shed. It was fully dark now, but the horrible noise continued. The dogs were barking on the other side of the fence, maintaining the noise and keeping the four bodies awake. Just like the teacher's wife and child, they were unable to move but were still active.

The shed door stood half open. There was no light coming from within.

"Honey? Mat? Mat, do you hear us? Everything's okay. You can come out now, sweetie," said Lili.

"Mat," called Andrei. "It's us, little man. Come on out. It's safe." Nothing.

As they entered, Andrei had an idea. He grabbed his now-useless phone from his pocket and turned on the flashlight.

The space was only ten by fifteen feet, with shelves lining the walls on all sides. And there, curled up beneath one of them in the far corner, was Matei.

He was passed out, sleeping. There was a puddle around him. The shock had made him lose control of his bladder.

"Oh, poor thing," said Lili, crying.

18 SEPARATED

Andrei cautiously entered the house. Lili followed, holding sleeping Mat in her arms.

It was a nice one-story house. Unfinished, but with a lot of potential.

Inside, the temperature was still above freezing. Not by much, but it was clearly better than outside.

"It's so warm," whispered Lili.

"They'd probably had strong fires in the fireplaces as the family got sicker by the day. I guess the walls retained some of that heat," whispered Andrei.

"But now the broken door is a problem, and the cold is creeping in fast. The house will freeze soon."

The family in the backyard had broken out through the back door. It was a flimsy, temporary one, so they'd managed to knock their way through it.

"Look," whispered Andrei, pointing. "The scratches on the metal front door. At some point, they tried to get out through here."

"Yeah," answered Lili. "Maybe because the dogs had been making noise on the main street."

Andrei nodded, continuing his advance.

As Lili and Andrei entered the building, the barking and growling from outside dimmed. When they approached the living room, though, their blood froze. A high-pitched growl could be heard.

Lili yelled, startled.

Andrei made a mental note to tell her to control her screaming. But that could wait until later. Now, they needed to see what was causing the noise.

As he stepped into the room, his chest tightened.

Inside, was a baby crib—one with high wooden sides.

Within the crib was a baby, probably around eight-months old, looking toward him.

He was white, and his blue clothes made him look even paler. And he was biting the air, growling.

* * *

"Oh," exclaimed Lili. "Kill it," she added, and she couldn't believe her own words.

"What?" asked Andrei. "He's just a baby. Like Mat was."

"Mat? How can you say that? I remember Mat at this age. He was such a beautiful baby, with the biggest, most beautiful eyes," said Lili in a soft voice, looking down to where Mat slept peaceful in her arms. "And he was so tiny and helpless and needed all our support. But not this one." She looked back at the baby in the crib. "This baby is dead, and it turned into one of those things. Do it."

"Well," mumbled Andrei.

"Pfft. It takes a woman to do a man's job," said Lili, and she passed Mat into Andrei's arms, while taking his bat. "Stand aside."

She took a few steps forward and swung the bat.

* * *

"Damn," Lili said, dropping the bat.

"Ugh, honey," said Andrei.

He'd hoped she would do it. But she hadn't, and now he'd have to take care of this. He then realized that, deep down, he was relieved she couldn't go through with it.

"What can we do?" asked Andrei. "We can't stay in the house with this creature inside, ready to wake at the slightest noise."

"Especially not with Matei around."

"Let's take it outside," said Andrei.

Lili nodded.

* * *

They carried the crib between them. The baby was small, barely standing, and always trying to bite them. He sometimes managed to grab their hands with his mouth, but their gloves were more than sufficient to keep those baby teeth away.

"Do you see this?" asked Andrei, as they moved through the snow. "See how it has issues standing?"

"Yeah. So?"

"So it is just like a real, normal child would behave in the same situation. I think it's clear that this change, this disease, isn't giving anyone extra abilities."

Could a person in this state evolve? Could this baby, with enough attention, grow up? Lili wondered, yet she didn't express her thoughts out loud.

"Let's put him out back with the others," said Andrei, pulling Lili out of her thoughts. "We need to get it as far away from the house as possible. And for God's sake, let's make sure we don't step on any of the other four," he added, shuddering.

* * *

Finally they were back inside. They'd retrieved their backpacks, cleaned the baseball bat in the snow, and got the fire burning.

"We need to fix that back door," said Lili, turning to Andrei a few dozen minutes later. "Cold air is coming through it and this fireplace is not enough."

Andrei looked for a few seconds at the couch where Matei was sleeping, before rising. "Yeah, you're right, but I don't know how to put the door back together. I mean, I could try to find some planks and then—"

"We don't need a functional door. We just need that opening sealed off. Not even properly insulated, just something so the wind is not blowing directly into the house, as it is now."

"Okay," said Andrei, "in that case, I think I saw a tarp in that shed. Let me go check."

He came back with the tarp, a hammer and a handful of nails.

Then, by employing some high-level skill, at least in his opinion, they managed to nail it to the doorframe from the inside. It was clearly not the best insulator, but it helped.

All that hammering woke the family out back, which in turn startled the dogs, who seemed to have moved back to the front of the property, on the main road. The commotion woke the entire village.

"We need to keep it down," said Lili. "We keep waking the village, and I feel danger is everywhere."

"Yeah, I know what you mean. And this tarp looks so flimsy, now that you mention it. Can these monsters jump fences?"

"I hope not. But maybe we should find something to block this entrance," suggested Lili, looking around the hall.

"How about that armoire?" said Andrei, pointing. "Let's push it against the tarp. We're going to use the front door from now on anyway."

Pushing the heavy armoire and blocking the door made them feel safer, allowing them to focus on the interior of the house.

Matei was still sleeping, and Lili changed his pants and knickers, to make sure he was dry.

They found food in the refrigerator, but all the cooked dishes had gone bad. Luckily, they also came across canned fish, canned peas and a couple of unopened pickle jars. It was enough to put together a decent meal. To their relief, there were also a few onions in the pantry. They were not very fresh, but they could use most of them.

* * *

With the morning light, they were able to investigate the house properly.

"Hey, Andrei," said Lili in a strange voice, opening the metal door of the house. "Come quick."

Andrei followed her into the front yard.

"Look," she said, pointing. "The poor thing."

There was a dog, medium-sized and a half breed, just like the ones outside, kept on a leash near the access gate to the main road, where a small kennel was situated.

"Ugh, the poor thing," said Andrei with a sigh, closing in. "He's so skinny and barely breathing. He's almost dead."

"The bastards," said Lili. "Why do they have to keep the dogs on leashes? Especially when the family gets sick and there's no one to feed him."

"I don't know."

"Let's feed him," said Lili. "I'll go inside and bring some food and a blanket. And then we'll take him in with us."

Andrei was removing the collar and petting the dog, who was not even able to wag his tail.

Lili returned and handed her husband a piece of meat, which Andrei started waving at the dog's snout. Yet, the dog was so weak he couldn't even open his mouth.

"He's done for," said Andrei, with a tremor in his voice, while Lili covered him with the blanket.

"Let's take him inside anyway, where it's warm. Maybe he'll make it."

"Yeah, okay," said Andrei, grabbing the unexpectedly light dog, "but I don't have too much hope."

Back indoors, they set the dog down close to the fire. Minutes passed and he seemed to relax a little.

Yet, a few minutes later, he took his final breath.

"Oh," said Lili, tearing up as Andrei folded her into his arms.

"Come on," said Andrei, kissing her head gently. "There was nothing we could do. Come on. Go, check the house for food and clothes. I'll take him outside, then I'll check the surroundings."

* * *

The house had three bedrooms and a living room, a kitchen, and a big hallway connecting the different areas.

"Andrei, I checked the rooms. Even if parts are still under construction, the living room and the bedroom seem well insulated," said Lili, meeting Andrei who was just reentering the house. "Their walls are covered with planks and I see some insulation in areas that are not completed."

"Nice," said Andrei, stamping his boots to remove any stuck snow. "I checked outside and there's a lot of firewood. We can keep a fire burning all day round until spring."

"That's good," said Lili, gently petting his shoulder. "I don't have the same good news in terms of food and onions though."

"What? Why?"

"We only have enough for one or two days."

"Damn." Andrei sighed.

"We do have a bathroom," said Lili, smiling briefly.

"Yeah, but I bet there's no running water or electricity. So we can use the outhouse," said Andrei. "There's one out back."

"Have you found a well?"

"No," said Andrei, shaking his head. "There's none, at least not in this yard. But we can collect snow in some clean pots and melt that by the fire. By the way, what's the kid doing? Still sleeping?"

"Let's go see," said Lili, and they both moved into the living room.

"It's rather late. I say we wake him," said Andrei, inching in. "Hey, little man, wake up."

"How are you, sweetie? Are you okay?" asked Lili, smiling at Mat when he finally stirred. "How did you sleep?"

"Well, Mommy, well. What... what happened yesterday?" he asked, yawning while looking around the house. "How did we get here?"

Andrei took over. "We jumped that fence, remember?"

"Yes?" answered Mat in a questioning tone.

"And then, do you remember what happened next?"

"No," said Mat, clearly puzzled.

"You fell asleep," said Andrei, glancing briefly at Lili. "You fell asleep, as you were very tired. And we had to carry you to bed. You fat rat!" He smiled. "You like being taken care of, don't you?" he continued, while trying to tickle the boy.

"Daaaddddyyy, no." Mat laughed, trying to push Andrei away. "You're... the... fat... rat!" he answered, squeezing laughs between each word.

"Truer words were never spoken," said Lili.

"Ha!"

* * *

"But I don't like this food," said Mat, grumpy. "I want mashed potatoes! Mom, please give me some mashed potatoes."

"Well, let me check the pantry," she said. The owners had a few potatoes left, and most looked fine. While throwing away the cooked food, she had even found some butter in the fridge, and she used all of that now, to put a bowl of mashed potatoes on the table almost an hour later.

"There," she said proudly. "Eat up, ogres."

"We're the ogres! Roaaar!" said Mat, happily.

"Don't you join us, cute ogress?" said Andrei, smiling.

"Of course, I will!"

* * *

As they sat watching the fire later in the day, things seemed a little better.

"Things are looking up," said Lili, snuggling next to Andrei. "We need food and onions, I agree. But we are together and we are healthy. I just hope Dad will join us soon."

"Plus we are warm and safe," said Andrei, kissing her cheek gently. "When Dan comes, it will be perfect."

"Well, I guess 'perfect' is too strong a word," said Lili, giggling. "But I know what you mean."

"I think we need to go out every now and then to check the road," said Andrei. "You know, to wave to your father when he comes."

"Do you think it worked?"

"What? Giving onions to your mother?"

"Yeah," said Lili, looking into Andrei's eyes.

"I really don't know. It sounds a bit far fetched. But if it did, then there is a way to go back to normal some day."

"I hope Grandma is fine," said Mat, who was sitting next to Lili.

"Ugh, I hope so too," said Lili, turning and kissing Mat. "How are you, little one? Is it okay by the fire?"

"Yes, Mom. It's great."

"That's good," said Andrei, sitting up. "I'll go check the road. I'll be back soon."

And for the next few hours, every now and then they went

outside, looking left, trying to see if Dan was coming.

* * *

"We need to find more food," said Lili, as night settled in. "We have to do something. We could then wait here for my dad. Maybe we can put up a sign or something. No, that's probably not necessary. He'll see the chimney smoke for sure. But until he comes, we need to get some food."

"True," agreed Andrei. "We should go tomorrow."

They went to bed, but Andrei barely slept. And when he did, he dreamed of being stuck under a big, huge piece of pork. He was sinking deeper under the weight of the meat. And the light was getting dimmer by the second, until he found himself in complete darkness.

When he woke, he was relieved to see light entering the bedroom through the window.

* * *

"Okay, then," said Andrei. "Where should we go?"

"To the house up front, a bit to the right," said Lili, pointing.

"Well, let's analyze first, shall we?" said Andrei, getting a scoff from Lili. "What, you just want to follow the first idea we have and go into the first place we see?"

"Ah, no. But it's the best course of action. But fine, let's analyze."

"So. Unfortunately, we are surrounded by an ocean of danger."

"Mm, I always thought you were, deep down, a poet."

"Ha," said Andrei, kissing her briefly. "Behind our house there's nothing—a hill, trees here and there, snow as far as the eye can see."

"Right. I stand corrected. That's some next-level analysis," said Lili, trying to control her giggles.

"Stop it. So, to our left is the road we came on. Basically there is nothing there. Stop it, I said! I climbed on a ladder and looked to the right. There are three other lots with crappy or even missing fences."

"Why do we need fences?" asked Lili. "To keep the dogs away

while we loot?"

"Yeah. But that's not even the main problem. The trouble is that all these properties have no buildings except small sheds."

"Yeah, I bet there's no food in those sheds."

"Indeed. That leaves us the properties across the street."

"Yup," said Lili, trying to stop her grin. "So, we go to the house up front and a bit to the right, right?"

"Wait," said Andrei, shaking his head. "We still have to analyze the rest of the properties across the street."

"Please do," said Lili, grinning.

"The closest building is the house right across from us. But it's under construction, it's even missing some windows, so it is highly unlikely we'll find any food there. Plus, it has that flimsy wire-mesh fence, which will not keep the dogs away."

"And what is the remaining option, then?" said Lili, raising her eyebrows.

"After careful review," said Andrei in an official tone, "I believe our best option seems to be the property next to that. It's an old country house, one story. And it looks like someone has lived there for a long time. Surely there will be food inside."

"Great choice!" said Lili. "So, we'll go to the house up front and a bit to the right."

"Indeed. Now, stop grinning," said Andrei, kissing her.

"And Matei? We take him with us?"

"Yes, of course. But he needs to listen to whatever we tell him to do."

"Right. And what do we do about those dogs?" said Lili.

"First, let's talk to Matei. As for the dogs, I have an idea."

* * *

"We have to go get food," said Lili in a calm voice, after she and Andrei had discussed the plan. "We have two options, and we want to tell you about them."

Matei was looking up at Lili, while Andrei caressed his hair.

"We can go together. But it's really important you are quiet and do as we say. Or you can stay here, all alone, and wait for us to return."

"Alone? No way! I want to come with you," said Matei.

"Are you sure you don't want to stay here, all *alone*, and wait for us?" Andrei pushed a bit.

"You're overdoing it," whispered Lili.

"No! I want to come with you. Mom, please take me with you!"

"Okay," said Lili, looking quickly at Andrei. "You'll come with us. But pay attention: they will be some noises, especially from the dogs."

* * *

The day was warm. Still below freezing, but it felt good. The sun was up, and Mat was running around the front yard, happy.

"Eeeee-oooo!" yelled Andrei. "EEEEEE-OOOOO!"

The village came back to life.

The growls started, and the pack of dogs showed up as expected.

Andrei stood at gate, near the main road. While banging on the fence, he started moving left, until he reached the left back side of the yard, where they'd barely escaped the pack two days ago.

The dogs followed, barking and sometimes even slamming against the fence.

"Now!" said Andrei, as he and Lili grabbed the family's dead dog and heaved it over the fence.

The dogs took the bait! They tore into the unexpected meal, snarling.

Andrei and Lili sprinted back to the house, where Matei was waiting.

"Quick, let's go!" said Andrei. "And zip up that coat, you little goat. You don't want to catch a cold."

They opened the gate to the main road and stepped out.

Upon reaching their target house, they had hoped to find the gate unlocked. It wasn't.

"Ugh," said Andrei. "Now what do we do?"

"Well," said Lili, "these gates usually have shitty locks. I could jump the fence, then open it from the inside."

"But what if there's a growling guy in there? Or more?"

"I'll have my bat," said Lili. "Plus, I really think I'll get the door open before they can reach me. It doesn't sound as if anyone is here right now. And if there is someone around, they are in the house."

"Fine. Do it."

And Lili jumped.

When she studied the gate from the inside, she realized unlocking it wasn't going to be the easy task she'd imagined.

"Damn it," she said to Andrei. "I need a key."

She started hunting around. Time was short. The dogs could return at any moment, and there could be dead people in the yard. She had to be fast, yet quiet.

"Could it be in the house?" she asked.

"I don't think so."

"Yeah," said Lili, taking a step back. "It wouldn't make sense. The owners would leave it near the gate, for convenience. Ah, there it is," she said happily as she spotted it lying in a small nook.

* * *

Andrei switched his weight from one foot to another and glanced around, mostly over his left shoulder, toward their current base camp.

"Come on, open it already." He whizzed closer to Lili, moving around nervously.

"Daddy," said Mat, "when is—"

"Shh," whispered Andrei, putting his finger to his mouth. "Be quiet. Remember what we said. You have to be quiet."

"But when is—"

"BE… QUIET!" whisper-snapped Andrei. "We don't want to attract the dogs."

But as he finished his sentence, the first dog appeared around the corner, pulling a dead one with him. Clearly the fight over the food had turned deadly.

Andrei panicked. That night at the fence would haunt him forever.

"Shit!" he exclaimed. "Let's go back!" And he started running blindly toward the first house. Matei followed.

The dog saw them, dropped its dead comrade, and raced toward its new prey. A few steps behind it, the rest of the pack appeared.

Lili finally had the gate open. "Come here! Matei, Andrei, come here!" she yelled.

Andrei was oblivious to her calls. He couldn't hear anything, think anything. All he could do was sprint desperately.

Matei, however, turned around.

As Andrei reached his gate, he opened it, entered, and spun in time to see the first dog bite Matei's back, right in front of the gate where Lili stood.

"No!" he yelled. Why had he run off? Why hadn't he stayed close to Matei?

* * *

Lili screamed as the dog leaped at Mat.

She grabbed a fistful of her son's sweater and yanked him forward, trying to free him from the dog's teeth.

That's when she realized the dog teeth had only sunk into Mat's winter jacket. The one Matei kept unzipped.

She shoved the garment off his shoulders and pulled him in, quickly closing the gate as the dogs ripped apart their useless trophy.

* * *

"Is he okay?" called Andrei.

"Yes, he is. But no thanks to you." answered Lili, crying nervously.

"What do you mean?" Andrei asked, but he knew she was right, and the feeling of guilt was crippling.

"What do I mean? What do you think I mean? You nearly let our kid become food for bloodthirsty dogs!"

"I didn't... I thought he was right there with me."

"You should protect our son, Andrei. You should protect him," she said, voice getting smaller, before being drowned out by tears.

Since the start of their exchange, the growling in the street had grown louder.

"We have to stop yelling," said Lili, trying to control herself.

* * *

"Wait here," said Lili, finally releasing Matei from her arms.

"I wanna come with you."

"No, you need to wait here. We don't know what's inside."

"But I can help."

"No buts. There could be anything inside that house, and I don't want to push our luck. Okay, little one?"

"Okay, Mommy. But I can fight too."

"I know you can, I know," she said, kissing his cute little forehead. "But stay here. We have to check the house, and I'm happier when I know you're safe, okay?" said Lili, squeezing her bat and rising.

Matei agreed and she turned around to face the house.

* * *

Andrei was restless. He'd failed. He'd failed miserably. So damn miserably.

He'd almost got his family killed. He'd panicked and forgotten about everyone else. He was a failure.

He paced the yard as if he were a caged wolf ready to pounce. Then suddenly it came to him. He knew what he had to do.

* * *

Lili crept toward the house.

The house was probably over a hundred years old. It had no fancy windows or other showy features. Even so, these houses were pretty well insulated. A country family could live decently in a house like this, despite the fact that the toilet was probably no more than an outhouse with a hole in the ground.

She peered through the first small window she reached, but she couldn't see much because of the drapes covering them. She moved around a bit. What to do?

She realized that if they stayed silent, whatever was inside would stay dead. Or asleep. Yes, asleep sounded better. That way, she could move and act.

She remembered that a knife in the heart would kill those things. And that they needed a few seconds to wake up after hearing noises.

That was enough time for her to do the job.

She moved away from the window, planning to go around to the back. Then she spotted a dog house in the far corner of the yard, near the main road, and went to investigate.

There was no dog, but there was a chain leash, with a collar at the end. The collar wasn't broken or chewed. It looked like someone had released the dog, but when and why?

She returned to the house and the main problem at hand.

* * *

Andrei found a good axe. It was a woodcutting axe, and probably everyone around here owned one. Or a couple, really.

This would make for a decent weapon. One good hit with it should be enough to kill anything, whether dog or one of those growling creatures.

Andrei looked at it, satisfied. "This will do!"

* * *

Lili held tight to the bat as she took small, careful steps. This side of the house had no windows, but she was anticipating a surprise when she turned the corner.

As she was proceeded and the angle of her view widened, the backyard slowly became visible.

To the back there was an old, rundown shed. As she closed in on the corner of the house, she could now see the outhouse. The same simple wood, blackened by the elements over the decades, had been used to build both outdoor shacks.

She paused as she reached the corner and took a deep, calming breath. As she peered around into the yard, she gasped and drew back.

She was finally ready to proceed when a cry rose up.

"That idiot!" she murmured and turned back.

* * *

"Lili!" yelled Andrei. "Lilli, can you hear me?"

The dogs started barking, and soon the whole village was filled with growls.

"Lili! Do you hear me?"

"Yes, you idiot! Yes! What do you want? Why do you keep yelling? Don't you think at some point some of these sleepers will manage to break a door and come get us?"

"One of these what?"

"Sleepers!"

"Why do you call them that?"

"I don't know, because they sleep when they're not bothered. And now a big idiot is bothering them and waking up the entire village!"

"I prefer 'growler', but who cares. Well, I'll have you know that I'm ready to come and save you!"

"What?"

"I'm ready to come save both of you!" said Andrei, not without some pride in his voice. "I've found an axe, and I will go out, kill one or two of these dogs, and get to you. I think the others will get scared and run."

"Don't do that! You cannot kill eight dogs. That's crazy!"

"Seven."

"What?"

"Seven dogs. One is dead."

"What do you mean?"

"They killed one of their own. There're only seven left."

"Well, good for them. Even so, you cannot kill seven dogs all by yourself! You could barely kill one, and even that sounds crazy."

"Well," said Andrei, starting to feel useless again. "I have to save you."

"You don't have to do anything yet," continued Lili. "Let me investigate this house. Let's see what I find here and then wait a bit. Maybe my dad will arrive. If so, we can do things together. Three adults would be better than two, don't you think?"

"Well, yeah, maybe." Andrei surrendered.

"Fine. Now shut up. I have to investigate and I need quiet."

Andrei mumbled to himself about the world being a bad place for well-intentioned people, who got no credit for their clever plans.

* * *

"Jesus," muttered Lili. She turned toward Mat and forced a smile "You okay, hon?"

"Yes, Mommy, but I'm cold. Can we go in?"

"Oh, poor thing! You don't have your jacket. Look, have mine. I know it's too large, but keep it wrapped around you until we get this house sorted out, okay?"

How could she miss that he needed a jacket? She was always so careful. This world was becoming too much.

"Yes, Mommy. But why isn't Dad with us?"

"Well, because he's in the other house."

"Moooom!"

"I'm kidding, Mat, I'm kidding. He's there because he had to run to safety. Those dogs were coming, and he would have been bitten if he hadn't done that. Now, I'll go around and finish checking the house. Then I'll come back to you. Okay?"

"Okay."

"You should be safe here; however, if anything happens, yell my name as loud as you can."

"Yes, Mommy."

"And whatever you do, do not open the gate. There are dogs out there."

"Yes, Mommy. Geez. I won't go to the dogs. I'm not a baby!"

"Fine, fine." She kissed him a few times and then moved, again, toward the back of the house.

She reached the corner, and there she saw, again, the thing that had made her gasp right before Andrei started yelling like an idiot.

There was a small terrace, walled on three sides. The back and left were made of some simple wooden planks as the shed and outhouse. The right was the house wall itself, which had a door leading inside.

In the middle of the terrace stood a plain wooden table, with two wooden benches and one old armchair.

And in the armchair, there was an old lady.

Dead.

Well, not dead, but sleeping.

A head scarf surrounded a very white face, and her blank eyes were open, her mouth as well. Her clothes looked old and flimsy, less warm than those an old lady should wear during winter.

She was frozen, but every time there was noise, she woke, hissing and growling. She couldn't move, being frozen, but still she made those horrible sounds.

It was clear to Lili that the old lady lived alone. Probably her husband had died a while back—judging by the state of disrepair to the outside buildings—and their children had likely moved out, for work or to build families of their own.

She must have felt she would die soon, so she'd set the dog free and then come into the backyard, where she probably spent a lot of her time, to die a peaceful death. One of the dogs outside might even be hers.

It was a nice story. Lili couldn't be certain that was how things had gone, but the explanation had a nice ring to it.

Her mind didn't stop questioning though. Had she gone outside because she didn't want the house to smell? Or maybe she'd wanted to be found faster? But then why was the gate locked?

Ugh, her story wasn't making that much sense now.

As she moved closer, a new detail caught her eye: the old lady's hands were tied to the armchair.

She couldn't hold back a little scream when she also noticed several crucifixes and icons spread out on the table.

Lili's scream had the expected result: the old lady started hissing and growling.

A few seconds later, a similar sound could be heard through the door next to the bench.

Who had done that to the old lady? And why? Were they trying to perform some kind of countryside exorcism? Boy, her imagination was going wild. Probably she'd never know the truth.

But who was inside? Was it one person or more? She'd have to find out. She needed that house to be empty, to shelter her and her son.

She slowly approached, touched the knob, then remembered something and stepped back. As she waited, the noise stopped, both inside and outside. Now she could move.

She turned the knob and pushed the door open. She immediately saw an old man, face down on the floor.

Unfortunately, the door made a lot of noise.

* * *

Well, this was stupid. Was he supposed to do nothing? It hurt so bad to feel useless. At least if he had his PC or even his gaming console, he could play a game and take the edge off. Of course, he would need electricity as well, but that was another subject.

He needed to do something, to find a way to get rid of those dogs.

He kept moving around, going in and out of the house, looking left and right.

And then he had another idea.

He went to the shed, looking for something. Something long.

* * *

The old man was on his belly, trying to look up at Lili. His eyes were white, his mouth open, and he was growling. He looked even older than the lady in the armchair. He kept attempting to move forward, pulling with his hands, and she suddenly realized he had no legs. Not from the knee down, anyway. His arms were weak, and even though he tried to push himself up or crawl, he only managed to crumple an old floor mat under his chest.

It seemed that this... disease definitely didn't give you extra strength, concluded Lili. Of course, if you didn't consider the ability to move even if you were dead or frozen as an extra strength.

She carefully entered, looking around for any other possible enemy, and then she reached for the mat upon which the old man lay and started pulling. As it unfolded, it grew to about ten feet long. The old man was still on top of it, chest down.

In this manner, she managed to pull him out of the house. She took him past the old lady and left him there on the terrace.

* * *

That was it!

There he was, up on the fence, sitting proud with a pitchfork in hand. If he could hit a dog from here, injure it at least, that would mean one less enemy to fight in his quest to save Lili and Mat.

The seven dogs were on the main road, ignoring him. Now they were well fed, they'd grown sleepy and had dozed off under the shiny winter sun.

None were very close, so he couldn't hope for a killing blow. But what if he hurled his weapon. Could he then kill one of those bloodthirsty dogs? He'd seen it in the movies: spears being thrown great distances yet hitting targets. If they could do it, so could he!

And so, he tried. He took aim and threw the pitchfork.

He missed. And that wasn't the only problem. He'd wasted a good weapon. Even worse, he lost his balance.

As he barely held himself aloft, up on the fence, he realized he'd have to spend the night alone.

He was afraid to yell again, not after Lili had specifically told him not to.

God, he hoped they were fine!

Well, they should be, as he could see smoke coming from the chimney of that old house.

He climbed down and returned to the house. There, he ate some canned beans with half of an onion and then fell asleep staring into the fire. He dreamed of knights in shining armor, the kind who always killed the dragon and saved the princess.

* * *

Lili managed to unlock the front door from the inside and brought Mat in, without him ever knowing about the old man and woman out back.

As night came, they curled against each other next to the fire.

They'd found some food, mostly vegetables and legumes, probably grown by the old lady in the garden behind the house. They'd also found two cans of peas, and a few apples and pears, so they had a royal dinner. It seemed the old couple was poor, as their food supply was barely enough for the two of them for a couple of good meals.

As they stared into the fire, Lili found herself feeling sorry for the old couple. They'd died helpless and alone. And from how little food they had, it was clear they'd lived from day to day, probably thanks to the kindness of their neighbors. Even the store of firewood was far less than the old couple needed to get through the winter. Andrei was right. What was happening in this country was not okay! She saw it now. She'd grown up around here and was used to seeing some poor people. But this was not right.

"I miss Dad. I hope he's okay," said Mat, and Lili, overwhelmed by her thoughts, started crying.

* * *

"Good morning, cutie," said Lili, kissing Matei. "Wake up, Mat. We need to start the day."

"Umm, Mom," mumbled Matei, yawning. "What time is it?"

"It's morning," said Lili, kissing him some more. "I guess it's almost nine. Come. Get dressed, and let's go to the kitchen."

A little while later, Matei entered the kitchen, just as Lili was foraging through some old, tilted shelving.

"Ah, you're here. Perfect. Take these and put them on the table," said Lili, pointing at some edibles near her. "We need to see what other food we've got here."

A few minutes later they had laid on the table all the food they could find in the old couple's house: the vegetables and legumes, the fruit, the remaining can of peas, and one jar of pickles. They'd found the latter only this morning on a top shelf.

"Now," said Lili, let's go out to the well, maybe we can get some water.

It was as they were trying to work the bucket and the rope that they heard desperate yells coming from the street.

"Maaaat! Maaattt!"

"Dad?" said Lili.

She ran to the gate and peered through the gap where it joined the fence.

"Dad, no!" yelled Lili, as she saw the dogs getting up to attack. Mat's old and shredded winter jacket lay in the middle of the road, covered in blood. "That's not Mat. That's just his jacket!"

* * *

135

This was his chance, Andrei realized when he saw the dogs go for Dan.

He flung open the gate and charged out of his yard, axe in hand.

The fight was on, and it was seven dogs against two men.

Two men and one woman. Moments later, Lili joined them, baseball bat at the ready.

19 TOGETHER AGAIN

Dan liked to fight. "What policeman wouldn't?" he asked every time the subject came up.

Jokes aside, Dan had always wanted to be a policeman. His mother, God rest her soul, had told him ever since he was a boy that we were here for a reason, and that reason was to follow God's plan.

When he met Maria, the messages he'd received as a boy echoed with what Maria was saying. She always looked for a higher purpose behind everything, and this had helped him a lot.

Dan wanted to help, so he'd enjoyed being part of the police force. He'd loved the structure, the respect, the organization. He'd appreciated being part of something bigger than himself, part of the group, part of a fellowship.

But there were a lot of bad seeds in the force, and temptation had been everywhere.

You could find the lazy ones, or those too stupid to do a good job. There were conniving ones, like his ex-C.O. he'd dreamed about a few days ago, who had their own agendas and didn't care about society or truth. And the worst: the ones on the take.

All eroded his trust and motivation, but throughout it all, Maria had been there, telling him that God had a plan for everything, and the only way to fight evil was to do good and punish those who deserved it.

This had given him confidence and strength he needed, and he understood he had to keep going, to train, and always be ready.

And with her support, that's just what he would do.

* * *

As the first dog jumped toward Dan's chest, Dan swung the bat, and the dog fell to the right, forever silenced.

He still had it, Dan thought. He quickly focused and assessed the situation.

The remaining six dogs arrived, and the dance began.

He loved this fight! It somehow reminded him of the good old days. And he wasn't afraid. He was fully alert, and his only possible regret would be, should he die today, that he had not lived long enough to help his family survive this plague that had come upon the world.

Dan turned left and right. He leapt in all directions, faster than he ever had. His body was getting old. Maybe he wasn't as fast as he used to be. But his mind was clear.

He gripped the baseball bat tight in his left hand. The right hand was too swollen to hold anything. Fighting with the right hand was clearly out of the question. Although he could use his forearm to cover his face, if needs be.

He'd fought multiple attackers more than once in his lifetime, but this was different.

Now, there were six enemies. And they had teeth and an instinct to kill. And to eat, one might add.

* * *

Andrei was closing in. His initial motivation, fueled by his wish to help and make up for past mistakes, was slowly eroded by exhaustion.

Running those 250 yards in deep snow, given his subpar physical condition, took its toll on his ability to fight. And the damn axe was heavy!

Step by step, though, he closed in, and finally got in range of the first dog.

* * *

"A pitchfork," said Lili, when she saw the tool lying in the snow. "How did this get here?"

Well, no matter. It might come in handy, so she picked it up and started running toward her father.

The dogs had surrounded Dan, and he was jumping and moving like she had never seen before.

She spotted Andrei's back as he ran toward Dan. But it was clear he was starting to lose his breath. He wasn't cut out for this. Heck, she wasn't ready either, and she'd been taking aerobics class every other day.

She'd soon be in range, however, and would put her bat to good use once more.

* * *

Dan was never going to win this. Not alone.

His energy was slowly but surely depleting, and the dogs had learned fast how to get out of the bat's way. What had happened to their comrade had made them more reserved, and now they approached with patience. They just needed to wait and wear Dan down. In the end the prey would be theirs.

Dan had to keep swinging the bat, even if he rarely hit anything. Otherwise the dogs would come too close, jump him and pull him to the ground.

That's when Andrei arrived.

* * *

His first strike went wide. It was way easier on PC games, that's for sure! There, he rarely missed.

Andrei had put too much weight behind the swing, and he fell to his knees, all his weight now supported by the axe, which had sunk deep into the snow.

The targeted dog didn't quite understand what had happened. It leaped away and landed on Andrei's right, clearly frightened. When Andrei stumbled, though, its instincts kicked in and it attacked.

As the dog charged, Andrei's instincts helped him as well. Dragging the axe out with a yell, he managed to take a horizontal swing. Not being proficient in axe fighting, he forgot to turn the weapon, though, and only caught the dog with the side of the blade.

Andrei stumbled again, this time to the left. He also managed to drop the axe, which flew away, together with the dog it hit.

The axe struck the side of the dog's head. The impact was strong and it dazed the dog, which retreated, wobbling, back toward the village.

* * *

Lili raced past Andrei, who had fallen while taking out one of the dogs.

Five to go, she realized.

Dan was doing a good job of keeping them busy, so this was their chance to take them out, one by one.

As she drew closer, she realized she couldn't wield two weapons at once. More comfortable with the bat, which was already in her right hand, she discarded the pitchfork.

With it, she managed to surprise a dog with a hit on its lower back. She must have injured it badly, as it gave a loud whimper. She almost felt sorry for it, but she had to save Dan.

Four to go, she thought. No, three! Across the way, Dan had managed to knock another to the ground.

As she tried a horizontal swing at one of the remaining animals, the targeted dog, alerted to the danger by its comrade's cry, saw her coming and jumped.

Had the swing hit its target, she probably would have maintained her equilibrium. However, just like Andrei, she'd put too much weight behind the strike, and because she'd missed, momentum made her turn midair and fall onto her side.

That's when the dogs saw an opportunity.

Two dogs jumped Lili. Their teeth were sharp, their bite was strong, and their breath smelled like putrid meat.

Lili used her hands to defend herself as they aimed for her face and neck. Their teeth ripped through her hoodie, scraping her skin, grabbing and bruising.

Now she could understand what Andrei had gone through when that huge man fell on him. But this was even worse, as her attackers were more successful, and she already felt pain in her arms and hands.

And the attack only intensified when the third and last remaining dog saw the opportunity and joined the assault.

* * *

Dan found himself suddenly alone. No dog was attacking him. Not anymore.

Then he saw the three animals mauling his daughter.

Not thinking anymore, he dropped his bat, charged forward and grabbed two of the dogs by the scruff of their necks, pulling them away from Lili. Unfortunately, the pain in his right hand hit violently and he only managed to get one dog out, unable to keep hold of the other.

He threw the dog to his right, as far as he could, and reached for the next.

He grabbed ahold and repeated the action.

But now, he had no bat. And the first dog he'd thrown, who had landed on some soft snow, wanted its vengeance.

Just like his daughter, Dan was soon on his back, defending his face against one, and then two, angry dogs.

* * *

Andrei rose with some difficulty. He was tired, snow was everywhere, and he was out of shape.

Upon getting to his feet, he saw events unfold as the remaining three dogs mauled Dan and Lili.

Lili. His beloved Lili!

He took a step toward her and spotted the pitchfork. *What is this doing here, so far from where I threw it? Well, who cares? This will do!*

* * *

When he was young, Andrei had spent most of his summers at

his grandparents' house in the countryside.

There, among other things, he saw the farmers pick up big piles of hay, turning them midair, and then throwing the piles back, upside down. This was, of course, done to help the hay dry, so it could be stored for winter.

As he got older, he'd been expected to help, so he'd soon got pretty good at the maneuver.

And the tool of choice? The pitchfork.

Lili was down. One dog was on top of her, biting her arms.

Andrei grabbed the pitchfork, and with one strong swing, he picked up the unsuspecting dog. Two of the spikes went through the animal, who let out a horrible cry.

With self-control he'd never thought he had in him, he raised the pitchfork, turned it midair, slammed it into the snow, and used his leg to hold the dog down while pulling the prongs free.

His moves were swift and accurate, as in a well-rehearsed sequence.

He then turned his attention to the two remaining dogs attacking Dan.

Stab. Turn. Slam. Pull.

One more dog.

Stab. Turn. Slam. Pull.

Well, he wasn't any good at throwing pitchforks, but he was clearly skilled at turning hay and stabbing dogs.

As he looked around, barely breathing, he saw his beloved Lili still on her back, tears in her eyes.

"How are you, honey?" asked Andrei, concerned. "Are you okay?"

"No, I'm not okay," said Lili, crying. "Those beasts! They almost killed me! Did you see that?"

"Yes, honey, I did. I did. You're okay though. Look," he said, touching her hoodie, checking for tears to see if she was wounded.

Parts of the hoodie had ripped as the dogs used their claws and fangs, but they hadn't punctured through to her torso.

Her arms were bleeding however. Not too much—she was in no immediate danger—but she needed patching up.

"You'll be okay, honey. Trust me. I know," said Andrei.

How could he know? But his words helped, and Lili relaxed.

Dan staggered to his feet, groaning.

"Hey, Dan! Good to see you. That was a horrible fight," said Andrei, genuinely happy to see Dan back with them.

"Yeah, Andrei. Hi. How's Lili? Lili! How are you? Those damn dogs! I would kill them all again if I could!"

"I'm okay, Dad… I think. How's Mom?" said Lili, still lying in the snow.

"She's… gone. The cure didn't work. She's dead for good," he said, his expression sad. "We'll talk about it later. Can you walk?"

"I guess so. Let's see." She got up with Andrei's help.

As they walked back toward the village, Andrei supporting Lili by the waist, she looked up at him, smiling.

"Well, what do you know. You actually saved my life."

"Well… yeah," he said, with a spark of pride.

"You realize that was a mistake, right?" Lili laughed. "Now you'll have to keep hearing my jabs about you looking like Jabba the Hut for the rest of your life."

"First," said Andrei, "as you already know, but choose to ignore, I'm not *that* fat. The doctor said, wrongly I might add, that I am borderline. And second, I'm starting to believe you're into chubby guys."

"I'm into buff bodies, not chubby."

"I see. Same here, I guess. I'm into cute, smart and funny girls. But somehow I got stuck with you," he said, and they both laughed.

* * *

"Mat? You can come out honey," said Lili as they approached the gate of the house where they had spent the night.

The dog Andrei had struck with the axe was curled up in front of the gate, dead. Dan pulled him away as the gate slowly opened and Mat's head, covered by Lili's jacket's hood, peeked out.

"Daddy!" He ran out and hugged his father.

"It figures," muttered Lili.

"Look who's here," said Andrei, a few moments after, as Mat hugged his grandpa.

"Where should we stay?" asked Andrei. "Should we go to your new house?"

"No. We were just preparing all the food to take back to yours. I don't like this house. It stinks inside, and the toilet is crappy. We can use the well, though, as it's only a few yards away."

She didn't say anything about the old lady in the armchair and how they would need to kill her, or at least smash her head in. The same with the old man. Still, her eyes watered.

And her self-control was put to the test even further when she realized the dog Andrei had struck had tried to come home, only to die alone in the cold, in front of the old lady's yard.

* * *

"Aaaahhh!" yelled Lili, as Andrei washed the wounds on her right hand. "By God, it stings!"

Her hands were all bitten. Deep cuts were visible. She was bleeding—enough to be concerned.

"Can you move the hand?" asked Andrei. "And squeeze the fist?"

"Yes, I can, you dufus," said Lili with a groan. "Look!" she added, waving her hands around and squeezing and unsqueezing her fists. "Happy?"

"Luckily, it doesn't look like you've taken damage to any major artery or tendon," said Dan, who was observing the exchange.

"That's good, I guess," said Lili, settling down and visibly relaxing. "But it hurts like hell!"

"Sorry, hon. We have to do this," said Dan, while washing the wounds on her left hand. "We cannot have these getting infected."

"Well, they got in pretty deep. Aren't we in danger of— Aaaahhh!—of just that?"

"Yeah, but if we clean them properly, you should be okay," said Dan, knowingly. "Okay, next one. You were lucky, I give you that."

He started pushing around the bite, to force some of the blood out. Lili screamed again.

"Sorry, hon, just a bit more. This should help keep the wound clean. There... that's good. Now, let's wash this one as well."

"Aaaaaahhh!!!"

* * *

Dan's wounds were lighter. He'd faced two dogs, but for a shorter time. And his jacket was thicker, all leather, which had helped.

As Andrei, now experienced and starting to feel like Dr. House, was cleaning Dan's wounds, he noticed the swollen thumb.

"This looks bad, Dan. This looks really bad. It looks like it needs…" Andrei stopped, not wanting to continue.

"Surgery?" said Dan, and Andrei nodded. "Yeah, I thought that. But it's not like we can go to the hospital. The good part is the blood vessels seem to be okay. It's just the extreme pain I sometimes feel. And if it starts healing… Well, I might have a deformed hand for the rest of my life. But that's probably not that long." Dan smiled.

"Dad!" said Lili.

* * *

Finally, they were together again, and more importantly, safe!

As they sat by the fire in the house under construction, talking, the hardships of the last few days began to dim. They had retrieved all the remaining food from the old couple's house, and now they could relax, at least for the time being.

Oddly enough, they were happy.

"Mommy, you look like a mummy!" said Mat, laughing at her bandaged hands. "Mommy the mummy. That's how we'll call you now!"

"Pfft," said Lili, smiling. "Cut it out."

"Okay… mummy."

"Hey!"

Everybody laughed.

"Right. Let's go to bed, young man!" said Lili, getting up. "Tomorrow is a big day."

"What do we do tomorrow, Mommy?"

"We gather resources, hon."

"What are resources?"

"Well, things we need. Food, onions, anything else we might find useful."

The two of them headed to the bedroom, while Andrei and Dan

remained in the living room.

"Look…" Dan tried to find the words. This wasn't easy for him, but it was the right thing to do. "What you did… That was… I mean, you saved my life back there. Thank you."

Andrei glanced at him briefly, then they both returned their attention to the fire.

They were both smiling.

A few moments later, Andrei broke the silence. "So… tomorrow we gather resources?"

"Indeed," said Dan. "We really need to find some onions."

That sounded simple. But Dan was concerned.

"But maybe even more importantly," he continued, "we got bit by dogs, so we also need to find some rabies shots."

20 THE ENEMY

"He fell asleep right away," said Lili, returning to the living room. "Poor kid. He should be outside, throwing snowballs, not on the run surrounded by monsters. He should have a childhood like we had."

"What are these monsters, anyway?" asked Andrei. "How did this happen? Was our country attacked? Was the world attacked? Or was it an accident? I still think it was the Russians!"

Dan smiled. As much as he liked to believe it was the big bear from the east, he knew better.

"Everyone got it. This thing," he said, "this disease, it's a full-blown pandemic. You've seen the news. And I don't think the Russians would have done this to our country. Not when they're so close."

"What do you mean so close?" said Andrei.

"I mean in terms of distance. They're only some thousands of miles out. They wouldn't risk getting infected themselves."

"I see," continued Andrei. "But is this a disease? Can we assume we pass it on to each other, like the flu? What if we just need to smell a poisoned flower or eat some infected meat. Or maybe burning the Russian gas our country buys frees spores into the atmosphere," he said, getting some brief smiles from Dan and Lili.

They all sat there, quiet.

"Maybe we need to talk about what we know, put all the info we have on the table and draw some conclusions about what we're

147

dealing with?" said Lili.

"That's a good idea, Lili," said Dan. "I wonder why I haven't thought of that. It's just like old times, in the force. We need to work up the profile."

"Let's see," said Andrei. "We know everyone is dead and that they turned into these growlers."

"You mean sleepers," interrupted Lili.

"Nope, I mean growlers," asserted Andrei. "They growl, so the correct term is 'growler'."

"Anyone can call a growling thing a growler," said Lili, checking her arms. No blood on the bandages, that was good. She'd have to change them again in the morning. "It takes smarts, however, to find a different attribute, one that is not so obvious but has a deeper impact. So, shortly," she concluded, "simple-minded folks talk about visible traits, while smart, next-level individuals consider more subtle ones."

"And which of those is calling a chubby yet sexy person Jabba?" asked Andrei.

"Hey," said Lili, hugging him. "You know I'm just pulling your leg with that. I always thought you liked these jokes."

"Yes, yes," said Andrei, kissing her. "You know I love how we sting each other," he added, as they both smiled and kissed. "Of course, I'm not sure you always get *my* jokes. You know, them being so next level and all."

"Ha. That's *exactly* your strength," she said, in a sarcastic tone, while continuing to kiss her husband. "The wit of your jokes." She then continued in a cuddly tone, faking a sad face. "But if it bothers you, I can stop mentioning your weight. You just tell me and—"

"We don't know everyone is dead." Dan interrupted their exchange. "This is an assumption. We always need to check our facts. And we should call them 'growlers', as it sounds menacing. It's more appropriate. Sleeper is too soft and vague."

"Yeah, a cute koala bear could be called a 'sleeper'," Andrei was kind enough to add, laughing.

Lili huffed and didn't look happy, but she moved on, while Andrei gloated for half the discussion, which continued long into the night.

"I remember they mentioned on TV that some research

institutes said it could be a bacterium," said Andrei, getting back to the main subject. "What if we can keep it at bay with antibiotics?"

"Does either of you have any medical training?" asked Dan. When both Lili and Andrei shook their heads, he continued. "So we can't know for certain. Whatever it is, it spread fast, without anyone having enough time to understand what it was and react."

"But what about the onions? Are they natural antibiotics? Why are they good for this? I mean, I know onions are really good," continued Andrei with a smile, while Lili rolled her eyes. "But why?"

"That we don't know either. Probably they have some substance in them, one that gets destroyed when they are cooked," answered Dan. "Still, it makes me wonder... I now remember what my mother used to do with the garlic and onion strings."

"What?" asked Lili.

"When I was a kid, and for all her life actually, she used to hang a string of garlic and one of onions next to the icons on the eastern wall."

"Yes, I remember now," said Lili, a little more enthusiastically. "I always thought it was because she liked them and wanted to have them close, not in the cellar. Why did she really do that?"

"She used to say the garlic was to keep away the Strigoi, while the onions were for the Moroi. I wonder if that's what Maria wanted to tell me."

"She wanted to tell you something?" asked Lili. "When?"

"Back at the cabin. She wanted to tell me something, something that the priest apparently told her. But she started coughing and I stopped her. What if she was going to tell me about the onions? She could be alive now," said Dan, descending into sadness.

"Hey, Dad," said Lili, touching his arm. "You're going down the wrong path. It's not your fault. It's not anybody's fault that Mom is dead. And she never considered eating onions to be the cure for what she had. She would have said it. She had every chance."

"I guess you're right," said Dan, taking a deep breath.

"Look," said Andrei, his eyes widening. "I've heard of Strigoi, they're vampires, but what's a Moroi?"

"The movies and books don't do justice to these things, but okay, Strigoi are *some sort* of vampire," said Dan, looking straight at Andrei. "The Moroi are dead people coming back to life. Their old self is gone, they just attack the living and the livestock. It is said a Strigoi can raise a Moroi, which then follows the Strigoi's will. It's probably just folklore and superstition, of course. Still, one can only wonder how come the people of old made the connection between these entities and garlic and onions."

"Don't tell me this is the work of some Strigoi," said Andrei, with a trembling voice.

"No, no. I'm not saying that. All I'm saying is, back in the old days, it sounded smart to have some garlic and onions around, and to consume them regularly. Today it sounds like a good idea as well, at least with regards to the onions."

"Look," said Lili peacefully, looking straight into Andrei's eyes. "Relax. Let's not dwell on the supernatural. All we know is we need to have a daily dose of onions for the rest of our lives."

They all sat there, quiet, thinking.

"Let's change the subject," said Lili, throwing a quick glance at Andrei. "I noticed something about the woman who lived here, the wife of the huge *growler* that attacked you," she said, doing air-quotes around 'growler'. "She smelled like a dead person. And she was very slow. All the others are more alert, faster, and they don't stink. Okay, they need a bath, but they don't smell like a rotting corpse."

"Yes, I've seen that too," said Dan. "It happened with Maria. I fed her onions, she looked dead, and then she woke again. But she was way slower than before, and rotting. What's up with that?"

"Maybe the way you die matters?" asked Lili. "The woman here was eaten, so maybe she died because of that and not due to the disease?"

"You mean if one dies due to the disease, it is a fast, non-smelling one, and if one dies from other causes, the body rots and then comes back to life as a slow, stinking one?"

"And by giving onions to Maria," intervened Andrei, "you somehow stopped the thing keeping her alive. She finally died, started to rot, and then the disease came back. I think that's why she was so different when she started walking again."

"Guess so…" said Dan in a whispery voice, staring into the fire.

"What about the head thing?" asked Lili, pulling Dan back. "I've hit, no, *we've* hit a few on the top of the head, cracking their skulls open. Hell, Dad, you even shot one. Still, they didn't die. They still move, squirm, and only die when stabbed through the chest."

"Ha! Another Moroi thing right there," said Dan, focusing on Andrei. "Killing a Moroi means digging up the grave, finding the sleeping body and nailing its heart. If they wanted to be one hundred percent certain, they would then burn the heart and scatter the ashes."

"Dad! Stop with this. He will never sleep after these stories," said Lili, as Andrei's eyes widened again. "Andrei, you wanted to say something?"

"Yes. So, clearly the brain is no longer the only CPU," answered Andrei. "The main CPU is somewhere else, and the communication bus—"

"English," said Lili, pointing to herself and Dan. "We're not computer geeks like you are."

"I mean, the brain is no longer the Central Processing Unit; it's no longer the place calling the shots. Probably it's somewhere in the chest. The brain might still be used for basic motor function, but the *alive* part is somewhere else. It probably communicates with the brain—"

"Through the spine!" exclaimed Lili. "That's how I stopped the huge growler outside, by smashing its spine."

"Right," said Andrei.

"But how come the alive part in the chest is still alive when frozen?" asked Dan.

"It probably keeps itself heated. I don't know. Some chemical reaction I guess," said Andrei.

"It's probably all about the calories," intervened Lili. "If it has a way to consume something, anything, it will generate heat."

"Can they eat? Wouldn't the mouth and stomach be frozen?" asked Dan.

"Lili might be right. Maybe that thing inside consumes internal organs around the chest. Maybe it's like a tumor, a tumor-brain, spreading all around, feeding off the body in times of need. I really don't know."

"Yeah, we can't know," said Dan. "But how come they can hear when frozen? One thing I remember since school is that noise is an electrical signal sent to the brain. But even with a smashed brain or a frozen body, it still hears."

"Maybe they hear with the new core? The chest is the one picking up vibrations and acting on them?" proposed Andrei.

"To me, it's more important to understand why they stop after a while," said Lili. "Why is the noise waking them, and then they fall asleep again? Why doesn't their own noise keep them awake?"

"Maybe it becomes background noise?" suggested Andrei.

"I don't think so," said Lili. "Then, when some background noise disappears, shouldn't that wake them again?"

"Remember what happened with Maria. When Dan turned off the generator, Maria woke. We thought she was far enough from the generator, but in reality, I think it became background noise for her. Background noise which finally disappeared and woke her."

"When did Maria wake?" interrupted Dan.

"Back at the cabin, Dad, right before we wanted to leave, all of us, together. We didn't want to tell you." She turned to Andrei again. "I don't think it's possible."

"Sounds farfetched," confirmed Dan. "How can you explain them not waking again after all the sound that becomes 'background noise' goes away?"

"It's the same explanation as for the 'why aren't growlers waking when they fall on the ground' question. Which is odd, as when it happens they make a lot of noise, plus they hit themselves."

Andrei jumped out of his chair as he spoke and started moving around. "Remember when you touched the teacher's wife, how fast she woke and then fell asleep, even while you kept holding her down? I think it all makes sense. Probably that touch became background noise, or 'background touch', if you will."

Dan and Lili looked at each other in disbelief. Andrei continued. "When they fall down, they have some sort of reboot. A full shutdown. Everything is off. You've seen the fall. It's uncontrolled. They just hit the ground. They don't try to break their fall, they don't hear or feel anything, not for a few seconds at least."

"Well, I don't want to test that," said Lili. "Fine. You think they will act up if a noise disappears. I don't. I just hope we're never in a position to have to test that."

"What about animals?" interrupted Dan.

"Can an animal turn into a Moroi?" asked Andrei, with disbelief in his voice.

"Would you stop with the Moroi already? It's just folklore. What do you mean, Dad?"

"What if rats can get this? Or cows? Or birds? Dogs seem fine, at least."

* * *

A short while later, their conversation exhausted for now, Lili, Andrei and Dan sat around the table in silence, save for the crackle of the fire in the fireplace.

"I guess you weren't completely wrong," said Andrei at last, looking at Lili.

"What do you mean?"

"Disease or no disease, these do sound like zombies."

21 THREE TEAMS

"Let's get organized!" said Andrei the next morning, enthusiastic.

"What's got into you?" asked Lili, with a smile.

"What do you mean? We have to do this."

"Yeah, I know. But why are you so hyped?"

"I'm not," said Andrei, chuckling. "We need to do this."

"He thinks he's back at the office," said Lili out loud, looking at Dan. "He *loves* to organize things, which basically means telling people what to do."

"Not true, pfft!"

"Well, after the discussion last night we're all missing our motivation and energy, while you seem to have found yours," said Lili. "And that's a positive."

"Okay, fine. Now, can we focus on what we have to do? Great. We need onions, food, rabies shots, and new clothes for the two of you," he said, pointing at Dan and Lili. "Am I missing anything?"

"We need a coat for Mat as well," answered Lili.

"Why? The family living here had a boy his age? The one you... I mean, we can use his coat, right?"

"That's the first thing I checked. I don't know why, but the only jacket I found was a worn-out girl's jacket. It's in the hallway, by the front door. Probably the boy didn't have a spare and was wearing his only winter coat when he turned."

"I don't want a girl's jacket!" squeaked Mat.

"Yes, okay, got it. We'll look for another jacket," confirmed Andrei. "Until then, young man, it's okay if you wear a girl's jacket. It will also allow you to go outside a bit. Wearing a girl's jacket just shows how much of a big boy you are. It shows courage and self-confidence," said Andrei, in a feeble attempt to convince his son to wear the available clothing.

"And that's why your dad wears girls' clothes too!" Lili clearly couldn't miss the opportunity to have a dig.

They all laughed.

"Is it true?" asked Mat, looking very surprised.

Now they all laughed again, but way harder.

"No, honey, it's just a joke. Mom likes to pull my leg. You should know that by now," Andrei quickly reassured him. "Okay, so, back to it. We'll look for a boy's jacket. Anything else?"

"Nope, I think that's it. Maybe a generator would be useful, as I would love to have a toilet I could flush. How about the firewood? Are we good or do we need some more?" asked Lili. "Andrei already said it's enough, but what do you think, Dad?"

"We're more than okay," answered Dan. "With the firewood we have stored at these two houses, we can get through the winter. And I bet there's enough in this village for twenty winters more."

"Cool," said Andrei. "Anything else?"

"Yup," said Dan. "We need a vehicle."

"Right!" exclaimed Andrei, with even more enthusiasm. "A nice 4x4 to go through this snow would be perfect. We could use it to bring the generator from the woodsmen's cabin, if we don't find another. And to bring enough fuel to last us for years."

"I don't think we'll find a 4x4 here that can drive in such deep snow," Dan cautioned. "But here's hoping. If you see a tractor, that might be better."

"True. So! We know what we need. How do we go about this?"

"Simple," intervened Lili. "We go and take what we need."

"Ha! That's a good plan. It covers everything. Shall we?" Andrei smiled and made a wide-handed gesture, inviting them toward the living room door.

"We should go to the other side of town. We'll scout left and right, identifying houses that look well taken care of. New fence, good roof. Those belonging to well-off people," said Dan.

"I don't think there are too many rich people here, Dad."

"Yeah, I know. That's why I don't want to break in randomly. Ideally, I want to hit just one—the one that has the most in it, as it will probably have a few times more stuff than all the poor ones put together. We also need to keep our eyes open for a vehicle. If we're lucky, we can then use it to go back to town. If not, we'll have to walk."

"What?" exclaimed Andrei and Lili together.

"Why?" Lili continued. "We barely got out of town! I don't want to go back to that apartment, without water, electricity or heat. Okay, we're missing some of those things here as well, but clearly we're better off having some firewood to heat our—"

"We need medical supplies," Dan interrupted "We need rabies shots for you and me."

"But, why don't we go to the village pharmacy? They should have rabies shots, given how many stray dogs there are around here."

"We'll look for that, yes," said Dan. "But as far as I know, they closed down the pharmacy over ten years ago."

"Okay then!" Andrei clapped his hands. "Let's go!"

"We need two teams. We have to split," said Dan, taking them by surprise.

"Again?" said Lili. "I don't want to ever do that again. You saw what happened last time. We almost died! And I keep feeling we were lucky. Too lucky. We will eventually run out of luck."

"What do we do about Mat?" asked Dan. "Do we leave him here alone?"

"Mommy, I don't want to be alone. I want to come with you."

"Why should we leave Mat?" asked Lili.

"He has no coat," said Andrei.

"No," answered Lili, sighing as she realized the answer. "We don't want to risk his life again. We don't want him to see what's out there. Or what we might have to do."

* * *

Dan and Andrei exited the main gate, waving back at Lili and Mat. They were armed to the teeth: one bat and one knife each. Dan also had his trusty gun in its holster. Two empty backpacks graced their shoulders, hopefully soon to be filled with all the food, onions and medicine they could find.

They started walking.

"We need to be quiet," said Dan, almost whispering. "There's plenty of growlers in this village."

"Yeah," answered Andrei. "We heard them whenever the dog pack started barking. Hopefully, they will remain dormant while we move around."

"Yeah, I guess it's up to us," said Dan marching on, his brows drawn together.

They continued their advance, looking left and right at fences and houses, sizing them up.

"My God," said Andrei after a while, "Lili was right."

"What?"

"There are mostly poor people around here. Look at the houses. They are in a poor state, all of them."

"Yes, I know. Now come, be quiet. We'll find something."

As they moved on, heading deeper into the village, they heard a weak growl coming from inside a yard. But it was a different kind of growl. It sounded like a dog. They moved on.

Strange that a dog had survived this long. *It must be a hell of a dog,* thought Andrei.

Suddenly, Dan stopped. He turned on his heel and started walking toward the yard.

"What?" whispered Andrei.

Dan paused and whispered back, "That dog survived. He deserves a second chance." His tone and posture said 'end of discussion,' so Andrei followed him in silence.

They entered through the unlocked gate and saw the poor dog next to his doghouse.

"It's a German Shepherd," said Dan, stopping a few steps away, by the gate. "And he's young, no more than three years."

Andrei said nothing as he looked around the yard, checking for possible hostiles.

"It's a miracle he's survived this long," said Dan, with a hint of pity in his tone. "Look at how skinny he is. He can barely stand. He doesn't even have enough energy to bark, although we just entered his yard, the poor thing."

Andrei looked at the dog. His eyes, which were still alive, followed the two men the entire time.

"When we return from town, I'll come back for this dog," said Dan, fire in his eyes.

Then, while Andrei looked on, he set to work.

* * *

As they left, Andrei looked at Dan, hoping to elicit an answer to a silent question.

Finally, Dan yielded and whispered, "I moved the doghouse onto the porch, for protection from the wind. I also put some mats I found on the porch inside. I didn't want to move him inside the house. There may be growlers in there, and we are in a hurry."

"Yes, I got that," answered Andrei. "What I don't get is why you didn't just set him free. And why you gave him all your food."

"Well, first, it's not safe for him to be out. There are probably no more stray dogs. However, Howler is in no position to defend himself at present, and wolves might come down from mountains. It's not unheard of, and they may get up the courage, since there aren't any people left to scare them off."

Andrei was listening, but only one word got his attention. "Howler?"

"Well, you call those things growlers, right? I'm going to call my new dog Howler." Dan smiled. "And, yes, I gave him all my food. I can easily go an entire day without eating, while Howler might have drawn his last breath tonight without sustenance.

"I know German Shepherds. I've had a few myself. They're a tough breed. And this one, except for the state he's in now, looks like he can carry his weight. With the food I gave him, he'll get stronger. And when we return this evening with all the food we can carry, I'll feed him some more. And probably tomorrow morning as well. I'll do a quick tour and feed him again before going back to town."

Andrei looked at Dan's determined face. *This man is actually something else,* he thought.

"It sounds like a good plan," he said a few moments later. "This way, Howler will surely survive. And having a dog of our own might prove useful."

The men moved on, continuing their quest to find a house that had what they needed.

As the village was about one and a half miles long, they kept walking through the snow, looking left and right.

Until finally they saw it.

* * *

"Tell me, honey, what do you want to do today?" asked Lili, smiling.

The day was, again, a little warmer, with a nice shiny sun in the sky. Still, temperatures were below freezing, and the kid had to wear the pink jacket.

"I don't like this jacket!" said Mat, crossing his arms with a frown.

"I know, sweetie," said Lili, "but you need something to keep you warm."

"But I want some boy clothes."

"I know. The other option is to stay alone in the living room," said Lili, smiling as Mat's expression showed what his choice would be.

"Okay, fine," said Matei, sighing. "I'll wear this."

"Come on, it will be a good day," said Lili, kissing him. "And we can wash some clothes later. Will you help me?"

As the day passed, they had fun. They carried more firewood into the house, increasing the stash to last them a few days, made more water by melting snow indoors, and then stored it in some bottles they found around the house. Later, they did the laundry. It was the first time Lili had had the opportunity for such a task, and in good time, as they were all out of clean clothes.

As the hours flew by, Lili realized it has been half a day since the guys left. She wasn't overly concerned yet, but a little nugget of worry started to eat away at her.

And when the whole village started to growl, as had happened when the dogs were roaming the streets, this quickly transformed into fear.

* * *

"The church," whispered Dan.

"The church? What could we possibly find there?"

"Around here, priests are some of the richest people. You can do without food and heat, but when you die, give birth or get married, you need a priest. Add to that Christmas, Easter, and a lot of other saints and celebrations. The priests usually live in the house next to the church, and they generally have plenty of food, wine, supplies and, of course, money. But we don't need the latter."

"Okay, fine. It looks way better than all the other properties we've passed, that's for sure. Let's do this."

The fence gate was wide open, welcoming people in. Thirty yards back stood the wooden Orthodox church. It was tall and newly painted brown.

Beyond that was a nice house, and between the church and the house a gazebo covered the entrance to a cellar, close to the fence out back.

The fence was only three or four feet tall, about half the size of the other fences in the village. It looked new as well, and the whole property seemed well taken care of. Although parts were covered by abundant snow, from the outside, it looked as if the church had a basement of its own, and the wooden part was a few feet off the ground. On the right-hand side of the property, at the corner of the church and close to the main street, there was a belfry—a small square gazebo really—held together by four nicely carved wooden pillars. In the middle of this there was a bell.

The one-story house was charming. Small, probably not more than two bedrooms and a living room, but with quality finishing. That's where the priest must have lived.

The gazebo out back did a good job protecting the cellar hatch from the snow. It was fully visible from afar.

"These guys sure love their basements and cellars," muttered Andrei.

"What?"

"Nothing. I see a few basements and cellars that are probably good places to look for food and supplies. What do we do?"

"Let's go in."

"I don't like this," whispered Andrei.

"Why?"

"I feel… uneasy. I don't like churches. And I hate the way priests have plenty while the poor remain poor."

"The good news, if you can put it that way," said Dan, "is that in death they are all equal."

"Yeah, well… check out the car parked there," said Andrei, pointing at a luxury sedan. "Okay, it has a few years under the hood, but how can a priest in a remote village own a vehicle like that?"

"What do you want to do, then? And what's this got to do with anything?"

"I don't know. There's something else here, and I can't put my finger on it."

"Come on," said Dan, controlling a quick smile. "Don't be afraid. We're together. We'll just go in, take the stuff we need, then come back out."

"Okay, fine," said Andrei, after a sigh. "Let's go."

When Dan passed through the gate, Andrei followed. They both surveyed the premises, looking left and right as they advanced.

Andrei was restless. He kept turning around, as if he was looking for something he knew was there, but he couldn't find it.

"At least the path isn't covered in snow," he muttered.

Andrei froze. He was almost in front of the church's entrance, about twenty yards from the gate.

To their right stood the church and the belfry, and in front were the little house and the cellar.

The long, winding alley connecting them had some snow on it. But still, it was visibly less than everywhere else.

"Dan," he whispered. "Dan. Dan!"

Dan stopped. He turned, raising his eyebrows.

Andrei moved his hands, indicated the alley.

As he realized what Andrei meant, Dan's face dropped. He spun around, checking their surroundings. Then he slowly set down his bat, opened his big winter jacket, and carefully unclipped the gun from its holster.

"Someone shoveled it before the last fall—"

"Shush!" said Dan, looking straight at Andrei and frowning.

They carefully climbed the five steps to the church's porch. Gun in his left hand, Dan pressed down on the door handle with his right palm, making sure his thumb didn't touch anything.

The church door was unlocked. Within, the light was dim, like in any Orthodox church, and after passing through the narthex, the church's lobby, they finally made it to the nave.

The first thing they saw was the side benches and chairs. They were moved around, some of them upside-down.

The second thing that hit them was the smell.

And the third thing they noticed, almost hidden behind an overturned bench, was the half-eaten body on the floor.

"It's the priest," whispered Andrei. "Look at his clothes."

It was impossible to tell his age, as his face was eaten. And not just his face: arms, chest, abdomen. There were deep teeth marks everywhere.

Next to him, all around, were signs of a struggle.

"Who did that?" whispered Andrei, taking a step back and rapidly turning his head, looking for an answer to his question.

Suddenly, he felt something underfoot. Then he heard the growl.

When he looked down, he saw a small hand, very white, emerging from behind the overturned bench upon which he'd stepped.

And then, the whole church began to growl.

Andrei let out a terrified scream.

A teenage girl was getting up. Her white dress was bloody, and crucifixes were dangling from her neck, tied with golden and silver chains. Her white face had blood around the mouth, and a black cross sign was drawn on her forehead.

As the dead teenage girl got up, he hit her with his bat. Once. Twice. Three times. He kept missing the head. He stopped, repositioned himself, aimed properly, and hit again. Four. Five. Six. The girl's head was smashed.

As adrenalin rushed in, he saw the priest. He was up. No face, and his guts were on the floor, still attached to his body. He was a slow one, coming toward Andrei, toward the noise.

Dan moved quickly and put his knife through the priest's chest. As he pierced the heart, a long growl came out of the priest's mouth, and then he fell down for good.

They looked around. There were no more oncoming enemies.

However, the whole church was growling.

And the sound was coming from below.

To the left of the altar there was a traditional, carved wooden door which led to the basement below. The door started to shift, being hit and pushed. It would soon break, and whatever was behind it would come pouring out.

Dan and Andrei exchanged glances, then they started to edge backwards, toward the exit.

The door gave, broken into pieces.

The first fast growler spewed forth. Then a second. And a third. There didn't seem to be an end.

Andrei and Dan turned and started running.

The growlers numbered more than a dozen, and they were all racing to get at Andrei and Dan.

* * *

"Into the house!" cried Dan.

But Andrei wasn't listening. He panicked. Again. As he got out of the church, he saw the alley leading to the cellar and bolted in that direction.

Since the house was closer, Dan went there. He tried to open the front door, but it was locked. And it was a sturdy metal one, so there was no chance of forcing it with his shoulder. "God damn it!" he yelled. Maybe Andrei had been right to go to the cellar.

People here usually had back doors, though, so he raced around the side of the house. He was now between the house and the church, the growlers fast approaching from behind. He continued to run, and as he turned the corner, he saw it.

There was a back door leading into the kitchen. It was locked, but the door was a simple wooden one, with glass windows on the top half. The growlers were right behind him.

Dan smashed one of the windows. A few pieces of glass pierced his hand, but fortunately his leather gloves prevented a more serious cut.

He turned the lock, dove inside, and closed the door behind him at the same moment as the first growler appeared around the corner.

Luckily, the growlers hadn't caught Dan's last move; they hadn't seen him enter the house. So they continued to run toward the back of the yard, where there were some apple trees. Dan peered cautiously through the broken glass window, and he managed to count eight, all adults.

He stood there watching, quietly waiting for them to fall asleep. That's when he heard the growl behind him.

* * *

The hatch was there, right in front of him.

Going into the cellar was simple: a metal hatch covered the stairs leading down. One would raise the hatch, secure it via a hook on a gazebo pillar, and then descend. Down there was another door, this time a normal vertical one, which was the actual entrance.

That's what Andrei tried to do. But being still in a state of panic, he pulled up the hatch and rushed down. He didn't think to secure it with the hook, or at least hold it with his hand, so it fell back, hitting Andrei's head as he scrambled down the stairs. The blow was powerful enough to make his head bleed. Adrenalin meant he felt no immediate pain though, and it spiked again when he discovered the cellar door was locked.

He was trapped!

The hatch was closed, it was fully dark, and the passageway was tight. He could barely stand near the door, and the stairs made the interior smaller toward the other side.

Above him, near the hatch, he could now hear the growlers.

He finally felt the sting on his head. He touched it and he could smell his blood.

That's when he started screaming in the dark.

* * *

Dan turned. It was a woman. A dead woman in her thirties, dressed in red and white cotton pajamas. As she bit the air, he could see some of her teeth were broken in pieces, as if she had used her mouth to bite metal or concrete things.

This was probably the priest's wife, Dan realized upon seeing the growler looking straight through him with its empty white eyes.

Dan was down, with his back resting against the door. He had his bat. But the growler was on the other side of the kitchen table. And it was a fast one.

It charged toward Dan.

* * *

The growlers were stepping and banging on the metal hatch. It was sturdy, made from several metal sheets welded together, but it wasn't built to hold the weight of a person. And certainly not more than one.

As the growlers paced upon it, the hatch door started to bend. Some of the sheets started to break apart, and the noise it made was terrible. Those screeching sounds, combined with the growls, made Andrei tremble. He was in complete darkness and his face was only a foot away from the metal hatch being bent and torn apart by those monsters.

He slowly sat, still screaming, his back against the cellar door. The darkness had him.

A gunshot sounded, waking the entire village.

This helped Andrei. It made him wonder what had happened and forced him to focus on other things. It put an end to his panic attack.

* * *

She attacked. It attacked. It was definitely not human anymore.

As it came close, Dan was in no position to strike a blow. All he could do was shove the tip of the bat against her chest, pushing her back. Which he managed to do successfully. The woman was slender and he forced her back a few steps.

But it came back. Again. And again. Relentlessly.

At one point he would miss his mark. And that would be it.

The fourth time it came at him, he decided to try something different.

He shoved as hard as he could, threw away the bat, and reached for his gun.

165

As it jumped him, he pushed with his right hand, ignoring the pain in his thumb, and he fell to the left, dodging the biting mouth.

The growler jumped toward him, trying to bite his face. But it hit the wooden door.

He pressed the gun to its chest, where the heart used to be, and pulled the trigger.

* * *

What to do? What could be done? What if they were dead? Could this be the end? Were she and Mat the only two people remaining in the world? And if rabies got her first, they would probably be dead too, sooner rather than later.

Andrei should have stayed home with Mat, Lili thought. What if she got sick? What would become of Mat?

As Lili stressed, pacing the living room, Matei started crying.

"What is it, honey?" said Lili, hugging him.

"What if Dad is dead? What if the bad people attack us? And where is Grandma? Is she dead? I don't want you to die, Mommy! We need to go save him! We need to go save Dad!"

"We can't go, honey. I'm not trained to fight these monsters. And you are just a boy."

"I can fight! I can help! Just give me a bat. I will hit them so hard!"

"Oh, honey… you are so cute!" said Lili, with tears in her eyes. "You are my big little man!" she said hugging him even tighter.

"Let's go, Mom, let's go!"

"Look, honey! Hey, Mat. Look at me. Look at me, baby. There! Good. Now listen. We cannot go out like this. It will be dark soon, and we'll risk getting hurt ourselves."

She needed to take care of Mat. She would do anything to keep Mat safe. Even if it meant letting the others die? That she didn't know.

"However," she continued, shivering at her last thought, "tomorrow morning, if they're still not back, we'll go to help them. Okay? Anyway, Dan is a policeman. He will take care of Dad and hold off any bad guys. I'm sure they're fine and that they'll come back shortly."

* * *

Movement above him ceased and the noise from the growlers grew distant. The hatch was no longer bending under the weight of people above.

A few seconds later, Andrei got himself together and finally stopped screaming.

This, however, proved to be unfortunate, as Andrei's theory was proven correct: the growlers were as attracted to sounds suddenly stopping as to new sounds. That meant, the disappearance of a noise was as attractive to them as the sound of a gun going off.

The five growlers turned and approached the hatch once more.

* * *

As the growler let out its final shriek and died, its head slumped against the door.

Dan pulled himself into a vertical position, still sitting on the floor, his back against the door. He moved to push the dead woman away. That's when the first hit came.

The other growlers were at the door.

The small square windows broke and pieces of glass fell on Dan's head.

The dead woman and his own body were the only things keeping the door closed, keeping him away from those monsters.

* * *

They were back, and the hatch would not hold for long.

Andrei slowly realized this was it. He would die alone in this godforsaken place. At the entrance to a priest's cellar. Perhaps God actually existed, and he had a twisted sense of humor.

"You never entered a church. You disrespected The Church and made fun of its representatives. You tried to steal food from one of them."

Andrei imagined God scolding him at their first meeting.

"Well, guess why you died in that place."

He suddenly felt serene. The noises around him faded and he began to feel... safe. That was the word: safe. So safe, he happily let his bladder go.

Warmth surrounded him. *"Now, that's good,"* he told God in his head. *"I really had to go. It's nice up here. Good thing I left that stupid world behind."*

The noise, the banging was far away.

As part of the hatch finally broke, one growler managed to stick its head through the gap. The opening was small, its shoulders couldn't fit in yet, but the growler was pushing.

The metal sheets were bending, cutting the growler's face and neck as the gap slowly enlarged. It didn't seem to care, as it continued to push forward, biting the air, leaning toward the helpless prey below.

Andrei opened his eyes and saw the growler. It was so close. An arm's length away maybe. He could feel its breath with every growl. He closed his eyes again.

Then the noise stopped.

As he waited for death, it seemed that death was also waiting for something, as it never came.

He opened his eyes.

All five growlers around the hatch, including the one with its head pushed through the opening, had gone dormant.

* * *

The door was hitting his back. Hard. The woman's head was pounded with every hit.

He leant hard against the door to keep it closed, the heels of his heavy boots scratching the floor.

The door was the only thing between him and those things.

And it needed to hold.

One growler managed to get its hands through one of the windows, as Dan had done earlier.

Luckily, it wasn't aware Dan was down there. Its instinct was go to the source of the noise, which it only knew was somewhere in that house.

The hands fumbled around. A few times, they almost touched

his head.

Until, suddenly, they stopped.

The eight growlers stood still for a moment and then fell. Some of them collapsed against the door.

So Dan still had to hold it closed.

* * *

Andrei came back to reality and tried to focus. He looked around, assessing the situation, so he could figure out what to do next.

He was sitting on the floor, his back against the door, legs resting on the lowest step of the stairs.

He noticed the liquid he was sitting in. He'd peed his pants! There was quite a puddle; all his behind was soaked.

He wasn't embarrassed though. Well, if the girls from work found out, that would be horrible. In that case, he would be petrified. But no. He wouldn't be embarrassed in front of Lili. He loved her, and he was able to tell her anything. Even this.

Plus, he could use this story as a teaching moment for Matei. Matei had peed his pants a couple of times and he might still be suffering. Knowing his dad had the same issue might help him. Andrei could be over-thinking it though.

Then there was that head. The growler was two feet away, facedown, and almost appeared to be looking at him. Its eyes and mouth were open. It was a fast one, so at least it wasn't stinking. But, boy, was that a horrible thing to see. Its neck and face were cut everywhere and some liquid was oozing down on him.

He couldn't escape, not with that thing blocking the way.

All he could do was wait for Dan to show up.

Oh, and he still had his knife. He'd panicked and forgotten to use it.

Should the growler wake, he would put the blade through its head.

But he hoped it wouldn't wake. He'd be very quiet.

* * *

Dan stayed there, back against the door, for a few more minutes.

When he looked up, he saw a growler stuck like glue to the door, its hands still poking in through the broken window.

He started to push the woman to the side, slowly, trying to keep quiet.

As he moved, his feet dragged over some broken pieces of glass on the floor. But, more importantly, the door shifted, together with the growlers leaning on it.

The growlers woke and started moving again.

And now they knew their target was down there.

* * *

Andrei heard a noise in the distance. Growling! What was going on? No matter. He was relatively okay down here.

But he was wrong. As the growling began near the house, it also reawakened the five growlers above Andrei, including the one with its head inside the hatch.

One thing that Andrei had misjudged was their intention.

Normally, they would have turned back, heading to where Dan was holding the door, seeking the source of the new noise.

But as the one stuck in the opening started to growl, Andrei immediately stabbed it with his knife. He hit the neck and face. The blade finally got through to the brain by piercing the temple.

The growler immediately started making horrible sounds, louder than usual. This triggered the other four to return.

The one with the knife in its head was now just squirming. It looked like the tumor-brain was not in full control anymore, but it was still moving and growling.

It slowly started to slip through the widening hole as its shoulders moved with the squirming. The growler was sliding in, and Andrei tried to push it back. Hands on its shoulders, he groaned and pushed, using all his strength to keep the growler from falling into the small space.

But his efforts were in vain.

As the growler wriggled downwards, Andrei pulled the knife from its head. He then tried to stab it in the heart, while sitting in that awkward position on the stairs.

He tried and he failed. He probably hit a rib, as the knife slipped on something hard. He needed to try again. This time, he almost cut his other hand, the one still holding the growler in place.

Stabbing someone was harder than he'd anticipated.

He made a third attempt and finally found the heart, burying his knife deep.

As the growler finally died, it made that terrible noise. Andrei shifted his head back as far as he could, repulsed.

Unfortunately, the growler then dropped in upon him, legs and everything. And through the opening, a new head appeared.

* * *

Dan raised his forearms. The growlers' hands were trying to get him, and they were relentlessly scraping and scratching. A few almost struck his face, and many more were shredding the arms on his jacket. Some hit his swollen, broken finger, which made pain run through his entire body.

He didn't yell. He held it in.

He'd seen it happen once and he could do it again. He would be quiet until they fell asleep.

And after a while, which felt like forever, they did.

He could finally put his hands down and think.

* * *

Andrei could see the new growler's face. Its shoulders were broader than the one who'd made it through the gap, but its mouth was close enough to start biting.

And it did. Snapping and biting.

Luckily, its teeth were only sinking into the other growler's pants—the one with the knife in its chest.

This was getting ridiculous. Seeing a growler eat another's growlers pants almost seemed funny, and Andrei had to focus a lot of energy not to laugh.

No, he needed to be quiet. He needed to wait for them to go dormant again.

Which, after a while, they did.

Now he could think.

* * *

Night came.

The dead woman was still leaning on him. He had his back against the door. Some growler hands and heads were only inches away.

Cold air was seeping in though the broken windows, but the temperature inside was still decent. Above freezing at least.

He couldn't move. Any movement would wake those creatures.

And the door was unlocked. Even if he tried to run, they would fall in and then block the exit.

The other door in the room was a flimsy interior one. It would never hold back even a single growler. Against eight it stood no chance.

No. His best bet was to wait for Andrei. He must be hidden in the cellar. He would eventually come and save him.

* * *

As the sun set, Lili and Mat sat inside, by the fire. They had no more onions, and this was yet another reason to worry about their survival.

They were not showing any symptoms yet, but something needed to be done.

More importantly, Lili's resolve to keep Mat safe at the expense of Andrei's demise had dimmed. She couldn't lose Andrei. Not like this. Not without knowing she'd done everything in her power to save him.

Tomorrow they had to go.

* * *

As night fell, Andrei realized that having the dead growler on top of him had its advantages.

Sure, some fluids and other things he didn't like to think about were leaking out of the body. That was disgusting, but it wasn't rotting. Not yet at least. And the body and its clothes were providing insulation, protecting him from the cold outside.

A chill air was coming through the hole in the hatch. But inside, the temperature was better.

He'd just have to wait. His best bet was to wait for Dan. He would surely come and get him out of here.

* * *

The next morning, Matei was up early. He woke Lili and immediately started talking.

"Let's go, Mom! Let's go save Dad!"

Lili looked around. Andrei and Dan weren't there. They'd never come home.

"But can we save them?" murmured Lili, blinking rapidly as she tried to wake up fast. "What if they're already... I mean... I don't know what I mean," she said, controlling herself.

"Come on, Mom! Let's go!" pressed Matei.

"I'm not sure, honey, if this... if this is the right thing to do."

"Yes, it is! Dad would come save us. We need to go save him. I will fight, you'll see, and I'll get him back!"

The kid was right. They had to go.

* * *

"Okay," said Lili, pointing to the ground. "There are two sets of tracks visible. See?"

"Yes," said Mat. "I think this is Dad."

"Right. All we have to do is to follow them. But we need to pay attention. Hey, Mat, listen to me. Pay attention! Whatever has got Dad and Grandpa could get us too," said Lili, trying to keep her voice light and calm.

"Yes, Mommy. I'll be careful."

"Okay. Now, let's go. Oh, and be quiet."

They walked for a while, and as they moved past a house, they heard a dog barking in the yard. Lili's heart stopped.

"Wait," said Lili, squatting by Mat, holding her axe. "Something happened here."

"Mom—"

"Shush!"

"Mom," whispered Matei, "look. The tracks go further. They didn't stop here. They just entered the yard but then they came out. Look, these are Dad's tracks," said Mat, pointing down the road.

"Oh, you're right," said Lili, visibly relaxing. "Okay, let's move out. I don't like that dog barking. It will soon wake the neighborhood, even if the barking is faint."

"Maybe the dog is tired," said Mat, as Lili started walking again.

They moved on, silently. Lili kept looking behind and was relieved when the dog stopped barking. Everything was quiet again, and nothing was after them.

They kept following the tracks. They needed to find the men and save them.

"There!" said Mat enthusiastically.

"Shush! Yeah, I see it. A lot of prints heading down that alley. They must have entered the church. Come, quietly."

They edged slowly along the pathway, and soon Lili saw the two piles of growlers. The situation became clear.

"Oh," she said, stopping abruptly and grabbing Mat. *They could both be dead. But they might also be alive. And if alive, they must be trapped.* She looked around, trying to come up with a plan.

* * *

"Ready?" Lili mouthed the word from near the belfry and waved.

Matei gave her a thumbs-up sign.

He stood about forty yards from her, out in the street, behind a large pile of snow.

Lili grabbed the rope and swung it.

The bell dinged, violently breaking the silence.

At the sound, the growlers near the hatch began moving.

The two on top of the pile had frozen backs. They could still move, but they were slower, their frozen flesh ripping with every move they made.

The two below had kept warmer, and they started running toward the bell, quickly passing the slower ones.

The same was true for the eight growlers coming from the backdoor pile.

All twelve were soon heading toward the bell, which Lili kept ringing.

The noise could be heard for miles. Church bells were loud.

Soon, the whole village was awake and growls can be heard from all directions.

This was the sign for her to stop and run behind the church. Now she had to save her family.

From her new position she could see the two groups coming. There was no direct path from their location to the belfry and all the growlers had to go around the church.

Most of them ran in front of the building, except the two fast ones from the cellar, who took a different route. They went past the back of the church, where Lili was.

That wasn't part of the plan, but luckily she was prepared.

As they came toward her, she stayed put, her back against the church wall, not moving and not making a sound. The growlers passed by without noticing her.

As they got three steps away, she let out a little shriek. It was the first time, since this whole thing began, that she had yelled on purpose.

The two growlers stopped and started to turn. One dropped quickly under a heavy blow to the side of its head. The other, a large woman in her fifties, attacked Lili, trying to scratch and bite her.

Lili jumped and pushed at the dead woman with her axe.

Maybe she wasn't that prepared, as the growler took a few steps back, unbalanced, but then came at her again with full force.

She would not be stopped now though. Not when she was so close to saving her husband and her father.

Her vision tunneled. Nothing existed except the growler in front of her.

It was coming at her, hands reaching out, trying to scratch, and teeth snapping.

She would end this now and then save her family.

Lili raised the axe and let it fall hard on the growler's head. The axe split open its skull, and Lili let go of the handle.

The growler staggered and fell facedown. Lili jumped back,

making room for the large body.

The axe handle struck the ground first and flew out of the bleeding skull.

Her confidence back, Lili picked up the axe, ready for anything. *Two down, ten to go.*

All ten remaining growlers were fast ones; however, five were moving slowly, being half frozen, and they barely managed to cover a few yards.

The five fast ones were already in front of the church, heading for the belfry.

Lili decided to move toward the two half-frozen growlers coming from the hatch, and taking advantage of their slow, spasmodic movement, she hit them hard in the head, one by one. Four down, eight to go. And she was just warming up.

She turned in time to see the remaining three half-frozen growlers coming toward her from the backdoor of the house. One. Two. Three hits. Seven down, five to go.

As she approached the backdoor, she saw her dad stand up from behind it.

He was all bruised and covered in blood.

She heard a noise behind her and turned to see Andrei emerge though the hatch, looking as beaten and worn as Dan.

"Let's do this," said Dan, with hate in his eyes. "Let's finish them."

"There are five left, but they're fast ones. We need to be smart," said Lili.

"Let's be smart then," continued Dan. "Andrei, are you ready?"

"Yes, I am," he said. She'd never seen him look so confident, so pumped when talking about doing something dangerous. She liked it though.

The group approached the growlers, who had gathered around the bell. But before they reached them, they started falling face down in the snow.

They were going dormant again.

At a silent signal from Dan, the group split, each moving toward the sleeping growlers from a different direction. Once they had surrounded them, they all swung their weapons down.

The strikes caught three of the growlers on the backs of their heads. As they started to rise, Dan, Andrei and Lili all swung again, and this time the strong blows destroyed their brains.

Then, the group turned to the two remaining growlers, who were already awake and up. They both tried to attack Dan.

As Dan jumped back, pushing one away, Andrei and Lili finished the job: they hit them from the side with heavy blows.

All the growlers were now on the ground. They were not dead, but their heads were smashed in. They were growling and squirming, but they would never walk or bite again.

As they looked at one another, a question popped up on Dan and Andrei's faces. Lili understood and answered quickly. "He's okay. He's right over there."

They rushed back to the main street and found Matei hidden in the snow, wearing the pink winter coat.

Dan bent down and picked him. Then they all started kissing the giggling child.

* * *

Between the four of them, they gathered a lot of food. The priest and his family were loaded, at least compared to the other villagers.

They found a lot of cooked, stored and canned produce. Plus, the priest had a huge pantry packed with fresh fruit and vegetables, including onions.

"Look here," said Lili as they searched the house. "That's his family," she said, handing them a framed picture. "They had a daughter. And I guess this," she said, pointing toward the dead woman, "was his wife."

"Yeah," said Dan, with a chill in his voice. "She almost got me."

"And the one in the church must have been his daughter," said Andrei, touching the picture.

"Yeah, probably. We have everything we need, but let's go check the church's basement before we go," said Dan, heading out.

The church basement held the biggest surprise though. Just like that old lady tied to her chair, they found quite a lot of people trussed up in a similar way down in the basement. All had transformed into growlers. They also found evidence of broken chairs and ties, probably from the ones who had chased Andrei and

Dan out of the church.

The noise was loud as the few remaining growlers tried in vain to get out of their chairs.

"I'll take Mat outside," said Lili, sprinting up the stairs with her child.

Andrei and Dan quickly followed.

"I bet they were trying some sort of exorcism," said Andrei as reached the front of the church. "Remember all the crosses, crucifixes and icons they had lying around."

"Yeah, it looks like it," said Lili. "They probably thought this was the devil's work. And who can blame them? And the priest, probably with the help of some locals, gathered the sick people in this basement. And then they tried the exorcisms."

"I bet they tied them up after they changed," said Andrei. "And the priest, he probably lost it when his daughter got sick. He probably tried his best for her. He kept the girl up in the church, trying to save her. Only to be eaten by her in the end."

"That's a horrible way to go," said Lili.

"He must have been eating lots of onions, since he was alive well after everybody else was dead," said Andrei.

"So, you think the priest is the one who cleared the driveway?" asked Dan.

"Yeah, who else?" asked Andrei, looking a bit frightened.

"I don't know. What if it was the wife?"

"I don't even think the priest knew his wife was dying," said Andrei. "Why wasn't she inside the church, like the daughter? No, I bet he spent his last days holed up in there, so the wife died alone, without him even knowing."

"That's another horrible way to go," said Lili, shivering.

"Look," said Dan, gently touching Lili's back. "We will never know for sure what happened here. Okay, all we said are good, possible explanations, but let's not dwell too much on this. Let's grab the things we need and be on our way."

They took as much as they could carry and went home. They focused on onions, but also on other fruit and vegetables, which needed constant attention to survive for a longer period. Still, plenty of food, fruit, and vegetables were left behind, and they would have to return for them later. But first, they needed to find some rabies shots.

"Ah, let me introduce you to Howler," whispered Dan as they approached the yard.

"We heard a faint bark when we came to save you," said Lili. "You mean that dog?"

"Yes," said Dan, approaching the gate. "I plan to save this one."

"Yay, we finally get a dog!" said Mat, fidgeting happily.

"Quiet, you," said Lili, as Andrei also shushed him. "We're not out of the woods yet."

"Ah, he looks a little better. I'll feed him now, and I'll come back tomorrow to check on him. When he can make the trip, I'll bring him back with me," said Dan, and he rummaged through his backpack to find some food. "Hand me that blanket, Lili. I want to cover him."

22 HOMECOMING

"We have to finish the job," said Lili that evening, back at their house. "We have to kill the sleepers in the backyard."

"You mean…"

"Yes, Andrei, I'm sorry. Growlers. We need to go back there and finish the job."

Interesting how the last few weeks had changed her.

Andrei immediately agreed. She didn't have to say anything more. He, too, knew what would happen come spring when snow melted.

They went out back, and Andrei pulled out his knife and approached the large man. It was still face down, and as he tried to turn it around, it started growling. It was frozen, so it couldn't squirm, yet Andrei took a few steps back, shaking.

"Relax," said Lili, approaching. "Come on, let's turn it together."

They turned the body, and Andrei grabbed his knife again and squatted near the monster. He held the knife over its chest and pushed.

"It won't work," said Lili, a few steps behind. "It's frozen."

"Ah," said Andrei, as he tried pushing the knife in. "Yeah, it's not working. I don't have the strength. Let's try the axe."

The axe got the job done.

"What do we do now?" asked Lili as they stared at the now-forever-silenced family. The large man, the wife and the children all had their chests cut deep by a few axe hits. "And what do we do with the toddler?"

"Let's pull all of them to the house across the street, the one under construction. I don't want them rotting here come spring."

"And the toddler?"

"I won't kill that," said Andrei, shaking his head. "Let's move him as is and just drop him and the crib as far away as possible."

"I'll call Dad to help us with the large one," said Lili. "After we finish moving the others."

They returned to the house a few hours later. They didn't speak for the rest of the evening, and Dan respected their silence.

* * *

"Let's go into town," said Dan next morning, as he entered the living room. He'd just returned from feeding Howler. And he had a surprise with him: Howler himself.

"We'll make up a fire and put the dog in one of the rooms. That way, he'll be warm for a few days. We'll leave him food and water. He'll probably eat everything on day one, but we'll be back soon enough.

"Why doesn't he come with us?" asked Mat, petting the dog.

"He's too weak. Look at him. He got tired just walking here."

"Just like you, Andrei," said Lili, giggling. "You, however, we'll take to the—"

"And he might bark and wake growlers," said Dan, interrupting Andrei and Lili's giggles. "He needs to be trained to stay quiet. It's better this way."

"Okay, we'll go," said Lili. "But we need to eat first."

Breakfast was different today.

It was a plentiful spread of food across the table. And they had their fill of onions.

"We now have enough to last us a few weeks," said Dan. "As time goes by, houses will start to freeze. Some might already be frozen. But there are also lots of cellars in the village, storing more provisions. For now, though, our biggest issue is finding rabies shots."

They finished eating and starting dressing.

The road back home was about ten miles long and they needed to focus on their mission.

"Even if the snow is deep, we'll go on foot," said Dan. "We didn't check the entire village the day before, but after our journey to the church, which is right in the middle, we didn't spot any suitable vehicles. I think there's little hope the other side will be much different."

"Yeah," said Andrei, "there's scant chance anyone owns a 4x4 big enough to drive through these twenty inches of snow."

They left, and the group quickly passed the place where they'd fought the dogs.

"It's easier today, I think," said Lili, breathing in the cold morning air. "We're heading downhill."

After a few hours, they were close to the cabin. The group was walking slowly, yet Dan was a few dozen feet in front of the others, seemingly lost in his thoughts.

"Maybe we should spend the night here," said Andrei, breathing heavily. "It's halfway, so it makes sense."

"Yes," whined Mat. "I'm tired, and my feet are cold."

"It's halfway to your car," corrected Lili. "It's only a third of the trip. It's ten miles total. Downhill. How out of shape can you be?"

"I'm not out of shape! It's just, you know, I'm thinking about the kid. We shouldn't push him too hard."

"I suspect you're thinking about the kid as much as I'm thinking about wearing shorts in this weather."

"Mm," said Andrei, grinning, "I would love to be those shorts covering your fine a—"

"Language!"

Andrei grinned wider. "Sorry."

"I can't move anymore," said Matei, stopping.

"If he stops, I stop," said Andrei, dropping his backpack.

"Hey, Dad," said Lili, calling to Dan, who seemed still mired in his thoughts. "Wait up."

"What's happening?" said Dan, turning around.

"You grandson is tired."

"I can carry him for a while, until he gathers his strength," said Dan, coming back toward them.

"Great," mumbled Andrei, reluctantly picking up his backpack.

* * *

The cabin was visible, from afar. As they got closer, Dan remembered something.

"Wait," he told the group. "We need to be careful. There's...something in the road." He set Mat down. "Go to your mom."

They understood. They continued single file, first Dan, then Mat, then Lili, and finally Andrei. They checked left and right, paying attention. Except for Mat, who was instructed to keep his eyes down—a rule he constantly tried to bend.

Dan stopped, and Lili, looking around him, let out a small cry.

* * *

They saw Maria. Or at least, what was left of Maria.

"What happened to her?" asked Lili, gasping.

"She's been eaten, I think. And look, there are tracks everywhere," said Andrei, pointing all around.

Bite marks were clearly visible on Maria's body, and her belly was open, her guts spilled over the red snow. Lili quickly pulled Mat's beanie over his eyes.

"Wolves," said Dan, looking at the paw marks in the snow, leading to and from the forest.

"Wolves?" asked Lili. "But I thought they lived farther up the mountain."

"Are there wolves around?" cried Matei with a scared voice.

"They sometimes come down here," said Dan. "They're just afraid to attack men. But now, since there are no people around, I guess they've gotten bolder. I've heard of a few wolf attacks in the past, but they mostly targeted livestock."

"Mommy! Are there wolves?" Matei was trying to get his beanie out.

"Poor Mom." Lili sobbed.

"Mommy! Mommy?"

And Maria woke up.

They heard a hissing sound.

Matei started crying, just as Andrei approached, hugging Lili and pulling Mat closer. "Don't look. It's okay, Mat. There are no wolves. Just don't look."

"We need to end this, Dad. We need to end it!" yelled Lili, crying. "We can't leave mother like this! It's so unfair and wrong! What has she done to deserve this?"

She was right.

This was worse than anything else.

And he had to fix it.

"We used an axe," said Andrei from behind him, but Dan didn't listen.

He approached Maria, knife in hand.

He crouched down beside her and pressed the tip of the large blade against her chest.

"Sorry, my love. See you soon," he murmured, and he pushed down.

* * *

"What do we do now?" Andrei broke the silence that had fallen. Mat was in his arms, crying, while Lili had moved away, toward her father.

"We need to bury her," said Lili, tears in her eyes. "But how and where I don't know." She started again crying.

"Who...do...we...need...to...bury?" asked Matei, crying with hiccups.

"Could you go talk over there?" said Andrei, moving away from Lili and Dan. "It will be okay, Mat," he added, not knowing what else to say.

"There are tools in the shed," said Dan to Lili, stepping farther away from the others. "However, we don't have time now. The ground is frozen. It would take forever."

"I cannot believe you want to leave Mother like this!" snapped Lili. "How could you say that?"

Dan's voice rang hollow as he spoke. "I don't want to leave Maria like this, Lili. All I'm saying is we need to finish our other job first. Until then, let's move her into the shed and lock it. Wolves won't be able to get to her in there. When we return, we'll have enough time to bury her properly."

Lili took a deep breath and then moved back toward Andrei and Matei. As she lifted a crying Mat, Lili, too, started crying again. They held each other while Dan and Andrei got to work.

* * *

"I'll try to start the car. It will start in half a second. You'll see. No, a quarter second," said Andrei proudly as they left the cabin. Dan was silent, looking a bit lost, so Andrei was trying to start a conversation.

"Yes, yes," answered Lili. "Sure it will."

"What? It's a perfectly good car! And in spring, we'll come back here to get it," said Andrei, with greater enthusiasm than was called for.

"Yeah, everyone needs a small car when the Apocalypse hits."

"Ha-ha."

* * *

They could see the town.

A few more steps, and, finally, the car came into view. It was there. It had survived.

There was a new layer of snow, so the vehicle was buried deep.

"Damn," said Andrei, sighing. "There's no way to move it until the snow melts."

"We'll walk," said Dan, coming back to life. "We'll go through Las Vegas, then cross the bridge near our apartment. I say we spend the night there. It's going to be cold, but I don't think it will have completely frozen. We'll sleep huddled together. We should be okay for one night."

Andrei continued to advance, impervious, but he gently pulled Lili, making her slow down until they lagged about a dozen feet behind Dan and Mat. He then leaned close and whispered in her ear.

"Whoopee," he said, trying to contain a smile. "I'll sleep glued to my father-in-law!"

Lili smiled and picked up the pace, but not before kissing him.

"Quiet, you two," said Dan, turning. "Keep the noise to a minimum!"

* * *

They slowed as they entered the town.

"Could we run into dogs here, in Las Vegas?" whispered Andrei.

"It's possible," said Dan. "Now that I think of it, it's most likely. There used to be lots of stray dogs in this neighborhood."

Andrei glanced at Lili, but said nothing more.

They were heading downhill, toward the bridge, the road winding left and right.

And then, after one curve, they saw something.

They halted.

About two hundred yards away, the snow was red. And there, scattered across that field of blood the size of a basketball court, were more than a dozen dogs, all partially covered in snow.

"They seem dead," whispered Dan.

"Mommy?" A tiny voice could be heard.

"Shush, honey. It's just some dogs. Remember the ones in the village? It's the same thing. Nothing to worry about. Just keep quiet and don't look too much."

They looked around. Nothing else seemed out of the ordinary. Just empty, silent houses and snow. They glanced at one other, and Dan waved his hand. Then they started moving toward the dogs.

"Are these dogs also sick, Mommy?"

"Yes, honey. Now be quiet. Andrei, take Mat and go."

Andrei picked up his son and went ahead. "It will be okay, Mat. Oh my, you're heavy. What have you been eating, rocks?"

"No. Rocks are not edible, Dad."

As they moved forward, whispering, through the dead dogs, Dan and Lili stayed behind and checked them.

"Look," said Dan. "Some bear bite marks. Here and here... see? Most look like animal bites, maybe dog or wolf. But see this one? This is different."

"Could it be growlers?" asked Lili.

"I don't know. I don't know how a human bite looks. Do you?"

"Nope."

"And see, over here? This is a cut. And this one looks like a blow form a blunt object. This is interesting."

"What does it mean?" asked Lili.

"It means nothing. We cannot tell what the cause of death was, not like this," answered Dan. "Look at this one. His head seems to have been hit. See the skull here? However, he's also bitten and eaten, so it's difficult to say if he was killed by an axe or by wolves."

"Well, who or what could survive an axe to the head?"

"The point is, there are many wounds, so we don't know the exact cause of death."

"But this looks like an axe wound," insisted Lili, shivering when she realized how she'd come to know that.

"Look, if a person killed this one in particular, that doesn't mean anything. Remember that priest. If a person killed this dog a week ago, he might already be dead himself by now."

"What? You think there are other people alive out there?" said Lili.

"I'm not saying anything. I'm not preparing you for some strange secret. But I've been thinking… Look, this is not the place." All of a sudden, Dan changed the subject. He looked around. "Let's get to the apartment and then we'll talk."

* * *

The bridge was there.

"Somewhere on it should be the man we saw from the window," whispered Lili close to Andrei's ear.

"Yeah," he answered in a similar way. "Strange. It feels like a lifetime ago."

They continued forward carefully. As they neared the middle of the bridge, Mat lost his balance and fell face down in the deep snow.

"Aaah!" he yelled.

Lili jumped and covered his mouth.

It was too late. A growling and hissing sound started in front of them, on the right-hand side of the bridge.

"Yes, you were right," said Andrei. "He's still there. He's covered in snow, but he's not dead. At least not in the general definition of 'dead'."

They crept past it, and soon it fell dormant.

"The current situation has some advantages," said Dan.

"What do you mean?" asked Lili.

"Come March, as the temperature rises, these things will be able to move around again, and our life may be very different."

* * *

When they reached their building, Dan used his key to unlock the main door.

"Cover his eyes," said Dan, as Lili again pulled down Mat's beanie.

"But I want to see."

"Shush and hold my hand. Be quiet, it's important."

They went in.

The teacher was there, a dozen feet away, his brains all over the walls.

"He's in a different position," whispered Dan, as the group stopped at the entrance. "He's been awake at least once."

"Maybe, like in the village, noise from the street sparked eruptions of growling all over town," whispered Andrei in response.

"The temperature is still above freezing, so he's not frozen," said Dan. "He probably crawled aimlessly, since his brain is destroyed. But, yes, he must have been awake at some point."

"At least he doesn't stink," said Lili. "Yet I do smell some rot in the air. Faintly, but I do."

"Yeah, there is," said Dan, inhaling. "Come. Let's be quiet."

They started up the stairs, slowly, and with every step the air became fouler.

"Mom, it stinks," whispered Matei.

"I know. Be quiet. It's okay," she whispered back.

When they reached the second floor, they saw it. And smelled it.

Outside their apartment lay the teacher's wife and their child.

The mother, the first growler they'd ever killed, was rotting. It was bad, really bad, worms and everything. Andrei vomited, making a loud noise.

"What is happening?" yelled Matei. "Mommy, what was that noise?"

Next to her was the young girl, head smashed in. The vomiting and Mat's yell woke her. Her head was almost completely gone, though, so she could only squirm.

Her left hand dug through her mother's entrails, spilling guts all over the floor.

The whole image was sickening, and Andrei felt like vomiting again.

The whole building woke then, taking the noise to a level they remembered only too well.

* * *

"Take the keys and go in," said Dan. "There's something I must do."

"What?" tried Lili.

"Just go! This is horrible. Think about Mat."

"Good point!" said Lili.

She picked up Mat in her arms and they hurried past the bodies, making sure they didn't touch anything. They unlocked the door and entered the apartment.

Home, sweet home! Everything was just as they'd left it. There was that painting, that vest, those pens. Everything they had, that they'd cherished, all their life was there. For a moment, it almost felt as if everything was back to normal.

"We should sleep in the kitchen," said Lili, bringing Andrei back to the dark, cold reality. "I think it's the most insulated room."

"Yeah, and it's smaller. Our bodies should be able to heat it a bit, since we'll all be sleeping together," said Andrei. "I say we bring in some mattresses too, for extra warmth and comfort."

Just as they'd finished preparing the kitchen for the night, the front door opened again and Dan entered.

"What have you been doing for so long?" asked Lili.

"Cleaning," he said, and the look on his face indicated the discussion was over. "Let's eat and then sleep. Tomorrow is a big day."

* * *

Mat was sleeping, his beautiful face turned up.

"How relaxed he looks," whispered Andrei, with a smile on his face.

"Yeah," whispered Lili. "He's so cute." Suddenly, her smile went away and she turned towards Dan. "What was that about? The thing you were about to tell us when we found those dead dogs, about other survivors?"

"What other survivors?" said Andrei, his eyes widening. "Are there other survivors?"

"Relax and wait for Dad to answer, dufus."

"Ah, yes. Well, as I said… I'm not preparing you for anything. I have the same info as you do. We all saw that priest, how he'd survived a little longer, how he'd managed to round up sick people in his basement. How he'd tried to save his daughter, only to be killed by her. And then, the most important example is us."

"Us?" asked Lili.

"Yeah, dufus, us," answered Andrei. "We survived. We're not elite soldiers, yet we survived. Maybe others did as well."

"Yes and no," said Dan. "We were helped by your onion obsession. And we were thus better prepared than others.

"But what I'm saying is this: there might be other survivors, just like that priest. Somewhere in this huge world, there might be other groups like us. I also think people might have better chances of survival in smaller towns or villages."

"Why is that?" inquired Andrei.

"Because there'd be fewer enemies around, giving the survivor a better chance of living long enough until they understood how to fight these things. The first few instances of contact are critical for survival. Oh, and imagine the craziness when thousands of people try to flee a big city, realizing there's an epidemic, the poor souls not even knowing they already have the disease."

They all lay there, quiet, thinking about the implications.

"However," concluded Dan, "these are just assumptions. Aside from the priest, we haven't seen any other survivors yet. And as time goes by, the probability of finding others decreases."

23 THE HOSPITAL

The morning found them sleeping in the kitchen. It was cold. Upon waking, they had a quick breakfast and then talked about their mission.

"Man," said Andrei, puffing as he fastened his jacket, "that was horrible. I froze all night."

"Okay, so gather round," said Dan. "We have three steps to clarify. How to reach the hospital, how to get in and secure the medical supplies, and finally how to get back to the apartment."

"Sounds about right," said Lili.

"How many hospitals are there?" asked Andrei.

"There's only one," said Dan. "It's fairly close to our building. There are some smaller clinics as well, some of them privately owned. However, there's a good chance none of them would keep rabies shots on hand."

"How come?"

"Well, in my experience as a cop, I know that ambulances have to take people bitten by dogs to the emergency room of the local hospital, so that's the safest way to go."

"Okay, got it. And where is the hospital?"

"You know the big park?" asked Lili, looking at Andrei.

"Which one?"

"The *only* one, dufus," said Lili, laughing. "The large, circular one, built around the hill. The one a few blocks from here."

"Ah, yes. You should have said 'the one with the palace'. I know

191

it."

"I guess I should have said 'the one where hundreds of years ago a king built a summer palace and used the hill as his personal garden'. That would have been clear for you, right?"

"Or that, yes," said Andrei, grinning back at her.

"You're at it again," said Dan, interrupting them. "I swear to God, sometimes you behave like children. Matei is the grown-up."

"Yeah!" said Matei from his corner, only to be immediately pounced upon by Andrei, who started kissing him.

"Okay, so, to answer the question," said Dan, shaking his head, "the hospital is right across the park. That means we have to walk for a few blocks and then cut through the park for about a mile to reach the hospital on the other side."

"And how do we get in?" asked Lili. "I guess we can't just knock on the door."

"Indeed, we need to find a way in. I know the emergency wing is easily accessible, but I don't know if it's safe to go that way. What if it's better to go in through the main entrance?"

"We should expect to find growlers in there, right?" asked Andrei.

"Yeah," said Lili. "I guess a hospital would be crowded when there's an epidemic."

"True," said Dan, pausing for a few moments. "It might be safer to approach the hospital and then decide on the spot which entrance to use. If it's the direct path, we can just continue our walk to reach the emergency room. If not, we can go around. We'll see what we find when we get there."

Everyone agreed.

"Okay, so next. When we're in the ER, we need to locate the rabies shots."

"They should be in a refrigerator of some sort, right?" asked Andrei, and Dan nodded.

"I propose," said Lili, "since we're going to all this trouble, we take some empty backpacks with us and grab as many medical supplies as we can carry."

"That sounds good, yes," said Dan.

"Okay, so once we have everything, we'll be ready to go. What then? We take the same road back?" asked Andrei.

"Maybe, but it depends on what we find on the way in," said Dan.

"Okay, sounds good," said Andrei, nodding. "Sound good you too, Lili?"

Lili nodded.

"Great. What do we do with Matei?"

"He's a liability. We can't take a seven-year-old into a hospital that could have hundreds of growlers in it," said Dan, calmly. "We need to split, just like last time."

"But I can fight, Grandpa."

"I agree," said Andrei, extra alert following the 'hundreds of growlers' comment. "He's too young. He could put the entire operation at risk. We need to take care of him, and one of us will always have to be on duty, guarding him."

"I'm not young. I'm almost eight. I can fight. You'll see."

"We're all on the same page," insisted Lili. "However, I know where this is going. You want me to stay home with him. And I'm telling you, last time I stayed home you two almost died, and we had to come save your sorry asses."

"Language!"

"Ugh! Yes, sorry, I apologize. But that doesn't change the fact that if Mat and I hadn't come to save you, you would both be dead!"

"Yes, me and Mom saved you. See? I can fight."

"Yes, you're right," said Dan. "But if all four of us had been there from the get-go, all of us would certainly be dead now."

"No, we wouldn't. I would have fought. I can hit so hard."

"Would you shut up already? You're not coming with us and that's final!" Andrei finally exploded.

"Don't yell at your kid! Tell him nicely and he'll understand!" said Lili.

"Sorry."

Silence.

"Fine." Lili surrendered. "How do we do this?"

"Well, it's simple, honey," said Andrei. "Me and Dan, we go together and bring back the stuff."

"We have two options, really," continued Dan right after. "Andrei and I could go, as he just said, or you and I. You're pretty good with the bat; I've seen it. And *that* might be the better option."

Andrei looked surprised. He turned his head, glancing between Lili and Dan, then looked down in numb silence, pursing his lips. A few moments later, he closed his eyes and drew a deep breath, then stared into the distance, thinking.

"I'm not sure, Dad," Lili finally answered. "Andrei is better at making decisions. He's stronger and heavier. I might not be the best choice."

"What do you think, Andrei?" asked Dan.

Andrei was still out, lost in his train of thought.

"Andrei!"

"Do we have walkie talkies?" Andrei finally spoke.

"I might have some. Why?"

"Well, we could form two teams," answered Andrei, "and I could be in the second team. We'll go together, and when risk presents itself, we'll wait behind. But we'd stay close, in case you need saving."

* * *

They opened the front door, ready to leave.

"What happened?" asked Lili. "The little girl is gone. And the mother is under a blanket, frozen. Oh, and yes, it's freezing out here. The temperature is way lower than yesterday."

"I removed the non-stinking growlers and I've opened the windows on each floor. Oh, and I covered that thing," whispered Dan.

"Good move," said Andrei. "We got rid of the squirming growlers, and the rotting ones will stop rotting as soon as they freeze."

"And I guess at that point they can be removed too. Good thinking, Dad."

They moved out silently.

They walked down the main street, checking their surroundings with care. Left and right, there was no one. Stores were closed, cars were parked. And there was snow everywhere.

"I think you were right out there on the bridge, Dan," said Andrei.

"About what?"

"We were lucky this outbreak hit during New Year celebrations."

"I didn't quite say that."

"Yeah, true. You said that it's good it happened during winter. But I want to add that I think the New Year celebrations helped a lot. Most people probably contracted the disease around Christmas, then were too sick to party and stayed home, or at least left early."

"True," said Lili. "I bet everybody in this town is inside. We are the only ones out and about."

"Except the one on the bridge," said Andrei, glancing at her. "But you're right, and that makes our lives easier."

"Yeah. Now, be quiet, you two," said Dan. "And stay focused." They soon reached the park borders.

"Oh, wait," said Andrei, stopping in his tracks.

"What is it?" asked Dan, as both he and Lili turned to look back.

"This town has a million stray dogs. And I remember there were quite a few in the park."

"Ah, right," said Lili. She peered toward the park and then turned to Dan.

"And I bet the mayor, who otherwise seems to be doing a good job, has a soft spot for them. But I bet it's more," said Andrei, with some spite in his tone. "I bet he and his friends make big bucks for each dog the city sterilizes. So, it's therefore good business to always have a few hundred dogs around, to provide a new supply of animals every year."

"Yeah, probably," said Lili. "But that's hardly relevant now. So far we've seen no dogs, except the ones in Las Vegas. Were are they all?"

"I don't think they can be in the park. They used to hang around here because people were feeding them. But now those people are gone," said Dan, moving his hand in a wide circle, "so they lost their food source. Everyone is dead, so the dogs probably moved out, looking for food. That, or they died."

Andrei and Lili looked at each other.

"I say we go through," said Dan, and the others agreed.

"But what do we do if we do run into some dogs?" asked Andrei. "I mean, I can kill five or ten," he added, trying to sound confident, "but what if—"

"The park is wide and the trees are far apart, as you know," said Dan. "We can see well into the distance. If we find a pack of dogs, we'll go around it, as wide as we can. If we are attacked, we'll go back to back, Matei in the middle, and slowly walk away. Should a dog come close, we'll hit it with the bats."

"But isn't it safer to just go around?" asked Lili.

"I don't think so. It would take four times longer, and it increases our chances of coming across both dogs and growlers."

Lili and Andrei looked at each other again, before eventually agreeing.

"Okay, so, straight through, as quickly and silently as possible, is our best bet."

The park was beautiful. It had majestic beech trees which had been growing there for hundreds of years. Most of those trees had no lower-hanging branches. They were either tall, with their crowns way up, or they'd been pruned back so that people could move around freely. The trees were not too close to each other, so during summer there was enough light for grass to grow as well.

All this made the park feel like the interior of a cathedral. The tall, straight, stout trunks stood there like columns. The foliage was like a high roof, and the sunlight filtered through the leaves, shining like stained glass. The air was breezy in the summer, and the trees protected people from the wind during the winter. Plus, kids loved it.

Especially in winter! remembered Lili. As a child, she'd liked to come here throughout the year with her dad, to walk and run. But during winter was the best. They would ride downhill on snow sleds all day long. The trees were far apart and there was no danger; it only made the rides wilder.

Those were good, simpler times, realized Lili, with a melancholic smile on her face.

* * *

As they drew close to the top of the hill, they could see the hospital. To their left was the side of the castle, the old 'summer residence'. Straight ahead, through the trees, they could see the tall white building half a mile away. It was built within the park boundaries, so it was nicely located. "A hotel could double tariffs with this location," Dan used to say.

They were looking toward the back of the hospital, where the emergency room was.

A second later, they froze, while Lili squatted and pulled Mat closer, burying his face in her chest.

Mat tried to say something, so she pushed his face harder, covering his mouth, whispering in his ear to be quiet. He tried to push back for a while, then he relaxed.

Luckily, from this lower position he couldn't see what was happening down there, or at least not enough to make a sense of it.

For the adults, however, words couldn't describe what they saw.

The whole valley, downhill, had the same type of trees: dozens and dozens of tall beech trees spaced widely apart. The snow beneath the trees on this side, however, was red. And here and there, bodies lay. 'Leftovers' was a better word for it. And 'scraped bones' would have been the perfect definition.

And in between them and this carnage were dogs.

Hundreds of dogs.

* * *

"We have to go back! We have to run!" hissed Andrei, his eyes wide with panic. "There is no way we can survive this."

Lili gave Dan a startled glance, as he squatted near a tree.

The dogs were calm. Most seemed to be sleeping, and they hadn't noticed the arrival of people.

"Relax," said Dan, eventually. "Just relax. And stay out of sight."

The others squatted near him, banding together.

"It's only a matter of time before they see or smell us. We're intruders in their territory. And judging by what they've been eating lately, they will kill us."

"Why are there so many human bodies in the park?" asked Lili.

"No idea. Let's go back," whispered Dan.

Silently, they started to back up, keeping their eyes on the scene, struggling to believe what they were seeing.

It seemed like the dogs didn't have a worry in the world. Sleeping or playing. There were some puppies as well, running around and bothering their mothers, while a few adult ones yet awake were trying to claim some final scraps of meat from the yellow bones lying around.

"How did this happen?" whispered Andrei. "Was there an epic fight between men and dogs? How come the dogs won? Why are there so many bodies? Why is—"

"Let's not stick around to find out," interrupted Dan. "We need to go back to the apartment and come up with a new plan."

* * *

By midday they were back at the apartment. The place was, of course, familiar territory; however, it wasn't friendly, as they had no running water and no heating. The reason why they'd left in the first place was becoming more obvious.

"If only we could burn some things," said Andrei. "But we can't. You needed somewhere for the smoke to get out, otherwise you'd suffocate and die. If only we had a fireplace. Or a generator. Or a small gas tank and a burner."

"A heat source would temporarily fix the water issue as well," said Lili. "We could do the same as in the village: put snow in big pots and let it melt."

"Is there anything that we could use to get warmer?"

"Remember, right before leaving the apartment, we discussed some heating options," said Dan.

"Yeah," said Andrei. "We were talking about a generator, if I remember correctly."

"Indeed," said Dan, with a smile.

"And I think the issue was that if we put that generator out on the balcony, the whole building would hear. The growlers would wake up and then..." Andrei brightened, while Dan kept on nodding and smiling. "But!"

"But what?" interrupted Lili. "Spit it out!"

"But now we know that, after a while, the growlers will ignore the sound! It will eventually become background noise," said Andrei triumphant.

"Exactly!" confirmed Dan.

"Okay. So, where do we find a generator?" asked Lili.

"There's the big hardware store," said Dan. "They'll have everything. We need a generator and a canister of gas. Oh, and a portable electric heater."

"But Dad, those things are heavy. And large. We would waste a lot of time getting all that equipment here and setting everything up," said Lili. "Wouldn't it be faster to focus on the real issue: finding the rabies shots?"

"True, but we're running out of drinking water. Our bodies generate heat, we can melt some snow, but we need food to keep our internal 'engines' running. And we don't have much left. We must take this one step at a time. We should postpone the rabies shots for one day and secure heating for this evening. We haven't been warm for a while now, and we cannot go on like this for too long."

* * *

They were up and running. Their destination: the hardware store.

Once again, they headed toward the town's central park. For the hospital you had to go straight through the park, while the hardware store was on the left-hand side of it.

"I suggest we go clockwise around the park to reach the store, not through," said Dan.

"Definitely. I don't want to get anywhere near those killer dogs," said Lili, while Andrei nodded his approval.

"What she said," he added with a raspy voice.

They reached the store as the sun was setting behind the hills.

The main gate of the parking lot was locked.

"They actually closed this thing," muttered Dan. "I'd expected to find at least the gate open. But someone has taken the time to lock it down."

"We jump?" suggested Lili.

The metal mesh fence was tall, almost ten feet.

"They surely fear thieves around here. I can't jump this," said Andrei, "and I bet Mat can't do it either. And even if we could hurl him over, he would get hurt on his way down."

"Yes, no way can we throw our kid over the fence," said Lili, shaking her head.

"Why is it so tall?" asked Andrei, with a hint of desperation in his voice. "Why would someone build such a thing? It looks like a prison."

"When it first opened, people tried to steal from this store almost every night," answered Dan. "They had no fence back then. And on top of losing merchandise, property got damaged during the attempts. Mind you, this is a huge hardware store, part of an international chain. It serves not only the needs of this town but those of people from half the county who come here for their supplies. Just look at the huge parking lot. It can take hundreds of cars. I guess the cost of putting up this fence was an acceptable outlay."

"And did it work?" asked Andrei.

"Well, they still have some attempts here and there. But not like before. It's difficult to go over the fence, plus they have a security system. The guard can call the police if he sees something."

"Okay, so it was necessary. But what do we do?" said Andrei, still visibly upset. "How do we get in? The gate is closed, with a metal chain and a big padlock. It's impossible to break. If we had the key, it would be awesome," said Andrei, with the tone of someone who hopes to win the lottery.

Dan instantly turned to him. From his expression, it looked like he'd had an idea. "This place is huge. It probably has dozens of employees. I bet there's not just one key, which some guy takes home in the evening." He got more and more enthusiastic. "I think the padlock key must be somewhere close. They couldn't risk having that key taken home by some employee who could be late or call in sick the next morning."

By the time he finished, they were all looking in the same direction: the guards' plastic booth, right on the other side of the fence, next to the main gate. That's where the key would be.

* * *

"Take care, honey," said Dan, clearly concerned.

Lili was getting ready to make the jump.

Andrei was facing her, his back against the gate. He held his hands together, palms up with interlocked fingers, making a one-step stair. The plan was for her to come running, step onto his hands, and then jump over the fence. And Andrei should help push her up.

If it weren't for all the snow, it should be easy. Running in deep snow, it was difficult to build speed and momentum.

But then Lili had another idea.

"You okay? Can you get over?" asked Andrei. He was again standing by the fence, gripping the metal mesh. Lili was standing on his shoulders.

She'd climbed first onto Dan's back while he was on all fours, then onto Andrei's shoulders, while he squatted. Andrei had then slowly pulled himself up with the help of the metal mesh. He'd barely managed it. But luckily, Lili was light.

Now, she could easily reach the top of the fence. She pulled herself up, put her left foot on top of the gate, then slowly leant forward. She held tight to the metal mesh for support as she went over.

But she pushed too fast and didn't manage to grasp the top of the gate to lower herself down. So, she fell, face up.

The good part was, the snow broke her fall.

The bad part? The plastic booth was locked as well.

* * *

Andrei was barely able to hold in his frustration. Why couldn't they get a break? Why did it have to be so difficult all the time?

"Throw me a bat," said Lili.

Andrei had what she wanted sitting next to him in the snow. He picked it up, took two steps back and threw.

As expected, he wasn't good at this either. The throw fell short and the bat hit the fence. The noise was loud, and they looked around, scared.

Andrei almost yelled in frustration; it took all his willpower not to do so.

"Idiot!" muttered Lili. "Use your brain."

Oddly enough, he loved her tone and voice when she called him an idiot; she was so tiny and cute in her rage. This made him relax a bit.

He moved closer to the gate, threw the bat higher, and it finally reached the other side.

Lili took the bat and promptly broke the window of the plastic booth. This made some noise as well, but clearly less than the bat hitting the gate.

As she was small, she managed to climb inside. And, yes, she found keys.

They were in!

* * *

They moved through the empty parking lot. Still, a few cars were scattered around, buried under piles of snow.

"What if the owners are inside the store, all turned into growlers?" asked Lili, but no one answered.

As they neared the doors, the stack of labeled keys Lili had found in the booth came in handy. They managed to open the door to the office and entered that way.

Inside, the growling began.

"Oh!" exclaimed Andrei, squeezing his bat.

"We can do this," said Dan with confidence. "Get him out," he continued, looking at Lili.

They entered and stood still. A man, probably in his fifties, now clearly a growler, started running toward them. He was dressed in office clothes, and probably the sickness had got him while he stayed behind to finish some work.

Dan and Andrei placed themselves two steps apart, while Lili backed out of the room, keeping Mat behind her.

Matei started yelling and crying again, and Lili tried to soothe him.

As the growler reached the men, they struck it in the head at the same time.

It fell, squirming and growling.

Dan took out his knife and pushed it into its heart.

"These knives come in handy," he said, turning toward Andrei. "We ought to look for some better ones, and this hardware store is the place to do it."

Crazy how fast you can get used to something like this, realized Dan, freezing for a few seconds while holding the knife deep in the growler's chest. *I've often wondered how people could do some of the horrible things they did.*

It put some of his strange and difficult cases from the past in perspective.

He'd heard a theory that if you saw the people around you as objects it became easier to do bad things. Evil things. And ever since they'd started seeing the growlers as creatures without a soul, they'd been capable of a lot.

"Hey, are you okay?" asked Andrei, making Dan come back from the mire of his thoughts.

Dan rose, then thumped his bat against a metal locker, making noise.

Nothing.

It looked like the man was the only growler in the offices.

They left the room and found Lili and Matei holding each other, a few yards from the entrance.

"We need to be smarter next time," said Lili. "We talked about having two teams, and you, Andrei, should have stayed behind with Mat."

"Yes, you're right," intervened Dan. "It's my fault. I am the tactical leader and I should have said that. You should go farther away while we clean up here. Andrei, can you help?"

Once Lili and Matei departed, he and Andrei pulled out the old man and stowed the body behind a large dumpster.

While Lili and Matei continued to wait outside, they then headed into the store itself—an industrial hall the size of a football field—and made some noise.

No growls could be heard.

They were alone, and Andrei went back to bring in his family.

"Let's look for the generators," said Dan. "They should be back there, down that aisle."

"We might need some flashlights first," said Andrei. "I can barely see now, and back there it's almost pitch black."

"Good idea," said Dan. "They should have some by the checkout."

They picked up some flashlights and then went in the back,

where they located the generators.

"Man, these weigh a ton," said Andrei, puffing as he tried to move one. "We need a bodybuilder to carry these for us."

"This doesn't look good," said Dan. "I could carry one, but not all the way back to our apartment."

"Plus, we need fuel as well. Another trip, another thing to carry," said Andrei, shaking his head. "What the hell can we do?"

While the group pondered, Mat had been wandering close by, gazing at the displays.

"Look, Mom! Look how cute these are," he said. "They look like wooden Lego."

"Yes!" said Dan, turning and inching closer to the child. "You guys know what these are?"

"Not really," said Andrei. "Small wooden thingies."

"The richness of your vocabulary never ceases to amaze me," intervened Lili, prompting a chuckle from Andrei.

"They're wooden pellets." Dan pressed on, as Lili and Andrei fought to hold in their giggles. "Pellet stoves use this as fuel. We can warm up with these."

"But where does the smoke go?" asked Andrei, still throwing fond glances at Lili.

"There's a funnel, an evacuation tube."

"Okay, then," concluded Andrei. "Let's pack one and go back."

"Not so fast." Dan stopped him. "These stoves are still quite heavy."

"Then... how is this helping us?" asked Lili.

Dan indicated the door to the offices through which they'd entered and the vending machines near the checkout area. "Why go back to the apartment? We have everything we need right here. If we manage to get the evacuation tube out, we can stay the night in one of the offices."

* * *

They set up camp in one of the offices. They installed a simple, non-electric pellet stove and drew the evacuation tube outside. They had to break a corner of the window for this, but they had enough duct tape to fix the tube properly in place.

They found sleeping bags, tents, pillows... everything they needed, inside the big store. They managed to break open a vending machine, too, so now they had plenty of sweet and salty snacks. And lots of carbonated drinks, plus enough drinking water.

A few hours later they had a comfortable setup and were getting sleepy.

They had everything they needed for the evening.

Everything except for a plan to get the rabies shots.

24 EMERGENCY ROOM

When morning came, they returned to their discussions.
"The hardware store is located near the park, as you know," said Dan. "If we go clockwise around the border, we will reach the hospital."

"But what about the dog pack?" asked Andrei.

"That one is blocking the entrance to the emergency room at the rear of the building. We'll reach the front of the hospital."

"Do we have any idea what's awaiting for us at the front?"

"How could we know, dufus?" asked Lili.

"We don't know," said Dan, "but I hope that's our way in."

"I see," said Andrei, in a fainter voice. "Could there be dogs? More of them?"

"Relax," said Lili. "We'll see when we get there."

"Andrei, you and Mat are to stay put in the hardware store. Now, more than ever, it's clearly not safe," said Dan. "But we have to do this."

"Maybe I should go with you," said Andrei, without a trace of enthusiasm.

"No," answered Dan. "Me and Lili, we're the ones with dog bites. If we die today, you two still have a fighting chance. You don't have any risk of rabies."

Seeing Matei getting ready to speak, Lili quickly said, "No one is going to die, honey, it's just the way Grandpa talks." She then turned to the guys. "You really need to mind what you're saying."

"I think he's old enough to put two and two together and understand what's happening," answered Andrei.

"He's too young, too fragile."

"We already told him that people died due to this sickness. And he knows what death is. He's seen all those stupid cartoons."

"Still, you need to take care how you frame it."

"It's not my place to tell you how to handle things," intervened Dan, "but we do have to help him grow, sooner rather than later. The world has changed, and he needs to adapt. We might be in a situation where he needs to act, and he needs to be ready."

"We need to stop talking about these things in front of him," said Lili, spitting out every word.

"We could find a nicer way to present things, you're right," said Andrei in a pacifying tone, trying to hug her.

"Don't touch me!"

"But I love you."

"I love you, too, but don't touch me."

"I know Grandma died," interrupted Matei. "She got sick and died. And then she became evil. And I almost died too. But Dad gave me onions. Are you going to die if you go to the hospital, Mom?"

Lili glanced at the others, before finally answering. "I hope not, but I might."

Everybody stood there silently. It was a difficult thing to do, to ponder the possibility of death.

"Well, let's make sure you don't die," answered Andrei. "We'll be right here, waiting, and if you need help just call me."

"Yes, Mom. I'll come save you," said Matei with a flicker of determination in his cute eyes.

Both Andrei and Lili hugged him.

As Andrei caressed her shoulder, Lili finally kissed him back. "You idiot," she said, visibly more relaxed.

"He, he."

"Before we go, should we get some walkie talkies, as Andrei suggested the other day?" asked Lili.

"Yes," said Dan. "We need them. They should be down that aisle."

They reached the place and looked at the various options.

"These look nice," said Dan, holding a pair.

"I think these are better," said Andrei. "They seem top-of-the-line, long-range. They have higher wattage and I think they will cover the distance between here and the hospital. Plus, the main advantage is they come with these earpieces."

"To hear better?" asked Lili.

"No. I mean, not just for that. When the earpiece is on, any transmission will go out only through that."

"Ah, and that way the growlers won't hear it," said Dan.

"Exactly! So, let's say I talk, asking 'Hey guys, how are you?'," said Andrei, mimicking a casual tone. "And let's say you have some growlers a dozen feet away. They won't hear my voice. Only you will hear it, through the earpiece."

"Yeah, that sounds like a really good feature," said Lili. "Any device that prevents people or things from hearing your voice is a godsend."

"Ha-ha," said Andrei. "This earpiece is a godsend. Now, remember: always keep the earpiece on and plugged into the walkie."

"Perfect," said Dan. "Everybody, grab one. And some fresh batteries. And let's go."

"Let's take just three," said Lili. "Matei doesn't need to hear whatever will happen."

Everybody agreed.

And about fifteen minutes later, Dan and Lili headed toward the hospital.

* * *

There it was, far away and surrounded by tall trees: the hospital.

Dan and Lili crept toward it. The park was to their right, and as they reached its border, they could see some dogs in the distance.

"Come," whispered Dan upon seeing the dogs. "Let's move a bit further away. Let's take a wider circle. If we can see the dogs, the dogs can see us as well."

"I agree," whispered Lili, and they continued their advance, putting a few more yards between them and the pack.

They were now near the hospital's main access gate.

Luckily, the path seemed clear. There were no dogs here.

"Look, just like at the church back in the village," said Lili, pointing. "The main street and the surrounding alleys have been plowed, up to a point. True, the last snowfall is here, but someone has taken care of the hospital up to the last moment."

"Yeah," said Dan. "It makes sense. They fought until the end," he added, pausing a bit. "Look, the entrance is next to those ambulances. And the best part is, there are no dogs. Come on."

A few ambulances were parked out front. Pretty old models, they were probably hand-me-downs from a richer city.

They went to the main door, which was unlocked.

"This is it," mumbled Dan.

Lili heard him and squeezed her bat.

They entered, passed through the reception, and reached what looked like a waiting room. The counters in the back were all closed. The chairs and benches were all empty. No one was here.

The room had three access doors: one right in front of them and two double doors on each side.

So far, so good. Before they could take the next step, Andrei interrupted them.

"Do you ... me?" buzzed through their earpieces. The walkie talkies were working.

"Yes," whispered Lili. "We're inside. Do you hear us?"

"I think I ... you, but we ... to be ... little to ..."

"Come closer! We can't hear you!" continued Lili. "Come closer. Come closer," she repeated a few times.

"Okay ... oser ... nn ...," crackled his reply.

"Hopefully he heard us and will shorten the distance a bit," said Dan.

"Where to now?" mouthed Lili.

Dan nodded toward the middle door. "That one connects to the ER. I've used it a few times in the past, as a police officer."

When he tried the handle, though, he discovered the door was locked.

"Ah," whispered Dan. "They used to buzz me in, via a button behind one of these counters. It was possible to open the door from the inside mechanically, by pressing the wide handle, yet there is no way to open the door from our side with the power out."

"We have no choice but to go around," whispered Lili.

He tilted his head again, and they slowly opened the door leading to the right.

* * *

"I think she said to come closer, right?"

"I think so," said Mat, after a pause. Andrei realized Mat couldn't hear what they'd said, since he didn't have a headset.

"Okay, then. Put on your coat and let's get closer to the hospital."

"Dad, do you think we can find a boy jacket in here?" asked Mat, hope in his cute little eyes.

"Well, we could," said Andrei, smiling. "But I don't think it's a good idea to do it right now. We need to be there for Dan and Lili, should they need our help."

"Okay, Dad," said Mat, and put on his pink coat.

* * *

It was a long corridor with no windows, like a tunnel, linking the two hospital wings. To the left and right, in the middle of the corridor, were two doors with toilet signs. At the opposite end, where the corridor made a ninety-degree turn to the right, was a restroom for people with special needs.

They advanced slowly, trying to be as quiet as possible. Some light was coming from the doors behind them and from the other end of the corridor, so soon their eyes adjusted well enough to see there were no obstacles in their path. Dan also had the flashlight he took from the hardware store, but he was afraid to use it.

They reached the turn, and Dan took a quick look around the corner. It seemed the passageway stretched for about another twenty feet before a turn to the left.

Eventually, they reached another waiting room, smaller than the last, with counters, benches and chairs, and an access door leading outside. The counters were all closed, just like in the other waiting room.

"This is probably another wing," whispered Lili.

"Yes. This hospital has more than one entrance, depending on the care you need. This is the polyclinic part. I think we should have taken the other door, as this wing doesn't seem to link to the ER," said Dan, looking around at all the doors and access ways. "But since we're here, let's check the offices for medical supplies."

"Have you ever been here before?"

"Yeah, but while on duty I've always entered the ER from its regular entrance. Or they would let me access it through that locked door in the main waiting room. Thank God, we never had to come here often with health issues of our own. The downside is, I'm not sure which wings lead to the ER."

They moved through different offices. They found some medicine here and there, and everything they came across went into their big, empty backpacks.

Each time they entered a new room, they feared finding growlers.

"It looks like we need to go back and take the other door," said Dan, whispering. "I still think they treat dog bites in ER only."

"But you don't always go to the ER for dog bites, right? Don't you need to come back for new shots, after the first one?"

"Yes, you do. There could be some rabies shots around here somewhere, in some storage cabinet or in an office, but we should be looking for a refrigerator. However, it makes no sense logistically for them to store such things in multiple places."

They went back along the corridor.

As they reached the main waiting room they looked around.

Lili had to try for herself to open the door leading directly to the ER. It didn't budge.

The double doors leading left, then, were their only remaining option.

They entered a corridor, shorter than the one leading to the polyclinic, but with a similar go-right-then-left layout. There were two elevators. One had its doors wide open, but there was nowhere to go, not without electricity.

This corridor was wider than the last, probably to allow wheeled hospital beds easy access. Like in the other corridor, light was scarce, but they could just about see where they were going. It was colder here too—far colder than the rest of the hospital.

They advanced silently, taking each blind turn with care, until they found themselves in the middle of another scene of carnage.

They were in a large and very long hall. The opposite wall featured tall windows, with strong metal grills on the outside. Light poured in, deepening the impact of what they saw.

To the left and to the right were doors accessing various wards and offices. Eight on each side, all numbered. These doors stood open. They couldn't see clearly into the rooms, but the area seemed deserted.

There was blood everywhere, and bloody handprints smattered the walls here and there.

Putting it all together, it was clear: this had been a battleground.

"What now?" whispered Lili, visibly scared.

They took a few cautious steps in, looking left and right.

Dan stopped and turned his back to the large windows. He peered back down the corridor along which they'd come. Beside it, a large staircase led up. To the left, he could see another corridor, wide enough to fit hospital beds.

"This way," whispered Dan. "This should lead to the ER."

"And the stairs?" whispered Lili, moving closer.

"They probably lead to more wards. This is the hospital area, so they have wards for different kinds of care spread across different floors."

"We need to go down this corridor then?" asked Lili, with a tremor in her voice.

"Yes," whispered Dan. The long hall was creepy, and he expected to see a growler coming through one of the doors at any moment. "Let's go."

As Dan and Lili advanced, they saw traces of blood everywhere. But no people.

The passageway was wide yet short, immediately turning left toward the back of the building. Then, just like the other two corridors, two right-then-left turns followed.

Dan finally stepped into the ER, Lili behind him.

It was a big square hall, with corridors and doors on all sides.

At the back a large access gate stood open. That was where the ambulances would drop off patients.

That's why it's so cold in here, realized Dan.

Through the gate they could see the park and the pack of dogs. They were still there, just like the day before.

As he crept forward, he realized the huge square hall was covered in blood.

"Stop," whispered Dan. Lili halted just before the turn. She hadn't seen anything yet. "I can see the dogs," whispered Dan.

"What do we do? Are we safe?"

"If we move fast, they might not see us," answered Dan. "I'll go first, you follow. There's a door to the right, leading to a room with glass walls. I enter, you follow quickly. Don't waste time, and close the door behind you. It's the main ER office, and if we're lucky, that's where we'll find our rabies shots."

"Let's get some tetanus shots as well," said Lili.

"Right."

The room with glass walls was large. There were a few desks in the center of the space and medicine cabinets lined the walls. In one corner stood a large refrigerator, where even more medicine was kept.

That's where they found the rabies shots. They managed to fill their backpacks with supplies, and then they were ready to move out.

This has proven to be an easy job in the end, thought Dan. He reached the glass door and inched it open. There was no change in their surroundings. Lili quickly followed, and they got back to the corridor leading to the large hospital hall.

Then, behind them, a dog started barking.

It was a different kind of bark, not too loud, with some inflexions in it. It was a mix of barking and whining.

They turned, ready to fight. But the dog didn't attack. It charged toward them, but stopped a few steps away, barking in that weird way before running off. Then it charged again, repeating the process. Charge, bark, run away.

What is this, thought Dan. *Could it be? ... Never mind!* "Let's move!" he said, and continued walking down the corridor.

The dog suddenly became aggressive. The barking was louder, reverberating along the corridor.

As Dan and Lili reached the halfway mark, the growling began.

It was loud. It sounded like hundreds of growlers had woken at the same time. They'd never heard anything like this before.

They started running, reaching the large hospital hall in time to see a few growlers racing down the stairs.

Dan hesitated for a moment. Behind them was the pack of dogs. A few were already in the corridor, barking loudly. To their left, growlers approached.

During his pause, Lili moved past him and entered the hall, heading toward the corridor linking to the main reception. She hadn't spotted the growlers on the stairs, and they took her by surprise.

She yelled, and instantly turned right, running toward the large windows at the end of the hall.

"No!" called Dan. "Come back!"

Lili stopped, turned around, but it was too late. The first growler—an old man wearing a bloody hospital gown—was already at the bottom of the stairs, right behind Dan.

"Run!" said Dan, and he took the lead.

They had no idea what awaited them in the wards. There could be dozens of growlers. They had no choice other than to fly through those wide-open doors.

They sprinted across the hall. Behind them, growlers followed.

They soon reached the large windows. There was nowhere else to go, as the wards were not safe.

They made a lot of noise while running, and about two dozen growlers were on their heels. The dog, however, had managed to attract a few of them in the other direction, drawing away the first, and thus the fastest of their pursuers.

This helped Dan and Lili.

When they reached the end of the hall, the remaining growlers were far back, still by the stairs.

Dan looked at Lili, pressed his index finger to his lips, his back against the wall, and waited.

Lili understood and followed suit. They stood there, keeping as still and quiet as possible.

The growlers were slowly approaching. Most were fast ones, yet they seemed slower than usual. Some had medical issues which prevented them from running. A few had tubes coming out of them, as if they'd started moving without someone disconnecting them first. Most wore hospital gowns. And the majority were old.

As they got closer, the growling got louder.

Seventy feet... fifty feet...

Dan realized they'd been lucky. Clearly there were no growlers in the wards, otherwise they would have come out already.

If only they'd known that in advance! They could have entered one of the wards, thus putting more distance between them and the growlers, giving these beasts more time to become dormant. But it was too late now.

The growlers were closing in. Thirty feet now.

For Lili and Dan, it was hard enough to see these monsters coming, but it was harder still to watch them advance so slow, prolonging their agony.

Twenty feet... Ten feet... Could this be it?

It didn't matter. He would attack the growlers, make noise and run, to get them away from Lili. His baby girl. He just hoped she would not join the fight, so she had a chance to go unnoticed and survive. He would tell her that. He would attack yelling "Don't move! Stay there!". That's what he'd do.

* * *

As they reached the park, Matei started to look worried. "What if Mom and Grandpa are in danger? We need to go save them!"

"No, they should be okay. We're just getting closer so they can hear us better. And please whisper. There's a pack of dogs nearby."

"They can hear us better now, can't they?" asked Matei, whispering.

"I don't know," said Andrei his patience wearing. "I have to check."

"Then why don't you check?"

Andrei opened the mouth, then realized he had no answer.

He pressed the Push-To-Talk button on his handset.

"Hey, guys, do you hear me now? I'm near the park. Guys?"

Nothing.

It should work. He was right next the park, and this was professional equipment. It was impossible for Dan and Lili not to hear him, unless something had happened to them.

215

"Guys? Lili, Dan, are you there? Over."

He was getting nervous.

"Is it working, Daddy?"

"Well, no. We're too far away." He had to lie to the kid.

"Then let's get closer," replied Mat, and started walking.

"Yeah," said Andrei, with a sigh. "Let's get closer."

* * *

Dan was ready to fight to save Lili!

He started to raise his bat and took a deep breath, ready to yell.

Suddenly, the growlers fell, one by one, facedown, accompanied by the horrible sound of broken teeth and smashed faces and noses.

Finally, the whole corridor was silent.

Silent save for the breaths of two living persons hugging the wall as they stared at the twenty or so growlers face down on the cold floor.

Dan slowly relaxed, lowering his bat.

That's when the walkie talkies came alive in their ears.

"Hey, guys, do you hear me now? I'm near the park. Guys?"

Lili looked at Dan. Dan looked at Lili. There was no way to answer without waking the growlers.

They were trapped.

It was a horrible place to be: backs against the windows, growlers so close to them. So close! Any move or noise, the faintest whisper, would wake the monsters.

All the doors nearby were dead ends, leading only to various doctor's offices and wards.

All the windows were closed, and even if they weren't, they had those damn metal grills.

Across the hall, however, far away, were three possible exits.

In the middle, the stairs led to the upper levels, filled with dormant growlers. Judging by the growls they'd heard, the other floor held many more. That route was out.

To the left of the stairs was the corridor leading to the ER, where the dogs awaited fresh food. Another strike out.

And to the right lay the corridor where they'd initially come from, leading back to the main waiting room and freedom.

That's where they needed to go.

Unfortunately, between them and freedom about twenty growlers were spread across the floor.

They'd never be able to run past them. They would die within minutes.

They couldn't risk sneaking past them. Any little sound would kill them as well.

What could they do? They'd just have to wait. Hopefully Andrei, who seemed to be closing in, could find a way to save them.

As Lili and Dan waited, they heard that low, whiney bark again. It was barely audible, but it was loud enough to wake a few of the growlers closest to the stairs.

The dog was baiting the growlers, realized Dan, reinforcing an idea he'd had when returning from the ER. Unbelievable! That's why there were no growlers on the ground floor.

The dogs had found a way to attract the growlers, luring them out, one by one, and eating them. Then they'd come back and take another. They knew exactly what volume bark to use, how to direct the sound so only a few awoke.

And that's why the dog had grown aggressive at the end, waking the entire hospital. It had seen they were not responding to its earlier call.

Finally, he had an explanation for the bones and the bloody field in the park.

* * *

Andrei and Matei were right in front of the hospital. It looked dark, although it was one of the whitest buildings in town. The windows looked especially menacing, with those strong grills on all of them. Andrei had said on many occasions that the hospital looked more like a prison.

As he pushed away this thought, he tried again to contact Lili and Dan.

"Guys, are you there? Dan? Lili? Come in. Over."

Nothing. Quiet. This was disturbing.

"Guys? Please answer. Give me a sign. Anything!"

Still nothing.

JOHN BLACK

"Lili?" His voice trembled. "You're worrying me sick. Please answer."

Then he heard a noise through the earpiece. It was the BEEP sound made when people press and then release the PTT button, followed by some crackling.

And then many more BEEPs followed.

Andrei gasped. The BEEPs were too regular—BEEP, BEEP, BEEP, like a clock. They were clearly being made on purpose, and it wasn't a communication glitch.

That meant only one thing: they were in there. They were alive. But they couldn't talk.

"I got the message. I'll come back to you. Over," he said, still with a tremor in his voice.

The night he'd spent under the metal hatch came to mind. He'd been in the exact same situation. He couldn't talk, move, or do anything. Maybe they were in a similar situation. But how could he tell? How could he find out?

And more importantly, how could he save them?

* * *

After what felt like forever, Andrei was again talking through the walkie talkie, begging in their earpieces.

"Guys, are you there? Dan? Lili? Come in. Over. Guys? Please answer. Give me a sign. Anything! Lili? You're worrying me sick. Please answer."

If only there was a way to answer him, thought Dan. Andrei was pleading. Hopefully he wouldn't give up, thinking they were already dead.

And then Dan heard a BEEP in his earpiece, followed by a few more, in sequence.

He slowly turned his head and saw Lili's hand on her walkie talkie.

Most importantly, Andrei understood the message. They were finally communicating.

Excellent! he thought, as hope started to fill his heart again.

* * *

Andrei was restless. He needed to do something.

He could come up with some sort of communicating algorithm. He used a lot of algorithms and protocols at work. He could start asking questions, and one click would stand for 'yes', two for 'no'.

But he couldn't do that here. He was right in front of the hospital, and he knew those horrible dogs were not far away.

He needed a place to hide. And he needed some paper.

He could go into the hospital. But that's where Lili and Dan were trapped. So it probably wasn't the best hiding.

As he looked around, he spotted the ambulances.

He approached one, and luckily, the door was unlocked. He even found the keys tucked into the sun visor.

He got in, secured Mat in the passenger seat, found a notebook in the glove compartment, and started communicating with Lili and Dan.

"Hey, guys. It's me again. We're in a safe place. Mat and I are fine. Let's use one click on the PTT button for 'yes' and two clicks for 'no'. Are you guys still there? Over."

Andrei loved those movies where people were using communication devices like these, and he loved to say 'over'. It made him feel in control.

After a few seconds, he finally heard the BEEP.

He relaxed a bit.

"Perfect! Are you alive and well? Over."

BEEP

"Can you come out?"

He sometimes forgot the 'over' part, as he wasn't really used to it.

BEEP, BEEP

"Okay, you cannot come back. Is there a way for me to save you? Over."

Stupid question, as he got a string of BEEPs in response. Probably the person on the other end—he suspected Lili—had lost his or her temper a bit.

"Okay, got it, stupid question. Let me think for a bit and I'll circle back."

What could he do?

Andrei had no idea. How could he plan anything unless he could find a way to understand what had happened and where they were?

Well, what could it be? First, they were probably stuck somewhere, with growlers close by, so they couldn't talk. The growlers were obviously present in large numbers, otherwise Dan and Lili could have easily killed them.

Hopefully the growlers could be attracted somewhere else, like Lili and Mat had done back at the church.

He needed to find out more.

"You' re trapped by growlers, right? Over."

BEEP

"Can you see them or are you locked in somewhere?" Again that hatch came back to haunt him. He realized this was not a yes-no question, so he quickly added, "Use one click for 'see them', two for 'locked somewhere'. Over."

BEEP

"Can you count them? Over."

BEEP

"How many do you see? Use clicks. Over."

BEEP, BEEP, BEEP, on and on. He almost lost track! Twenty-six growlers. Wow!

"Twenty-six? Over."

BEEP

"Are they all sleeping? Over."

BEEP

"I'll think some more. I'll come back soon. Over," he said.

There was no way for him to save them! How could he lure twenty-six growlers away and live to tell the tale?

Andrei still needed more info.

"So, you said there are twenty-six growlers. Can you move past them? Over."

BEEP, BEEP, BEEP, BEEP.

"Okay, okay, sorry," he said. "I've asked that before, I know. It's just I'm still thinking. I have no idea yet. Over."

Silence.

BEEP, went Andrei's walkie talkie about half a minute later.

"Ah, 'yes'? 'Yes' what? I haven't asked anything. Over."

BEEP

"What? Over."

BEEP

"What?"

BEEP, BEEP, BEEP, BEEP

"Umm. You want to say something? Over."

BEEP

"Great! What is it? Over."

BEEP, BEEP, BEEP, BEEP

"Okay, okay. Do you have an idea?"

BEEP

"Something I can do to help? Over."

BEEP

"Wow, great! Tell me!"

BEEP, BEEP, BEEP, BEEP

"Damn it! Sorry! I'm so stressed! I don't want to lose you guys! If I lose you, I don't know what I'll do! It will be just me and…" He stopped, realizing Mat could hear him. "But all will be fine, clearly!"

After a quick pause, he had an idea. "Let's do it like before with the 'yes' and 'no'! What if we assign a number for each letter of the alphabet? Can you then send a few words, so I can try to understand?"

Morse code would have probably been way faster, but he didn't know it.

BEEP

"Perfect! This is perfect! So, use 1 for A, 2 for B, etcetera, up to 26 for Z. Okay?"

BEEP

"Perfect! Start now!"

He counted the numbers, at the end of each set asking, "Okay, that's a five? Over."

In the end, he got the numbers 5, 18, 14, 15, 9, 26 written on his paper.

Which translated to 'ERNOIZ'.

"Ernoiz?" he said, distrustful. "That's what you sent, 'Ernoiz'?"

BEEP

"What the hell is an ernoiz?"

Silence.

"Ernoiz… ernoiz… sounds like noise, I give you that. Over."

BEEP

"Ah! It's noise?"

BEEP

"Hmm, so 'er'-noise?"

BEEP

"What's that 'er'... is it 'err' with two R's, like to err, to make a mistake? You made a mistake by making noise? Over."

BEEP, BEEP

"Damn! Okay. 'Er'... 'er'... I have no idea what this E-R means."

He suddenly realized it.

"I'm such an idiot!" he exclaimed, releasing the PTT and smiling at Matei.

BEEP

"Yeah, yeah," he said using the walkie talkie, laughing. "So, I guess it is 'E. R. noise', right? Over."

BEEP

"You need me to make a noise in the ER?"

BEEP

"Do I have to come to the ER?"

BEEP

"Okay then, I'll come to the ER. Do I go through the front entrance, like you did?"

BEEP, BEEP

"Okay, so no. Do I have to go through the back?"

BEEP, BEEP

"Ugh! Where do I have to enter the building?"

BEEP, BEEP

"No? 'No' what? I don't have to enter?"

BEEP

"Aha! Hmm, but you said to come to the ER. Now you say I don't have to enter? Over."

BEEP, BEEP, BEEP, BEEP

"Okay, okay. So, I will come close to the ER, but not enter. I will then make noise there?"

BEEP

"Cool. Where should I come then?"

Silence.

"Did you hear me? Over."

BEEP

"Ah, you don't have an answer to that. Do you know where I should come?"

BEEP

"Do you want to tell me using letters?"

BEEP

"Okay. Do it, go!" he said as he prepared to write down the numbers.

BEEP, BEEP, silence. BEEP, silence. BEEP, BEEP, BEEP

"2, 1, 3? Over."

BEEP

"So… B, A, C, 'bac'… Back?"

BEEP

"You want me to go to the ER's access, out back, and make noise?"

BEEP

"That place with a thousand dogs?"

BEEP

"Noise… noise… We need to make some noise at the ER behind the hospital. But how?" Andrei spoke aloud inside the ambulance.

"Daddy?"

"Not now, Mat. Daddy needs to think."

"Daddy, do you want to—"

"No, Mat, I do not want to! I want to find a solution to save Mom and Dan. So, please, let me think."

"But…"

"But what? Huh? But what?" said Andrei, turning toward him aggressively.

"Daddy," tried Mat once more.

"What?" barked Andrei.

"Don't ambulances make a lot of noise?"

Andrei stopped short. He really needed to behave differently with the kid. He'd treated him wrongly so many times.

"Come here," he said, and leaned over to hug Mat. "I'm so sorry. I truly am. Every time I get stressed or busy, I treat you badly. I tell you mean things and then I dismiss you. Please forgive me, little doughnut."

"It's okay, Dad."

"I love you, Mat."

"I love you too."

"Now, let's see what this baby can do!"

The ambulance crept past the front of the hospital. The layer of snow was thinner here and getting access to the back of the building would be a piece of cake.

The ambulance was big, tall, and there was easy, direct access between the front seats and the back, all the way to the rear double doors.

Andrei had spent a few minutes talking to Dan and Lili, explaining his plan. In the end, he got a BEEP as a sign that they agreed.

He took a left and reached the side of the hospital where the polyclinic was. Another left and they were right behind the hospital.

To his right, dozens, maybe hundreds, of dogs stared at this strange apparition.

To his left, stood the large, open gates of the ER.

He backed up as close as he could get to the ER doors and turned on the siren.

* * *

What is taking him so long? thought Lili.

Their feet were getting tired and her back was killing her. But, most importantly, the stress was getting to them. The fear that any move they made could wake the growlers collapsed a few steps away.

What was that sound? Could it be?

Finally, Andrei had come through.

An ambulance siren could be heard, coming from the ER.

About half the growlers on the floor woke, and their noise in turn disturbed most of the others.

In the end, twenty-two of them started moving toward the ER.

The remaining four, those closest to Lili and Dan, remained dormant. The sounds weren't loud enough to rouse them.

Lili and Dan exchanged looks and silently agreed. In the same moment, they attacked the nearest of the remaining growlers.

* * *

Hell must be a nice place compared to this.

Andrei watched through his side mirrors, keeping an eye on the corridor connecting the ER to the hospital wing. As soon as he saw the first growler coming, Andrei cut the sirens, though he kept the engine running.

The growler advanced toward the open gate.

In front of them, the dogs were closing in. They started barking, startled by the commotion. And that was the perfect lure for the growler, which immediately attacked the dogs.

Soon, about twenty other growlers followed, all coming down the corridor to joining the fight.

Every growler had at least four dogs on it. The dogs were biting and ripping the meat off the bones, while the growlers were doing almost the same thing to the dogs.

Dan pulled Mat's beanie over his eyes and told him not to look. Then he used his walkie talkie.

"If you can go, guys, now's the time. The dogs are fighting the growlers. If the coast is clear, tell me. Over."

* * *

"Let's go!" said Dan to Lili, catching his breath, immediately after Andrei told them to move.

The four growlers were on the floor, heads smashed in. Two of them had never managed to get up in the first place, while bat hits had put down the others.

They dashed across the hall, toward the corridor leading to the main waiting room. They were halfway there when suddenly a new group of growlers appeared, coming down the stairs, running and growling. They were pushing against each other. Some fell, but others immediately followed, coming in implacable waves.

Lili shrieked and started to slow. They were so close to escape, and this new group would ruin everything.

The first of the growlers reached the ground floor, and attracted by the noise Dan and Lili made, headed toward them. This blocked Dan and Lili from their escape route.

There was no way to get to the main waiting room, not anymore, and other growlers were pouring in from the stairs.

For now, they still had a free path to the ER, where Andrei was. "Go! Go!" said Dan, in a commanding tone, instantly boosting Lili's confidence. "Get to the ER," he added, and they turned left, sprinting past the stairs, barely escaping a growler's aggressive grab.

"We're coming to the ambulance," he yelled, pressing the PTT.

* * *

"We're coming to the ambulance!"

Andrei heard Dan through the walkie talkie.

"What? To the ambulance? Should I open the rear doors?" answered Andrei, taken by surprise.

"Yes, open it. We're coming," yelled Lili.

They both sounded out of breath. And scared.

Andrei opened the rear doors and there they were! Dan and Lili jumped in, Dan yelling, "Close it!"

Andrei happily obliged.

Behind them, the new group of growlers was closing in fast, just a few steps away. Some slammed against the doors of the ambulance, hitting, biting and scratching.

Luckily, they soon forgot about the two running people and instead joined the big, noisy fight outside. As they departed, some bits of flesh and teeth remained clinging to the metal mesh protecting the small windows of the rear doors.

By inching the ambulance forward, so as not to make too much noise, Andrei drove them out of the war zone.

In their wake, growlers continued to spew forth from the hospital. The fight was on.

But the four of them—Lili, Dan, Matei and Andrei—were back together again and in a relatively safe place, making their escape.

25 THIS CHANGES EVERYTHING

They took the ambulance close to the hardware store. The snow was getting deeper and soon the ambulance got stuck. "Let's abandon it. We only have a quarter of a mile left to our destination anyway," whispered Dan, tapping Andrei's shoulder. "Good job back there, by the way."

As they entered their improvised quarters and sat down, Lili started crying. Dan was fighting back his tears, while Andrei was losing the battle.

"This world is shit! It's shit!" said Lili, sobbing.

"I know, honey, I know," said Andrei softly, stilling her hands with his own.

"Oh, I know, language," added Lili. "We almost died! If it weren't for you being there to save us, we'd be dead!"

"It's okay, honey. You saved us last time."

"I know! I know! That's the problem! What if next time there's no one to save us? What if next time we all die, like we almost did today? We cannot live like this," said Lili, letting out all the accumulated tension, fear and despair.

Matei started crying, alone in his chair, until finally Andrei noticed and went to him.

The stress was too much for her. For all of them.

* * *

"There," said Dan, as he pulled the needle out. "We need to repeat this every three days, three more times. But maybe we'll add one more, just to make sure. It's been a while since we were bitten."

"Yeah, five days," interrupted Andrei.

"As far as I remember," Dan continued. "Ten days is the limit. We should be okay."

"Honey, do you feel any urge to be aggressive?" asked Andrei, smiling.

"When you're around, always."

"Yeah, I suspect you've had rabies for more than ten years already," continued Andrei, prompting a few smiles.

"Now," said Dan, "we have to go back to the village. I want to make sure Howler is okay."

"Yes, Dad. Let's go save the dog! Can we go now?" asked Lili.

"No, no," said Dan. "It's late, and we're shaken. The dog will be okay for one more day. We'll go first thing tomorrow morning. We'll make a quick stop at the cabin. And then, depending on our energy, continue to the house." He smiled. "And maybe, after that, we'll finally reach Grandma's house."

* * *

The next morning, they were up and running.

They returned to their apartment, where they'd left a few things they wanted to take to the village.

"You go in," said Dan, stopping in front of their apartment door. "I want to clean up here."

They all agreed, and while Andrei and Lili prepared their backpacks for the road, Dan managed to take the teacher's wife out down the stairs. In a few days, the smell should be just a bad memory.

Later, as they moved out, they once more approached the bridge. Everyone remembered the frozen growler, the first one they'd seen that night from the bedroom window. They moved as silently as possible, hoping not to awaken it again.

Dan was leading the group, followed by Lili and Mat, and then Andrei, who kept looking back, feeling unsafe.

As they reached the middle of the bridge, Lili stopped.

She was looking toward Las Vegas and let out a soft gasp.

"What is it, honey?" asked Andrei, waking the growler.

Dan turned, looking toward Las Vegas, then he froze too.

"What's going on?" asked Andrei, looking at them and then into the distance. "What is it?"

"Look." Lili pointed. "Look… smoke!"

Andrei followed the line of her hand. And at last he saw it. Smoke was coming from a chimney about two miles out, right in the middle of Las Vegas.

"What does it… Does it mean that…" stammered Andrei.

"It means," said Dan, "that we are not alone."

* THE END *

ABOUT THE AUTHOR

John Black has spent most of his adult life working in the
entertainment industry and helping create virtual worlds.

He is a gamer, husband, father, pancakes enthusiast and more
recently he followed his life dream of becoming a fiction author,
writing in the horror thriller genre. His approach to writing is to
go all in, keeping it fast paced and immersive.

John likes to think a lot of 'what would happen if' scenarios, and
he will continue to explore the genre.

* * *

If you would like to get in touch with John, or be notified about
the release of future books, drop a line at
john.black.author@gmail.com.

* * *

Readers trust other readers.
If you enjoyed this book please leave an honest review on
Amazon. Thank you!

Made in the USA
Columbia, SC
05 July 2021